DATE			
	ˮ		

About Yvonne

ALSO BY DONNA MASINI

That Kind of Danger

About Yvonne

DONNA MASINI

W. W. NORTON & COMPANY

NEW YORK • LONDON

The author wishes to acknowledge
Selected Poems and Two Plays of William Butler Yeats,
edited by M. L. Rosenthal, Macmillan, 1962.
All rights reserved
Printed in the United States of America
First Edition

For information about permission to reproduce selections from this book,
write to Permissions, W. W. Norton & Company, Inc.,
500 Fifth Avenue, New York, NY 10010.

The text of this book is composed in Garamond Number 3
with the display set in Ribbon and Copperplate
Desktop composition by Gina Webster.
Manufacturing by Quebecor Printing, Fairfield Inc.
Book design by JAM Design

Library of Congress Cataloging-in-Publication Data

Masini, Donna.
About Yvonne / Donna Masini.
p.   cm.
ISBN 0-393-04091-7
I. Title.
PS3563.A7855A64   1997
813'.54—dc21   96-45125
CIP

W. W. Norton & Company, Inc., 500 Fifth Avenue, New York, N.Y. 10110
http://www.wwnorton.com

W. W. Norton & Company Ltd., 10 Coptic Street, London WC1A 1PU

1 2 3 4 5 6 7 8 9 0

For generous criticism, unfailing encouragement and insight I would like to thank Tim Tomlinson.

I am indebted to Jan Heller Levi, Carol Conroy, and Rita Gabis for their indefatigable support and many rereadings.

For support and encouragement of various kinds I would like to thank Tom Wolfe, Barbara O'Shea, Karen Backus, Dani Shapiro, Martha Gallahue, Elisa D'Arrigo and Jim Stoeri, Wesley Gibson, Karen Masini, Gail Hochman, Jill Bialosky, and the Corporation of Yaddo.

I could not have begun or imagined this book without the support and enthusiasm of Judd Tully.

for my parents

For if the will is left without employment, and love has no present object to occupy it, the soul remains without support or activity, solitude and dryness give great pain, and stray thoughts attack most fiercely.

—St. Teresa of Ávila

It's all too horrible: Whatever will happen?

—*The Marriage of Figaro*

About Yvonne

· 1 ·

I have been stalking my husband's lover. I'm not sure exactly how long this has been going on. Twenty-two or twenty-three days, I think. I could check. I've written it all down.

Yvonne. Her name is Yvonne. I thought she'd be exotic. A belly dancer, a singer, a beautician. Yvonne. I only had her name for a while. Her first name. When I finally met her— *saw* her really—at an opening in my husband's gallery, I was surprised at how ordinary she looked. I mean, she could have been me. The clothes were wrong, though, the style. Not wrong for her. They looked pretty good on her. They just didn't look like me at all. I'm sure of that now that I've seen her whole wardrobe. A closet full of elegant dresses and skirts, some still in their dry-cleaning wrap. Little moth crystal hearts on hangers in each corner. Dressers full of stacked, color-gradated sweaters. Fourteen boxes of shoes— all good names and well cared for. I think she's obsessive. I couldn't even find much of interest in her wastebasket.

This afternoon was my first visit to her apartment.

I didn't come up with much but at least now I know what kind of toothpaste she uses. I bought it. And a toothbrush the same color as hers. Green with those little silver sparkles.

The kind that tapers at the tip to fit easily into your mouth. I like it better than the kind I've been using. The square kind. She uses Opium perfume, the same as me. So I guess I would never have detected the new smell on him. I wonder if he bought it for her. He bought me my first bottle for Christmas, the first year neither of us went home to our families, the Christmas we lay in bed all day, making love, drinking Chevalier-Montrachet, opening gifts haphazardly.

Mark is extravagant. That year we outdid ourselves in the choosing, wrapping, and presentation of gifts. He had quite a time getting at the tiny gold ring I'd strung on a red ribbon and wrapped, so to speak, inside me. His tongue was numb for twenty minutes after that. There was no order to the gifts. A silver box etched with scenes from Orpheus and Eurydice followed a Patty Duke coloring book and crayons. I hung a framed picture of Curly, his favorite Stooge, beside the bed and waited for him to notice. The Opium he laid on my stomach—unwrapped, save for its engraved Oriental case—at the very end of the day. I think he must have planned that. "I always want to smell you on me," he said. "Always and everywhere." I guess everywhere eventually included his lover.

"What are you eating?" Mark asked this morning, grimacing at my plate. He poured a cup of coffee and refilled mine. Our mornings are like that. Snatches of conversation as he's getting dressed, I'm doing my yoga headstands, putting on coffee, writing notes for the lit classes I teach in the afternoons at NYU. I'm an adjunct.

"Pastina," I said.

"You okay?"

"I guess."

I always eat pastina when I'm depressed. This morning I was depressed and excited. A deadly combination. I was shaking and jumpy and I needed to calm down. Last week I'd found the keys to Yvonne's apartment—I knew they were her keys—in the top drawer of Mark's desk at the gallery. In an enamel box I gave him three years ago. I had the copies I'd made in my pocket.

He wrapped his arms around me, kissed my hair. "What, baby?" he asked. I love the way his dark hair falls across his face. "Want me to stay home for a while?" He slipped his hand down the neck of my black tank which was covered with cat hairs. "Want to go back to bed?"

We used to do that a lot. Some days he'd never even make it to work. Some days we'd go back to bed, then spend the rest of the day wandering around the city, looking at art, going in and out of galleries, or just wandering and talking. All day. Then we'd come back to the loft, make love again, and order in for dinner.

"Honey," I said, "you have to leave. My lover's coming by in a few minutes." He didn't even wince. I wanted to see him wince. "She's *very* jealous," I said. Then he laughed.

"Call me later," I said. I kissed him. "And tell Glenda thanks for that catalog." Glenda is his assistant at the gallery.

He was out the door. Just like that. Like things were normal and he wasn't fucking Yvonne to death in a room full of mirrors. (Actually, there's only one mirror in her bed-room and you can't see your reflection while you're lying on the bed.)

After the initial thrill of following her through the halls at Columbia where she teaches English lit (I don't know how she can afford those clothes on an adjunct's salary), sitting in on one of her lectures on the poems of Yeats, I wanted to see more of Yvonne. Where she lived, who she met, what she ate for dinner. I followed her home one evening up Broadway toward 103rd Street. It was one of the first dark fall nights after you put the clocks back. The streets felt sluggish and dull. Yvonne walked into a Korean vegetable store and I waited outside by a sidewalk stand that displayed sneakers and sheets and household cleaning products. She picked up a plastic container and began to circle the salad bar with those long silver tongs upright in her hand like a wand. She looked pale in the bright fluorescence. I think she stuck mainly to the raw vegetables. Didn't take any of the fried stuff or Italian-style greasy concoctions. I tried to see if she took a vegetable sushi like I used to, but a stack of cartons was blocking my view. She filled the container.

I gave a quarter to a woman who asked and watched as Yvonne handed back the plastic fork and spoon and napkin the Korean woman had slipped under the rubber band on the container. I guess they made her feel lonely, as if the Korean woman thought she was going back to an office or something to eat. I started to feel sorry for her. She was pretty, but she looked pathetic in that harsh light. Everything did. I started to feel sorry for the Korean woman whose skin looked like she lived on all that salad bar food. Everything that didn't sell during the day. Yvonne was taking her change. She smiled at the Korean woman. I liked that.

On the way out she leaned into a bunch of tiger lilies and breathed them in. I wondered if she was thinking of Mark. Mark at home having dinner with me. If it made her feel sad. I wanted to rush over to her. Tell her I'd left a message on our machine telling Mark I'd be late. To start dinner without me. I thought of Mark being lonely and me being lonely and Yvonne and the Korean woman. All of us lonely. I thought how easy it would be to walk up to her, say I remembered her from the opening. I was Mark's wife. Maybe we could have a drink. That she would tell me to pick up a salad, she'd buy some wine, come to her place for dinner.

She walked toward the door. I moved behind the man selling sneakers until she was enough ahead of me, then I followed.

Broadway uptown can feel so desolate at night. Dark and shabby and unfamiliar with the occasional remains of a once-elegant hotel. Miserable-looking people leaning against buildings or walking alone. Slowly. Not hurrying. Old women sitting in Blimpie's. Children out later than they should be. Maybe it's just that my therapist's office is on 95th Street. I'm used to feeling sad up there. Wanting to weep up there. I was beginning to weep. I held it back. I wanted to jump in a cab down to Soho, walk into the kitchen with a bottle of Cabernet, and pretend I'd never learned my husband was having an affair.

Yvonne crossed Broadway at 103rd and walked to Riverside. I went as far as her building and waited. The rest would be easy as long as her last name was on the box. It was. Adams. I found it out last week. Yvonne Adams. A WASP, apparently. Her dark hair had thrown me. I always assume WASPs are blond. What WASP names their child Yvonne? I remembered she hadn't taken any condiments for her salad and wondered if she ate it plain or kept dressing upstairs. Bottled, probably. Probably Paul Newman. She couldn't even make her own salad dressing.

"What are you thinking about?" Eric asked.

I still can't believe I have a male shrink. Sometimes I hate him. How calm he is. He never gets ruffled, never shows any visible sign of passion, never coughs or twitches. On his desk, facing away from me, is a picture of a wife and young child. "I wonder if you have the capacity for great love," I asked him once. What did he do? He smiled.

"Yeats," I said. "I'm thinking about Yeats." When I'm feeling ornery I sometimes quote long passages of poetry. I know he doesn't have the kind of soul to really hear into a poem and it gives me an edge. He was waiting for me to begin. Maybe something about the foul rag and bone shop of the heart. Foul enough. "His wife, really," I said.

He looked approving. "What about his wife?"

"Oh," I said, "that stuff about her starting to do automatic writing on their honeymoon. On their *honeymoon* for God's sake."

Eric glanced at the clock. I never know if he is thinking

I'm avoiding the issue or wondering when the session's going to end. Actually, I spend enough energy entertaining him so I'm pretty sure I've won some small place in his enthusiasms.

"I mean, here all Ireland knows Yeats has been panting after Maud Gonne for half his life, and her always putting him off but wanting to be good close friends and political allies." Eric was frowning. "Here she is gorgeous and passionate and elusive, refuses three times to marry him and then marries some handsome war hero she barely knows. I mean, God, he even proposed to her *daughter* the last time Maud declined. And then he marries this gentle Englishwoman and how's she going to hold him? It's *ingenious*." He does jump slightly when I bang my fist on the armchair. "When I think of the love and devotion it must have taken, making up all that automatic, unconscious stuff, year after year, and him making those beautiful poems out of it . . ."

"Theresa . . ."

"I mean, God, it's really sad. And he probably always loved Maud Gonne." Fuck if Yvonne hadn't lectured about just this part of Yeats's life.

"Have you dreamt about Yvonne again?"

He was sitting the way he often does, with his hands pressed together against his lips, like he's praying for me. It always makes me think of the ceramic statue of the Praying Hands my mother made when I was a kid. I just stared at him.

"Why don't you tell me what you're thinking," he said.

Eric Anderson rarely uses the word "fantasies." I think it embarrasses him. Like he's asking me to tell dirty secrets. Ever since the time I told him I'd thought about him spanking me.

"Well," I said, and pulled my feet up onto the chair, "this afternoon I was imagining Mark and Yvonne fucking in our loft."

"How did that make you feel?"

When I first started seeing Eric I asked him how he saw himself. Did he see himself as a mirror? Another version of me? He just sat there watching me, staring the way he does. A blank screen? I asked. He looked like a blank screen. "I see myself as a prism," he said finally. "I see myself taking in what you say and refracting it back to you in a whole spectrum of meaning." He actually said that. For a while after that I couldn't look at him without seeing an enormous crystal hanging from a pink ribbon in a sunny kitchen window.

"Horny," I said.

He didn't say anything.

"I was thinking of him fucking her over the banister outside our loft. She had her pants down and his cock was moving into her from behind." Actually, I was embellishing this. In my fantasy they'd just been on the bed. "He was slamming into her and I was watching from the doorway. His hands were on her ass and he kept telling her to lean forward." I was really getting into this. "'I said, bend *over*,' he kept saying."

"Does he do that to you?"

I felt myself starting to cry. I tensed everything to keep it in. I held my breath, imagined I was a statue, marble and immovable. I guess it was the first time it really hit me. What my best friend Sarah had told me. About Yvonne. I think I've just been numb. Or scared. I still can't believe it. Of course he does that to me. Mark loves me. I know he loves me. We have great sex and great fun and it just doesn't make sense.

Eric looked concerned. If I had jumped into his lap and begged to be held he would have gasped, I'm sure, put me firmly back in my seat.

I need a new therapist.

It happens in every session. Twice a week the tears come up and I imagine myself a rock, a statue. Eric's moved the tissues closer to my chair, to tempt me, I guess. But I will not cry.

I dream about Yvonne. Our clothes mixed up together in big laundry bags. Yvonne and I swimming together. Eating together. Flying in small boats across elaborate sunsets. Yvonne in exotic veils and costumes, bent over windowsills. Only now it's *me* behind her. Sometimes she just holds me. Takes off my clothes and dresses me in colorful silk robes. She brushes my hair. Gives me a bath. Dabs Opium at my neck and wrists and armpits. I'm not unaware of the irony of *my* fear of calling out Yvonne's name in my sleep.

It was in a particularly bad session that I hit upon the idea of going *into* Yvonne's apartment. Eric was going on about investigating the self, the key to rooms you didn't know existed—something like that—and it just hit me.

But it was in my session this morning that I knew I would do it. Normally I'm a coward when it comes to things like that. I'm a sneak, but a coward. I don't like to take chances. I cringe at the thought of being caught.

She gave him her keys, Sarah had said. *I saw them. At the gallery.* She said she'd seen them together at Bar Pitti the week before or she wouldn't have thought anything. Sarah is Mark's friend, too, and as we plotted and planned, as she hesitated and apologized, tried to backpedal and reassure me, I think she felt nearly as bad as I did. Sometimes I wish she hadn't told me.

After my session I walked around Yvonne's block several times. I knew she was in class but I kept wondering what I would do if she or Mark showed up. I started laughing when I thought of that. I walked back to the Korean vegetable stand. The same woman was sitting at the counter, eating an ice cream. It seemed too cold for ice cream, too early. I bought a pack of tissues and smiled at her but she wasn't looking at me. She rubbed her fingers on a cut lemon and thumbed nine singles and change from my ten. Nine dollars could get me downtown in a cab before I did anything crazy. I walked to Yvonne's.

In the elevator my legs were shaking so much I thought I was going to faint. I got off on the fifth floor. 5C. C for cunt, I thought. I never use that word. It made me feel stronger. After that it was easy. I tried each key and found the right locks. I walked in the door and switched on the light. A woman's voice startled me and I froze until I heard the familiar beep of the answering machine.

"God, I'm really scared and you have to help me," I started to pray, but when I thought about God helping me break
into my husband's lover's apartment I started shaking again.

I sat on the couch. One of those futon couches with a
wooden frame. I wondered if this was where they fucked
until I saw beyond the telephone table to the bedroom. But
I wasn't ready.

I flipped through the papers on the table. It was just
some junk mail, but it reminded me of the time last year
when Eric left his office for a minute and I got out of my
chair and walked around, looked at the papers on his desk,
that picture of his wife and young boy. How anxious I'd
been.

Yvonne's place was neat. Not a pillow off its angle. A letter from India on the desk beside a silver letter opener, as if
she'd arranged it. I thought of her trying to arrange it all to
please Mark. There was no sign of him yet. I went into the
kitchen which was large enough for a refrigerator, oven, and
sink. Immaculate. Two bottles of Dos Equis in the refrigerator. Mark's favorite brand, but a lot of people like Dos
Equis. English muffins. Jam. And salad dressing. Paul
Newman.

There was a glass in the sink and I examined it for traces
of lipstick or mouthprints. I filled it with tap water and
drank three glasses. I was ready for the bedroom.

I knew it would be neat and beige. A picture of a man
that was not Mark sat on her bureau with a few pins and
bracelets scattered around. Maybe it was her father. A
brother. Not a hint of Mark. Not a T-shirt. It's hard with

men, no treacherous earrings to drop loose and give them away.

There wasn't a strand of hair on the bed. I sat on it. Bounced. The mattress was pretty firm and the box spring didn't squeak. I laid down on the pillow. I curled up and rocked and took in the scent. Opium. It might have been me.

I checked for mirrors. Just a modest wooden one above her bureau which didn't reflect the bed area as far as I could tell.

Gradually I went through every drawer. I wasn't looking for anything in particular—handcuffs or anything like that. Mark and I had already gone through that phase. I just wanted to see what she was like. I wasn't even particularly careful not to mess things too much. I tried on a string of pearls, wrapped a scarf around my shoulders. When I saw the bottle of Opium and dabbed it on my neck it reminded me of nothing more than sneaking into my mother's bedroom and dressing in her clothes. The only difference was that Yvonne was about my age and my husband's lover. And I was in her apartment.

After a while I wasn't even worried. When the phone rang I had an urge to answer it. The machine picked up. I prayed it wouldn't be Mark. I wanted it to be Mark. It was a hang-up.

The bathroom adjoining her bedroom was softly lit. A small makeup table was strewn with lipsticks and powders, the only sign of disorder in the apartment. The white wicker wastebasket was empty except for a few tissues and an empty bottle of contact lens solution. I sat at the mirror. I don't wear lipstick myself, more because I've never been able to figure out the right color than anything else. Also, it's uncomfortable. I picked a dark red. Scarlet Memory it was called. I still had on the pearls and green scarf over my black T-shirt and it was hard to look at myself in the mirror. I started to make faces. Little kissing movements. I widened my mouth the way I see women do all the time and drew a dark line of Yvonne's Scarlet Memory across my bottom lip. I pressed my lips together, then filled in the rest. The face looking back looked like my mother. I took a tissue and began to blot. I applied the lipstick again and blotted and blotted until there were several tissues covered with my lip prints. Then I threw them in the wastebasket. Right on top. Give her something to think about if she noticed. I have to laugh thinking about her blotting and trying to compare the lip shapes. Come to think of it I don't even know what kind of lips she has.

After I'd gone through her closets and drawers I was almost bored. I had an urge to call Eric and tell him where I was. To call Mark. I took another look through the medicine chest. There was a package of condoms on the top shelf. What a place for them. I'd checked the drawer beside her bed already. *That's* where they should be. Well, see what happens next time, sweetie, when they're not here. I put them in my bag.

It was time to go. I took the red plastic alarm clock by her bed, popped open the back panel, and emptied the battery out. I don't know why I did that. I put the pearls back but kept the scarf. It smelled of Opium, just like me.

On the platform for the Broadway local at 96th Street I began to feel chilled. I pulled the green scarf closer around my throat but when it hit me whose scarf it was I started shaking. I've always thought New York is the place to be if you are going to cry in public. Most people just ignore you. I mean they *look* at you, but no one approaches. I was weeping. First gently. Then I was sobbing. Violently. I was sobbing, doubled over by the edge of the platform, holding my stomach and saying things like "oh God, oh God" and hoping the train would come quickly so I could sit down. When I got myself quiet I tried to look down the tunnel for the lights, but I thought of Mark and Yvonne and I began to cry again. I leaned against a pillar and started looking for the pack of tissues I'd picked up at the Korean place. I never have things like tissues and tampons when I need them. I pulled a packet from my bag. The condoms. When I pictured myself wiping my face with a condom I almost laughed. But I was crying too hard.

A woman walked by me. She was stooped over and smelled awful. She pushed a broken cart with plastic bags bulging out of it. I thought she would say something. Something wise or meaningful, something that would help me know what to do next. She stopped. I thought for sure she would speak. Then she moved on. She needed a bath. *I* needed a bath. A long bath. And after that I'd clean up the apartment. Get some order. Then I'd be able to think. I'd stop and pick up some things we needed around the house. Toothpaste. Soap. Stock up. The thought of the drugstore near our apartment cheered me. Our drugstore. So familiar with its friendly cashier and fat old Mrs. Weisbaum who owns it.

I was cold. The train was coming. The front of it looking like the face of some ancient god. It's a funny thing, the subway. The way the tracks run under and through the city, connecting everything. Places. Lives. The way the trains run back and forth across the boroughs. Year after year. Over decades. Through wars and tragedies and terrible depressions. Carrying thousands, millions of bodies under the long snaky spines of Broadway, Lexington Avenue. Millions of lives. A long house connecting us all. Sometimes thinking like this makes me feel better. I was thinking about me and Mark and Yvonne. What connected us. What would happen to us. I knew the train would take me home. That I would have dinner with my husband. That our life together would be filled with hidden pockets of desire and mystery and possibility. That you can never really be certain of anything. I get these moments sometimes. I feel bigger than myself. Wise and rational and compassionate. And then I start to cry.

· 2 ·

You can tell a lot about a person by who their favorite Stooge is. It's significant. Mark and I both love Curly the best. Some people pick Larry and I can understand why. Larry's pretty funny, and he can take care of himself better than Curly can. Mark's brother David says Moe is his favorite. I would think a long time before getting involved with someone who said Moe was their favorite Stooge.

I was involved with Mark before I knew it. I met him at a dance party somewhere in Tribeca. I love to dance, to move from partner to partner. For hours. It was late. I'd been dancing with the same guy for a long time. We were at that point where your bodies anticipate one another. When you lean and twist and yield and turn and it's all perfectly timed. The man pressed against my hip, leading, turning. I was so hot my dress was sticking all the way down my back. When the dance was over I said I needed a drink and went over to Sarah.

"Girl, you can *dance,*" Sarah said.

I took her glass and held it to my neck.

"It's like sex," she said. Sarah hadn't had sex in a while. She was standing with a guy who turned out to be Mark's brother, David.

I laughed. "It's *better* than sex," I said.

"Who you been having sex with?"

I looked toward the voice. It was a thick voice, a rich voice. At first all I saw were his lips, which were large and almost startling in the way they curled in that smile. I remember thinking that they reminded me of the drawing of the Devil in my First Holy Communion prayerbook. His hair looked black in the dim light and his eyes were the color of his hair. He leaned against the wall, smiling. I couldn't say anything. That was Mark. That was it. I was hooked.

He could dance, too. But I found that out later.

Mark can dance, he can whip up an incredible late-night frittata, do fifty consecutive push-ups and a perfect imitation of Curly. *Nyuk-Nyuk-Nyuk* he says, snapping and wriggling his fingers the way Curly does. Sometimes when I get moody he sneaks up behind me and does his Curly until I laugh.

Mark's the only one I know who's read all seven volumes of Proust. He says that's why he's such a good lover. He is. Mark not only taught me to like sex, he made me crave it. I'd had lovers before him but I could barely name the parts of my body. Not the way lovers do.

"Where?" he'd ask, running a finger up my thigh.

"I don't know. You know. Down there."

"I want to make love to you all day long, and all night long, and through the night into the morning," he said once. Something like that. I was enthralled but the idea horrified me. I mean I couldn't imagine what we'd do after the first twenty minutes.

"I don't come," I said, to get it over with.

"Me either," he said. It's hard to catch Mark off guard.

Once, after we'd been together about a month, he called from a pay phone. "I'm downstairs," he said. "Take off your clothes, go into the bedroom, and wait for me. And Terry"—there was a long pause—"don't say a word when I come in." Poor Sarah had to run up and hide on the next landing, and spend the rest of the day at a friend's.

When I think about those times it seems as though we were in some kind of rolling erotic daze. Hours, *weeks* went by in his tiny West Village apartment. The two of us moving, whispering. On the bed, on the floor, on the table, in the shower. Mark would call, sometimes at three in the morning, and ask what I wanted. "Think about it all day," he'd say. Or "What do you think about when I'm not with you? When you're going to sleep?" He'd suggest something that sounded awful and after a few days I couldn't stop thinking about it. He taught me the French word for every significant part of my body and I'd never been with anyone who found more parts significant. Our talks were sexy and our books were sexy. Mark gave me Nietzsche. I gave him Baudelaire. He was painting then and the apartment reeked of oils and turp. Abstract landscapes leaned against the walls. Tacked to a bulletin board was a photo of him and an old girlfriend—Isabelle—in front of the Sorbonne where he'd gotten his degree in art history and philosophy. *Whatever is done for love always occurs beyond good and evil* above it in big block letters. Mark had quotes from Nietzsche posted all through his apartment.

Sarah, it turned out, started seeing Mark's brother, David, a few months later. It was before she realized she was actually more into women than men, but they weren't such a great match anyway. Sarah said David could spend an entire night narrating interminable synopses of movies she'd never heard of. And he says *film* instead of *movie*, which she thinks is pretentious. They just didn't click.

Mark and I did, though. I expected it to cool down. But even after we got married—five years ago—things stayed pretty hot. Maybe it's the Proust. Mark says he learned everything from Proust, that it's because of Proust he'd know immediately if his lover were having an affair. Well, he could have saved a lot of time. All he'd need is someone to tell him.

Sarah says I have to stop thinking about it, but what I can't understand is *why*. Does he love Yvonne? Does he think about her when he's with me? Does he think about me when he's with her? Does she know things about me? I can't stand the thought of him touching her. Talking to her the way he talks to me. I wonder if she's as eager a student. So willing to be conquered. So quick to catch on.

"I can't believe you let me do that," Mark said once. I was on the floor, "coming to." He held me, kissed my shoulder. "It's incredible," he said, "how you're changing. You'll do anything."

"You *asked* me to," I said, suddenly embarrassed.

"You *could* have said no."

It never occurred to me to say no to Mark. I was deeply in love or deeply charmed. Something.

"Do you think I shouldn't have done that?"

He straddled my hips and began to tickle me. "There's nothing more impossible than an Italian Catholic," he said.

Now he acts like things are just fine. Yesterday I bought a tube of Scarlet Memory and wore it to dinner.

"Do you think I should wear lipstick?" I asked him.

He frowned. "It doesn't look like you, Treas."

Who *does* it look like, I wanted to ask. So much for memory.

He was spooning spinach onto his plate.

"Do you still love me?" I asked.

"With or without the lipstick?" He tore a piece of bread off the loaf, then looked up at me. "Come here." He reached over and pulled me onto his lap. "Of course I love you." He kissed me. "What's going on? *Treas*, come on. What's up?"

"Oh, I don't know. I'm premenstrual, I guess."

"You just had your period last week."

When I was a kid I had a game called Fascination. Two plastic mazes with steel balls at the bottom and notches at the top. The boards were attached by a wire. At the word "Go" both players would begin to work their board, trying to get the balls through the maze, into the notches. When one of the players worked all three balls up a green light lit their board. The trouble was, if you started one of your balls down a dead end it was almost impossible to change course without knocking out your other balls. You had to maneuver the board very carefully. I played this game endlessly with my sisters. It sometimes seems to me marriage is a lot like that. And I'd just lost one of my balls.

Last night I dreamed of the Korean woman. She was at the bottom of three long sets of rickety stairs that led into a cavern that was also a beach. She stood in a line of identical women wearing white diaphanous dresses. She was waving those silver serving tongs, carrying Yvonne's red plastic alarm clock.

"Who is the Korean woman?" Eric asked.

I don't know why I mentioned the dream. I wasn't ready to tell him about going to Yvonne's. Usually I don't hold back. I spill everything. Sometimes even to strangers. Once I told a woman interviewing me for a teaching job that I first realized I was in love with Mark while he had me handcuffed to the headboard. I don't remember how it came up. I was surprised myself that I still hadn't told anyone about Yvonne's apartment. Not even Sarah.

"I don't know," I said.

"Who does she remind you of?"

"Maybe one of those huge weddings in Korea. You know. When thousands of Moonies marry strangers in one big ceremony." I had to say something. Sometimes I think about how much money I waste taking Eric down the wrong paths.

"Do you think you married a stranger, Theresa?"

Two years ago when I started seeing Eric I introduced myself as Theresa. I don't know why. To sound more mature, I guess. No one calls me Theresa, not even my mother. Mark calls me Treas or Terry. Tree when he's really excited. I keep wanting to tell Eric to call me Terry but I feel stupid after two years. Every session I have to remember to sign the right name on my check.

"Who's your favorite Stooge," I asked.

Sometimes when Eric looks at me I can feel his eyes moving over my face, inch by inch, like a fly crawling across a table looking for crumbs.

"Excuse me?"

"Moe, Larry, or Curly?"

"Theresa . . ."

"Why can't you just answer me?"

Eric looked at the clock.

"God*dammit* why do you keep looking at the clock? Am I boring you?"

"Who are you angry at?" Eric stared at me over those praying hands which were pressed, as usual, against his lips. Like he was afraid he would say too much.

I put my feet up on the chair. I couldn't see the clock but I guessed we had about another half hour. Water was running in the next apartment. A phone rang. Eric's shoe tapped the rug. He has three pairs of the same exact shoe. Black, brown, and oxblood. Loafers with these little fringy tassels. There's not a whole lot to look at in his office. A plant. A blue couch. Three blue pillows on the couch, always in the same configuration. My last therapist had paintings all over and tiny animal statuettes. The guy I'd interviewed before Eric had a room full of heads. All kinds of heads. When I made a joke about it he didn't even crack

a smile. I thanked him and left in the middle of the inter-
view.

"Maybe I should just go," I said. I think there should be
some kind of therapy where you curl up in the therapist's
lap for fifty minutes and get held.

"Do you want to lie on the couch?"

"Could you shut the light?"

He shut the light. I lay on the couch. It was softer than
it looked and soon I was feeling calmer and a little tired.
Neither of us said anything for a long time. Eric's comfortable with silence, that's how he puts it. There are many
kinds of silence, he said once. A lot can happen in silence,
he said. But it all feels the same to me.

"Does your clock glow in the dark?" I asked finally.

Eric didn't say anything. I wondered what kind of silence
he thought this was.

"I'm scared," I said, after a long time.

"What are you afraid of?"

"I don't know," I said.

"Do you remember why you started seeing me?" he asked
all of a sudden.

Cello music was coming from somewhere in the building.

"No," I said. The cello had a lonely, mournful sound.

Mark had gone to the Venice Biennale and I'd spent two
weeks alone, hardly sleeping at all. I was nervous and jittery,
convinced someone would try to break into the loft, convinced Mark wouldn't come home. I'd finally started staying with Sarah. I've never lived alone and didn't realize until

then that I'd hardly ever slept without someone else in the room. Even when I was a kid I'd always shared a room with my sisters.

"I feel so alone," I said. "I feel so alone."

"That's good," he said.

"That's good?"

"It's a start," he said, "but I'm afraid we have to end."

This morning I called NYU and canceled my class. The second one this week. I couldn't get out of bed. I couldn't think of standing in front of thirty students discussing the concept of irony and hyperbole in Marvell. I'm as far away from irony as I can get. I keep wanting to go uptown to Yvonne's but I can't leave the loft. I've just been lying here listening to Maria Callas's Mad Scenes and thinking about Yvonne.

That's her, Sarah had said that night at the opening. She pointed across the room, through the crowd, and I saw Yvonne. Laughing. Smiling up at Mark. I saw her casually hold his arm as she bent to fix her shoe. I saw Mark laugh and bop her over the head with a rolled stack of flyers. I saw that. The way she looked at him. And I keep seeing it.

It's cold in here. Lofts are always cold. Yesterday afternoon I made two bowls of pastina and sat and watched the video-tape of Olympic figure skaters I made a few years ago. I kept fast-forwarding through the commercials and slalom to Victor Petrenko. He was skating to Chubby Checker's "Twist Again," a song I used to dance to with my mother. He did three triple axels and a triple toe loop. Every once in a while

I got up and danced with him. Moving around cheered me up a bit. Got me a little warmer. But mostly I just watched. When he leaves the stage after his encore, my favorite part comes on: Klimova and Ponomarenko ice-dancing to what the announcer calls Bach's *Sacred and Profane Love*. I think I've watched it a hundred times. I still can't believe the timer screwed up. Somehow the recorder stopped and cut the dance three-quarters of the way through. After hours wasted on skiing and hockey and slalom. At the most important part. I mean some things just shouldn't end. Moments of music. It's almost excruciating to feel them break off. It keeps you hanging out there, waiting. And the two bodies moving together, never breaking contact, falling and turning grace-fully, passionately, over and around one another. I've watched it so many times I know the exact moment when the sound will stop, the bodies disappear, and the screen go black with that white snow shaking all over it. And then the bald black-and-white head of Isaac Bashevis Singer comes on, its mouth moving but no sound for a few seconds. "You read the story. You get the meaning," is the first thing he says. Then "You must believe in free will. You have no choice." I kept play-ing his head backward and forward as though he would tell me something important. As if there would be a special meaning in what he was saying. Then I'd rewind to the skaters. I watched them all afternoon.

Mark wasn't at the gallery. He said he was meeting a client for an early dinner. I called Yvonne's. I didn't expect him to be there, I guess I just wanted to connect with Yvonne. To hear her voice. To see if she screened her calls or answered breathlessly, hoping it would be Mark. If she would pick up quickly, being lonely and wanting to talk.

I found her number in Mark's Rolodex. There it was, ordinary and plain. In Mark's tight handwriting. Yvonne Adams. Not coded or written lightly in pencil.

"Hi. This is five-five-five six-two-three-two. Please leave a message." She sounded like a robot. She has one of those machines where the beep lasts forever and fades into a couple of short beeps depending upon how many calls have come in. There was only one short beep. I called three times but left no message. I imagined her on the other side of the machine, barefoot in her neat apartment. Eating salad out of a plastic container. Perhaps my husband was beside her.

I made another bowl of pastina. It's the only thing I can eat now. I've lost three pounds this week which is just about the only cheerful thing I can think of.

My cats circle me and lie in my lap the whole time I'm home. They know when I'm sad. Maybe it's the Maria Callas. I was thinking about Medea. How she killed her two children when she learned Jason was having an affair. I thought of Mark coming in to find Tony and Chico dead in a cloth sack. There's no way I could do anything like that. I love Tony and Chico. But I wonder how long Medea knew about the affair before she hit that pitch of passion.

I called Sarah. I always call Sarah when I'm upset. She's the kind of person who'll listen to you worry and complain for hours, then take you out and buy you a lace bra she really can't afford, and never get annoyed if you end up not taking her advice. Sarah's always saying things like "Life hands you the comb after you've gone bald."

"Why don't you try saying the Serenity Prayer," she said after I told her about Medea. Sarah had started going to Al-Anon meetings when she decided her lover was an alcoholic. Karen, it turns out, was not an alcoholic, and they split up soon after, but by that time Sarah had met another woman at the meetings and was in hot pursuit.

She read me the prayer. "Just ignore the God stuff," she said. "It's really helpful."

Asking a Catholic to ignore God is like telling a thief you left your door unlocked. But Sarah is Jewish. Jews can ignore God. Mark can.

I wrote the prayer down. *God, grant me the serenity to accept the things I cannot change, the courage to change the things I can, and the wisdom to know the difference.* It's no poem, but the rhythm's nice. I tried saying it. Kept the paper in my pocket. Personally I like Catholic prayers a lot better. *Precious Blood of Jesus, Devoted Mother of the Holy Womb, Strength of Martyrs, Wash me of guilt, Cleanse me of sin.* Now those are prayers.

Anyway, Sarah convinced me to go to a meeting. "Keep the focus on yourself," she said. She can pick up lingo in a minute.

I went to Al-Anon. I went after my session on Friday. I still haven't told Eric about going to Yvonne's but I did say it had been hard to leave the house.

"Make yourself go out," he said. "Make plans."

Sarah took a long lunch and brought me to a meeting called Midday Keeping Faith at St. Barnabas Church midtown, not too far from the *Elle* offices where she works. The basement was dingy and crowded and filled with aluminum folding chairs and bright posters. I was terrified I'd see someone I knew. Sarah was afraid she wouldn't. People—it was mostly women—kept smiling at us.

"I've got to run back right after," Sarah whispered. She was bent over an article she was editing on contemporary women sculptors. "I'm on deadline." I knew she was doing this for me, so I tried to seem enthusiastic.

The leader was reading what she called Steps. Latecomers were finding seats. Everyone looked kind of rueful and pathetic.

"Some meetings are better than others," Sarah said. "Don't get turned off too soon."

Actually it was the first time I'd felt like laughing in days.

The leader was asking if there were any newcomers. Sarah poked me. I stuck my hand halfway up.

"Hi, I'm Linda and I'm co-dependent," said a plump woman in an awful pink dress.

"Hi, I'm Sandy and I'm in recovery," said another.

One after another. It was getting closer to me.

"Hi," I said, trying to sound upbeat, "I'm Terry"—I hadn't thought of what I'd say—"and I'm just visiting." No one laughed. Sarah just shook her head. I guess it wasn't really funny.

One story was worse than another. The plump woman, Linda, stood up and started to cry. Her husband had hit her, she said. Last night. She knew it was the liquor and not him, but he'd *hit* her. He'd come in late and drunk and he'd *hit* her. She was rubbing her little hands up and down the awful pink dress that stretched tight around her hips. I couldn't help thinking that if I were her husband I'd have hit her, too. Anything to get her to stop whining.

"And the worst thing is," she said, "I was so upset I had a glass of wine."

"Well, you *needed* a drink," I said. I stood up, inclining myself toward her. "Don't be so hard on yourself."

Sarah yanked me down.

"No crosstalk. No crosstalk," someone shouted.

"That's not going to help."

"Ssh."

"*Please* don't offer advice."

"That's our problem, everyone's always trying to fix fix fix."

"Let's get out of here," I whispered.

We had to climb over all the women and pocketbooks and folding chairs. Sarah murmured apologies all the way down the row.

"Look," the leader was saying, "you can't buy oranges in a hardware store."

Sarah kissed me and ran back to work and I walked all the way downtown to Little Italy. I stopped in the old St. Patrick's Church on Mott Street to light a candle. I was glad they still had real ones and not the electric kind a lot of churches have now. A youngish priest was shuffling papers by the altar. He smiled.

And I wondered who his favorite Stooge was.

· 3 ·

"Are you there? Are you asleep?" My mother's voice. "Sorry to call so early."

"Disaster," Mark said, shaking me. Grieving Gloria, he calls her. And sometimes Gorgeous Gloria. *Gawjis*, he says, the way she does.

"What *time* is it?" I stood over the machine watching the tape turn, listening to my mother stall. It was seven o'clock Saturday morning. I'd been wanting to talk to her, which is unusual.

"Mom?"

"Aunt Anita died last night," she said. I yanked Mark's T-shirt from under Chico and tried to pull it over my head and the phone receiver. I got a flash of Anita's doughy arms. The pincurls she kept in all day. She had just begun to have that old woman smell.

"Ma, I'm sorry," I said. Anita is her oldest sister.

I covered the receiver and mouthed the news to Mark.

"The wake is Monday and the funeral right away Tuesday," she continued. "I have to arrange everything today. Of course it's all left up to me." Mark pulled me against his chest and rubbed my neck and shoulders. "You and Mark can spend Monday night out here. So you won't have the trip."

Out here is Brooklyn.

"It's okay, Mom. It's a quick cab ride." I can get to Flatbush by subway in under an hour, but I rarely visit except for Christmas and Easter.

I'd miss class. My session on Tuesday. And I'd been planning to go to Yvonne's.

"The girls'll be here. But Carla says she won't come to the wake."

Though they're thirty-three, my mother still refers to my twin sisters as "the girls." At least she stopped calling them "the twins."

"Well, you know how upset she gets."

"It's her aunt."

My mother has an idea of how things should be and she spends her time arranging the way other people will be made to see how she's right. But I went home without Mark. The deaths of older aunts is the kind of thing we're both allowed to skip.

Deep in Brooklyn I always feel like I'm starting to disappear. The way you almost forget you have a life when you visit your parents. The place you were born. The voice you changed. Most of what I remember from the neighborhood is gone. Key Food. Stride Rite. The Granada theater. I went out of my way to walk past Holy Cross, my old grammar school. Several West Indian workmen were ripping out the convent. I guess all the old nuns are dead, but I kept expecting Sister Dominica, my third-grade nun, to rush out of the wrecked shell, shrieking and pulling my hair. "Theresa

Spera," she said once, in her thick, Irish brogue, "you're the Devil's own child." It was Halloween. Everyone in our school had to dress up as their name saint, which was confusing as there are two St. Theresas—the visionary mystic and the humble drudge. I wore a long brown robe, belted with one of my mother's curtain tassels. I held rosary beads and was supposed to carry a broom to symbolize St. Theresa cleaning out her Interior Castle. Spiritual Housecleaning, Sister Dominica called it. In this way, she said, I could be like both St. Theresas. The thing was, I didn't want to carry the kitchen broom all the way from home, so I just stuck some Ajax and a sponge in my schoolbag and used that. When Sister Dominica saw the Ajax, she started pulling my hair saying that stuff about being the Devil's own child. She said I needed to do some very serious Spiritual Housecleaning. I ended up having to carry this big dirty pushbroom the janitor let us use. It was a terrible place that school, and yet I feel kind of nostalgic for it. For believing in things. In some kind of order.

I was almost glad to be home. It was the first time I needed to see my mother in years. To talk to her. I followed her around all day trying to lead into it, but the shifting arrivals and departures of relatives at the funeral parlor made it impossible to talk. I called Eric from a pay phone by the bathrooms to arrange a phone session for later that night.

"So, you're wearing lipstick," my mother said, when we were finally back at the house.

We were sitting in the living room which she has recently redecorated into what Mark calls postmodern pandemonium. A piece out of every period. Eighteenth-century lavabos and colonial pewter mugs, sky-blue ceramic ducks deployed around an imitation fireplace bricked up with Con-Tact paper. She works for a small interior decoration store on Flatbush Avenue. I imagine her erecting setting after setting in which nothing will ever happen.

"Yeah," I said. I waited to see if she liked it. I still wasn't sure of the color. "A friend of mine wears this color. Yvonne." I liked saying her name in my mother's house.

An arc of straight pins stuck out of her mouth like some kind of medieval torture implement. She was raising the hem of her funeral skirt, filling me in on the details of Anita's death. Once my sisters arrived I knew I'd hear it again.

"I just can't figure it out," she said through the pins, picking up a thread of an earlier conversation. Talk in our family has always been like this. Long arcs that cross but rarely connect. She'd been alluding to some mystery ever since I arrived but she hadn't elaborated. I guess she was waiting for the right setting. She picked the pins from her mouth one by one and stuck them in a tomato-shaped pincushion.

A scratchy recording of Renata Tebaldi singing "Un bel di' vedremo" blasted from the kitchen. *Madame Butterfly*, my father's favorite opera. I must have heard it hundreds of times while I was growing up. Last Christmas I bought him the Maria Callas version but I don't think he's ever played it. I think he thinks it would be disloyal. My father's voice blended with Tebaldi's. My mother smiled and shook her head. "Your father," she said, and I could see how much she loved him. That familiar kind of love. Married love.

"Ma, what about Aunt Anita."

The gist of it was that Anita died holding an envelope of old photographs. No one knows who the man is, squinting and grinning out of a series of blurry landscapes.

"It's a mystery," my mother said. She broke the thread with her teeth. "This one looks like Coney Island." She handed me the snapshots.

They were mostly black and white. And sticky. The one I liked best was torn and had bits of what looked like chocolate stuck to the corner: an angular-faced man with a slight sneer and sex in his eyes. An unusual choice for any of the sisters, especially Anita. The kind you couldn't hold on to for too long. Definitely an improvement on my Uncle Tony who died last year.

Anita was a sweet, placid woman. Unevolved you might say—like a giant amoeba, vague and shapeless in her flowered housedress. It struck me how there can be this big mystery at the center of the most ordinary life.

Renata Tebaldi hit that high, heartbreaking note at the end of the aria—that terrible mixture of hope and hopelessness. My father hit it with her.

"Ma, do you think Daddy ever had an affair?"

She laughed. She turned to the sewing drawer and replaced the pincushion, shoving the drawer in and out to jam it closed. While her back was turned I took one of the photographs.

"Your *father*?"

I have to admit the idea of my father having an affair is ludicrous at best. The most passion I've ever seen my father display was when I was eight and he caught me playing his *Madame Butterfly* record, shifting the speed up to make Carlo Bergonzi sound like a woman, and slowing it down to make Renata Tebaldi sound like a man. It was the only time he ever hit me.

The aria ended. My father lifted the needle and set it down and it began all over again.

"Ma," I said, "I wanted . . ."

The phone rang.

"Could you get that, honey. I don't feel like talking. I don't think I can tell the story one more time."

I picked up the phone. *Aunt Mary*, I mouthed to my mother. She motioned to me to hand her the receiver.

"*Ma*ry," she said, in the woeful voice she uses on sad occasions. "Another sad day."

It was the first time I'd slept at my mother's since I moved out. I was in the guest room, which was crammed with knickknacks and stenciled wallpaper and furnished with odd pieces from the bedroom I'd shared with my sisters in our old apartment. The streetlight threw a knife shape across the "antiqued" bureau. The top two drawers had been mine. When I was twelve my mother had gone through those drawers and discovered my diary. I forgot what she found in there, but I remember being dragged into the kitchen by my ponytail, then not allowed out after school for two weeks.

My mother was like that. There wasn't a drawer she wouldn't open. A place she couldn't reach. "I can read you like a book," she used to say. *Now* I know that all mothers say things like that. Thing is, I believed her. "People who live in glass houses," she'd say, eyeing me suspiciously, and I'd feel as transparent as one of her Jell-O molds—the gray, wrinkling grapes and miniature marshmallows bloating under the tough skin.

It was three o'clock. It occurred to me that my being away gave Mark and Yvonne a chance to spend the night. I dialed Yvonne. I knew her number by heart.

Most people, even if they have machines, jump to answer their phone if it rings at 3:00 A.M.

"Hello?" She sounded alarmed. "Hel*lo?*" I wanted her to say *Mark?* or *Fuck off*, or something emphatic. She just said *hello* again and then hung up. I dialed again but she didn't pick up.

I dialed Mark.

"Terry? Jesus. What time is it?"

"Three."

"Are you okay?"

I couldn't talk.

"Honey, what's the matter? You fight with your mother?"

"I want to come home," I said. I tried to quiet down but I was breathing hard.

"Treas, calm down. Tell me what happened."

The ruffled comforter stuck to my legs. I kicked it off.

"My mother found these photographs," I said. I started to tell him the whole story.

"Honey, hang on a second, okay?" I knew he was going for a glass of water. Mark always wakes up with a dry mouth. "Now talk to me," he said when he came back.

"They were pictures of this guy nobody knows," I said. "He looks a little like you." I wrapped the cord around my foot. "Do you really love me?"

"Terry, you know I love you."

"Remember you used to call me like this in the morning?"

"Honey, call a car service and come home," he said. "I'll take care of you."

"I can't," I said.

"Lie down," he said. "Are you lying down?"

"Yeah."

"What are you wearing?"

"Nothing," I said.

"Good," he said. "Pull down the blankets."

"They're down," I said.

"Okay. Now imagine I'm lying on top of you."

I'm still amazed at how easily he turns me on.

"Can you feel me?"

"No."

"Well, then I guess I have to get a little rough," he said and waited. "Now, I'll ask you again. Can you feel me?"

"Uh-huh."

"What am I doing?"

"You're licking my neck," I said. "Your hands are on my ass."

"One hand," he said. "The other is inside you. Can you feel me? Tree?"

I flashed on Yvonne. I felt guilty. Like I was having an affair with my own husband.

"Yeah," I said.

"You feel pretty wet."

"Yeah."

"That's good," he said.

"I wish you were here."

"Treas, do you really want me to come?"

"No," I said. "Just make *me* come."

He whispered and talked me into it while I rubbed my finger inside myself and softly over my clit. His voice still had some sleep in it. I could imagine his hands, his long fingers, the callus inside the left knuckle. I could feel his weight on top of me. By 3:45 I was calm and ready to sleep.

My sisters were at the kitchen table when I woke up. They'd come in late the night before. Both of them worked double waitress shifts and couldn't get off. Actually, Carla had lied. She's always hated wakes. The dead body lying there as though it were just sleeping. I kissed them both.

"Hey stranger," Carla said. "How's your gorgeous husband?"

She pronounced it the way my mother does. *Gawjis.* Sometimes it hits me that if I hadn't worked so hard to change my voice I would sound just like them.

"Gorgeous," I said. I looked for some regular coffee. It was useless. My mother only uses instant. I'd have to get take-out on the way to the funeral parlor.

Carla lit a cigarette.

"Isn't it a little early," I asked. I fanned away the smoke. I stopped smoking six years ago when I read an article in the *Times* that associated smoking with the undereducated.

Carla inhaled deeply and continued flipping through the *News*.

"Bad dreams?" Lisa asked.

We have five sets of twins in our family. In no pair do both have the same disposition. Lisa and Carla look almost exactly alike, but as flip and distant as Carla is, Lisa is gentle, loving. You can hear the difference in her voice. Lisa rubbed my shoulder. "I heard you moaning when I went by the guest room."

"Must be the ghosts of our childhood coming up," I said.

"Christ," Carla said, "with the crowd that'll be here later, there won't be room for all *those* ghosts."

"See Gloria yet?" I asked.

Carla raised her eyebrows. Each of us has taken acting classes at one time or another and we've all capitalized on our mother. Carla has her down the best. She struck a pose.

"As usual," she whined in Gloria's unmistakable voice, "everything's been left up to me."

"Another sad day," Lisa choked out, but was laughing too hard to continue. She put her arms around me.

Sometimes I think the three of us could have been a lot closer if it hadn't been for our mother. Infiltrating. Instigating. She has a genius for setting one person against another and her three daughters have given her a large playing area.

Though I'm two years older, people always mistook us for

triplets. Until I was ten we wore identical clothes. I think it was my mother's way of making me feel included. Actually, it was the time of mother-daughter dresses and we have photographs of the four of us dressed in the same orange print skirt and white blouse.

"Don't feel bad, honey," my mother said one time, "I'll be your twin." She had come into the bedroom after my sisters and I had been fighting. I was crying because whenever we played Patty Duke, Lisa and Carla got to play Patty and Kathy, and I always had to play Richard or Poppo. Everyone said that it made sense that they should play the twins since they *were* twins, but I didn't think it was fair. My mother laid on top of me. She held me and kissed me. Her perfume had a dark smell that rubbed off on my arms. "You're just like *me*," she said.

In our family I was special, my mother said, because I was not a twin. I was just myself. Unique. But there are so many sets of twins in our family that I've always had the vague suspicion that I'm half of a set. That my twin sister died early in the pregnancy but was carried to term. Stillborn. That I'd lain for months curled around my dead twin.

My mother had this book on twins someone gave her. I don't think she ever opened it, but one summer I read just about all of it. I read that at least one in eight pregnancies begins as twins, that the only sign of the vanishing twin is a little bleeding. I remember how shocked I was to see something in print that corroborated what I'd felt for so long. That I was only half of something.

I discovered all sorts of freakish facts—that some of us are actually twins walking around in a single body, that one twin had just absorbed the other, just merged in the womb. That was called a chimera. You can tell because there are people who actually have two different blood types. (I checked. I have only one.) The book had captions and illustrations that characterized twin pregnancies as these intense intrauterine battles for space and food. It said that sometimes only the stronger twin survives and is often plagued by lifelong feelings of terrible guilt.

Well, I can definitely relate to that.

The three of us went into the guest room to dress. Carla was still clowning and mimicking our mother. She went into the dresser behind a room divider I made twenty years ago out of balsa wood and rice paper. She came out in an embroidered denim mini-skirt and batiked halter I wore in my brief stint as lead singer in a neighborhood rock-and-roll band. For a minute I could see myself in her—exactly the way I had been. Under the strobe lights. Clutching the mike.

Lisa picked up a hairbrush and hiked up her robe. I put some beads over my black slip, knotted Yvonne's scarf around my head, and grabbed a perfume bottle. Carla stood on the bed. Without a word the three of us went into "Piece of My Heart," dancing and bending. Jerking back and forth into our mikes.

I took the lead, just like I used to. "*I said come on, come on, come on, come on,*" Carla leapt from the bed, "*and take it,*" the three of us screamed, "*Take another little piece of my heart now, baby.*" We fell into one another laughing.

"*What* is going on in here?" Our mother stood at the door.

We couldn't stop laughing.

"What is wrong with you? What in *God's* name can you be thinking of?"

"Sorry, Ma," I said. I pulled Yvonne's scarf off my head. I was still laughing.

"We're leaving at nine," she said and walked out.

We dressed in silence. Every once in a while one of us started to laugh. I stuck Tristan—that's what I named the man in the photographs—face to my stomach, just above the crotch of my pantyhose. I wore emerald stockings and a black velvet skirt. Death is one of the most exotic things that happens in our family and we've always dressed for it.

We've been through this a lot. The morning of the funeral the family sits alone with their corpse in the funeral parlor until it's time to go to church. Then one of the McFeeley brothers (we always go to McFeeley's) comes over and discreetly closes the coffin lid, a white handkerchief in his hand.

Anita looked scared, all alone in her box. I tried to pray for her but I was thinking about Yvonne, wishing it were Yvonne lying in that box. As soon as I thought that I said a little prayer to counteract it—but I can't help the way I feel.

My mother slid in beside me. She has a way of entering a room so quietly everyone takes notice. People have always said I take after her, but no one had ever looked at me the way they looked at her. Even my boyfriends used to fall for her. Once I heard our next-door neighbor say she could make a dead man come. I didn't understand it at the time, but I did know she could make just about anyone do just about anything. They'd even think it was their own idea.

She smiled at Jimmy McFeeley. An overweight, balding funeral director. My mother can't look at a man without trying to seduce him. She drove my father nuts—his words—but he was crazy about her. His words again. It's hard to imagine my father nuts *or* crazy. When I think of him, he's hunched over a broken toilet or kneeling beside a bathtub screwing in a copper pipe, singing an aria. My father's a plumber. We used to joke that he fixed things so they worked and my mother made them look good when they didn't.

Even as a kid I knew they were mismatched. Most kids can't picture their parents having sex. I couldn't stop. Even now I see him rolling, groping, and imprecise. Gloria trying to keep her hair neat and fixing their clothes when they took them off. Her pile. His pile. It'd make it easier in the morning. It's so awful it's almost beautiful.

She was whispering to Father Finnegan, tilting her head. A wide smile. Too wide for the occasion. She realizes it, tilts it down, frowns. The wistful, funeral smile. He follows like a pilgrim being led to heaven, his eyes resting just above the line of her V-neck. She really could have *been* something. An army recruiter or automobile dealer, a politician.

She turned to me and pushed the hair out of my eyes, the way she's always done. "You look so nice when you get dressed up," she said. She rearranged Yvonne's green scarf around my neck. My mother is big on improvement. "Don't just sit there," she used to say, "you could be doing your stomach pulls, pushing your teeth in." Dentists find it hard to believe now, but we closed a half-inch gap in my front teeth. Ten-second press three times a day. I kind of miss it. The gap I mean. The way my tongue rested in there when I was just thinking.

"Ma, do you think we could talk later?"

"Why don't you stay over tonight," she said. "Then it won't be so busy."

But I knew I wouldn't. I wouldn't even know what to say. What to ask.

Anita looked so sorry in her box, so alone. Like Yvonne, eating salad in that immaculate apartment and dreaming of Mark. I liked the idea of Anita and Tristan. That there had been someone she'd loved deeply, passionately. That she'd saved things up to tell. Felt his touch when he wasn't there. Waited for him, lost him, then carried him around inside her all these years. Like St. Theresa and St. Lucy she'd lived for something bigger. Moved toward the light no matter what was in front of her face. All those years with Uncle Tony and she'd been living for something else. For herself. Fifty-eight years of interminable barbecues, christenings, Irish Nights, and she'd been there with Tristan. Tristan by the watercooler, baptism font, Tristan by Sears Automotive at the mall. Touching her, tugging her hair the way he did, his mouth on her. Anywhere she wanted it. He knew. She didn't have to figure it out for him. She'd lived for something. I felt relieved. I wished I'd met him. That she'd died calling his name. That he'd show up for the funeral. Soon. Before Jimmy McFeeley shut the box. So he could see her creamed and powdered, puffy but still smooth. A fifty-eight-year fierce and faithful receptacle for his love. It gave me some kind of hope. Made me think you could escape anything, you just had to live for something big enough.

Jimmy McFeeley was fumbling with his handkerchief. My mother was flirting with Father Finnegan, and I was thinking about Yvonne. Yvonne in the coffin with Mark, fucking on top of the rosary beads and prayer cards, behind the condolence arrangements and flower stands, before the entire roomful of aunts and uncles and cousins. Yvonne rolling in a flowered housedress, Mark's mouth on her neck, arm beneath her waist, raising her up onto the red velvet pillow.

"Terry. *Theresa*." My mother has a way of whispering that's like onions hissing on a high flame.

"What?"

"Do you want to go up there one more time?"

I shook my head.

"Are you okay?" Lisa whispered.

"No," I said. "No, I'm not okay."

Then I remembered I'd forgotten to call Eric for my phone session.

· 4 ·

My mother says my first sentence was *I broke it*. I was eighteen months old. I think I've always had a very special relationship to guilt. It's familiar. If someone rushes into a room and announces their car's been stolen I start to sweat. I feel an urge to shout *I didn't do it*. I don't even drive. Last night I heard the word "affair" on TV. The word reverberated inside me sending little shocks up and down my spine. *Affair affair affair* I kept repeating, until the word split apart, fragmented into soft little pieces. Puffs of breath. Then I thought about Mark and Yvonne and it slammed back together.

Affair. The word conjures visions of my parents at a dinner dance. Everyone dressed up. Their children at home with babysitters. It's something you do when you're married. Single people do not go to affairs. And they do not have affairs. They have relationships. If you're married and involved with someone else you don't say I'm in a relationship, you say I'm having an affair. Usually you don't say anything at all.

I'm thirty-five and married and I've never been to anything I'd call an affair. And I've never had an affair. I've never had a relationship *or* an affair with a student. I mean it's just not something I would ever do. Not that I haven't been tempted. Fantasized. I mean I've had affairs with

ABOUT Y V O N N E

whole classes in that way you tease and seduce students into their best work. That power you feel as they laugh together, stay after class for advice, learn to love a difficult writer. Because you do. From time to time they bring in little gifts: a poem, a tape of music they thought you'd like. Brian did that yesterday. A tape he made of old Irish ballads. I've been playing it all day.

I love Irish music. The sadness. That plaintive, wistful knowledge of loss. Voices naked and unmoored. Suffering without any note of bravado. My father always played Puccini. That's the kind of suffering we listened to: passionate and operatic. Italian suffering. Blasting out of the living room, through the apartment, throughout my childhood. I love Puccini, but these voices leave you room for your own sorrow. There's no big fat star taking up all the emotional space. I've been playing the last song for the past half hour. "The Cliffs of Dooneen."

"I made this for you, Terry," Brian said yesterday. He's from Ireland—only been here eight months. He's got a voice just like the singer on the tape. Tender. "Terry," he said. He's been in my class all semester, but it's funny the way you can feel when someone says your name for the first time. And now I've been walking around all day, his tape in my Walkman, his music filling me up, and it feels like I've always known him.

I feel so connected to him that it's hard to believe I hadn't much noticed Brian before last week. He's quiet in class. Now that I think of it, he has a way of listening I'd been vaguely aware of. You can feel him taking you in.

What with a couple of sick days and Anita's funeral I'd missed several classes and was trying to make it up with an especially rigorous lecture on prosody. I discussed the different ways to enter a poem. Easing in with a loose iambic. Or opening with an attack. A hard stress on the first syllable. I can always come up with the perfect illustration on the spot. It's one of my strong points.

"*Others*," I began, stressing the trochee, "*because you did not keep / that deep sworn vow have been friends of mine / yet always . . .*"

The poem caught inside me. Out the window the traffic on Broadway whizzed by. Horns, sirens, a bus shooting out its exhaust. The falafel vendor wheeled his cart to the corner. Somewhere uptown my husband was sleeping with a woman who taught classes not very different from mine. My throat closed and my eyes went blurry. Damn if I hadn't picked Yeats. Tiny pieces of plaster were falling from the old ceiling onto the desk in front of me. The class had gotten really quiet.

"*Yet always . . .*"

I tried to continue. I knew the class thought I'd forgotten the line. I think they did, anyway. After all I've said about it being impossible to forget a line of Yeats. Not a word out of place, not a syllable. I was leaning forward onto the desk. Big tears were dropping onto the *Norton Anthology of Modern Poetry*, making a little puddle on the cover. I don't think they could see I was crying because my hair is thick and was falling forward over my face.

"*Yet always when I look death in the face, / When I clamber to the heights of sleep, / Or when I grow excited with wine, / Suddenly I meet your face.*"

It sounded like the voice of an angel. A soft Irish voice. Gentle. I was looking down at my desk. *Hallucination.* The word floated up into my head. It sounded like a younger, sweeter Yeats reading his own poem. A heartsick Yeats.

Of course it was Brian.

"Are you all right?" he asked later. Not pushy. He stood by my desk after everyone had gone and waited as I gathered my books.

"Sure," I said. I looked at him. That was a mistake. There was such sympathy in his look. Concern. "Just a rough moment. You know."

He rubbed an orange paint stain on the arm of his leather jacket. "Can I walk you somewhere?" he asked.

I have been thinking about what drew me to poetry. At the beginning. My family has never been big on books or reading. I'm the only one who went to college. But I've always loved the sounds of words, the feel of them in my mouth. As a kid I walked around repeating prayers, incantations. Sounds that made me feel good. I'd lie on my bed, roll and rub against the blankets, whispering words that excited me. *Tongue* or *naked* or *loins.*

In high school I discovered symbolism. Mr. Parisi stood by the window reciting Dylan Thomas and Bob Dylan. Yeats and Keats and Joni Mitchell. He had a beautiful ass. Tight jeans. It intrigued me, the way a straightforward line, about birds, say, or parking lots, could connote death or rebirth, lust or love or decay. You could hear it. The word would pulse, seem to collect all this energy around it. It was as though I was hearing something confirmed. The reason it had always embarrassed me to hold the Host on my tongue. The body of Christ. The naked body. Jesus in my mouth. How I tried not to think of the different parts. Thighs. Loins. Or the undercurrents that rushed through the rooms when my mother said something simple like "You are not leaving this house." Hidden things. The way you feel drawn or attached to a person you barely know. Feel them tugging at you. The way a rhyme in the third line links back to the first and makes a kind of gluey bond.

Brian walked me to Houston Street. The next day we walked together again. Saturday we went to the Museum of Natural History and wandered through reconstructed dinosaur bones, the Hall of Evolution, dioramas showing what happens underground during each season. By the glass cases of Asian peoples we chose our favorite figures. Two men squatting by a fire. A woman hanging bones outside her door.

Usually with students I keep a kind of arch and flirtatious distance. Teasing and helpful. But everything about Brian—his musical voice, wavy reddish-blond hair, soft lips, the way his eyes linger around mine and then look away—I don't know, it gets to me.

"Feelin' a bit under it?" he'll ask. It's sweet.

The museum's closing bell rang while we were in the South Asian Hall imitating poses of Siva and Kali. Brian was staying uptown and said he'd walk me to the subway. Both of us stood looking at one another. Below West 4th

Street I know myself a little better. Know what to do. If we'd been below West 4th Street I would have kissed him. No question. Below West 4th Street you kiss anyone you've met at least once before. Except one of your students.

When we got to the subway I made the first move. I held his arm and kissed his cheek. He's your student, I kept thinking. I told him my theory about West 4th Street. He laughed.

"So," I said. I get positively inarticulate when I'm attracted to someone. Either that or I talk myself into a tangle.

"Well, I'll be seeing you, Terry," he said.

"This was nice," I said.

"So, next time maybe we should meet downtown." He rubbed at the orange paint stain on his jacket.

"Downtown?"

"Below West 4th Street."

I laughed. I was relieved he could take the initiative.

Yesterday he told me he'd never seen the Three Stooges. Never even heard of them.

It's been almost two weeks since I went to Yvonne's apartment. This morning I stopped in the Korean vegetable stand on Spring Street near our loft. I don't know if it was the vegetables or my mood, but as soon as the young Korean woman touched the lemon to count out my change I thought I was going to throw up. I stuffed the change in my pocket and ran three blocks over to Dean & DeLuca to use their bathroom.

I threw up. I hate to throw up. It terrifies me. That feeling of your whole middle opening up and ripping apart. I stood in the tiny bathroom reading the graffiti on the wall above the toilet. *Obey God, Go to Church, Read the Bible. What do you think dickface?* scrawled across a crude rendition of a penis with eyes. That did it. I must have thrown up two weeks' worth of pastina. I washed my face, brushed my teeth, and reapplied my lipstick. *Yvonne's* lipstick. I stood by the sink for a few minutes. Then I went upstairs for a cup of tea. It was a relief to be so empty. So light. I was still dizzy. As if there were a big hollow space inside me filling up with ether.

Dean & DeLuca is like a giant playpen in the middle of Soho. You can't walk in there without meeting half a dozen people you know and ten more you recognize. With its frosting-white brick walls, high ceiling and skylight, the neat stacks of tiny sandwiches and perfect-looking cinnamon rolls, gingerbreads and poppyseed cakes, cappuccino and fifteen varieties of tea, it's like a scene out of *Mary Poppins*. I rarely have anything but coffee or tea but I always leave there feeling like I've been at a feast.

I stood at the counter and watched the busboy rearrange rows of bottled water. Blue. Green. Clear. I love watching people make order. When I turned I noticed Mark waving to get my attention. He was by the side wall with his assistent, Glenda. Right where Mia Farrow and Judy Davis sit in *Husbands and Wives*.

"Ciao bella," I said and kissed Glenda on both cheeks.

"You look awful," Mark said. He leaned over and kissed me then pushed my hair back. "Your hair is soaked. Are you okay?"

"I think so. I was feeling kind of woozy."

Glenda stood up and started brushing powdered sugar off her black leather skirt. "We're celebrating," she said, still chewing. She had on the clunky black combat boots she always wears.

I looked at Mark. I wondered if Glenda knew about Yvonne. If she was feeling sorry for me. Or superior. Or guilty. Maybe she was sleeping with Mark, too. We've known her for two years and she just moved in with Mark's brother David last fall. Right after Mark and David opened the gallery. I'd told her about Moe. Warned her. I looked at her boots. Maybe Moe is *her* favorite Stooge, too.

Glenda would have to know if Mark were having an affair. So would David. And who else? I looked her in the eyes but she just looked the way she always does.

"I'm doing Iago at the Public next spring," this guy was saying in a loud voice at the next table. He had that actory tone.

"We sold the Rauschenberg," Mark said, rubbing the lemon rind around the rim of his espresso cup. He said it quietly, not loud enough for the whole place to hear.

"Great. Who bought it?" I remember the night he bid on it. At Sotheby's. The first painting he bought at auction. We'd been there together.

"Trust fund baby," he said. "You don't know her."

Yvonne. He didn't have to say it. I knew it was Yvonne. A trust fund. Teaching to do something between shopping trips. I tried to picture where she'd hang it. No, she'd have it locked in a vault. Couldn't risk having someone break in and slash it.

I pressed the point on my arm that's supposed to be for nausea.

"Treas?"

"Great," I said. "You have to work hard to sell it?"

"Usual," Mark said. "Lunch. A few phone calls. Inspired talk on the rise of the art market." He was wearing a short-sleeved, cream-colored silk shirt and a black silk vest I gave him last year for his birthday. I love his arms. "I kept the Elizabeth Murray," he said. "I know you love that one."

Iago was putting on his leather jacket with a flourish and saying some very loud goodbyes. "Ciao, bellissimi," he said, blowing kisses.

"Terry, are you okay?" Glenda asked.

"Why?"

"You look kind of pale. Your eyes look funny. Maybe it's just that lipstick."

Mark put his hand to my forehead. "No fever," he said.

"I'm going home," I said. I dipped my finger in the tea and sucked it.

"Honey, wait a minute. I'll walk you." He stood up.

"I'm fine," I said. "We'll celebrate later." I kissed both of them. "Bring home the bill of sale and we can have it mounted."

"Ciao," Glenda said and held up her fingers to wave.

Turned out it wasn't Yvonne. Maybe Sarah was wrong. Maybe Yvonne is just a prospective client. Right. And

Mark has her keys in case he needs to check out her wall space.

Brian and I were meeting for dinner. Below West 4th Street. I made another trip to Yvonne's to borrow something to wear. I was tired of my own clothes. Everything black. Yvonne looked about my size, and she probably wouldn't miss a blouse or two. I still thought of her as a trust fund baby even though she wasn't the new owner of the Rauschenberg. Once I get a fact I can't part with it. I use everything I can find to piece her together. She's become a kind of project—like those enormous jigsaw puzzles people start and keep on their dining room table for weeks.

After my session with Eric I walked up Broadway toward Yvonne's. I passed her street and walked two extra blocks to the Korean vegetable stand. For good luck. Or ritual. Catholics have a habit of doing things exactly the same way every time.

The sneaker vendor smiled. I could see him telling the police he'd begun to see me hanging around.

"I'm from the neighborhood," I said.

"Verdad," he said.

The Korean woman was not at the register and I took that as a sign. Maybe Yvonne was home. Maybe I should call first. But she probably screens her calls. Besides, according to her schedule, she was supposed to be teaching.

I took a box of saltines to the register. The store's smell was getting to me. Every time I see a Korean I think of Yvonne. Every time I see vegetables.

"Where's the woman that's always here?" I asked the old man at the register.

"Yes," he said smiling broadly, trying to push the box into the bag. He had big, clumsy, arthritic-looking fingers.

"Is she sick?" I asked.

He kept smiling and shaking his head up and down. He ripped the bag. I hoped she wasn't sick. I pulled off the bag and left it on the counter, then opened the box and took a few crackers to calm my stomach.

Yvonne's apartment looked exactly the same except the letter from India was gone. I'd been stupid not to read it.

Not a glass in the sink. No half-drunk cups of tea or coffee scattered through the room. Not a stray paper on the desk. It amazed me a person could be so neat. I thought maybe she has someone come in to clean the apartment. I slid the chain lock into its groove.

It didn't take long to find what I wanted. A black silk boat-neck top and a black skirt, size four. The skirt was straight so there would be no playing around with size. It would either fit or not. It fit. Even the length was okay. Yvonne's probably a touch taller than me. The top was a little tighter across my breasts than it was supposed to be. WASPs have an easier time affecting that blousy look.

I checked the drawers. Yvonne is the kind of woman who would have several unopened packages of stockings on hand. Not like me. I keep a pair or two around and have to dash out in a panic if I get a run. I don't know what makes me know her so well. There were nine slim cardboard envelopes. Opaques. Evening Sheers. Control Top.

Sandalfoot. Varying shades of black though there was one hideous green pair. And taupe. I never wear taupe. I chose Jet Black Evening Sheer. Donna Karan.

I'd planned on bringing it all home but I got an urge to shower and dress at Yvonne's. Her clock said one, but it was three. She'd never replaced the battery. Anyway, if she was teaching it would be a while before she got home.

"*You may travel far far from your own native home,*" I started singing "The Cliffs of Dooneen." My voice sounded strange in the apartment. Not like my voice at all. I thought about Brian. The shy way he'd offered to show me his poems. I took off all my clothes and laid Yvonne's clothes out on the bed. My shoes weren't exactly right, but I never borrow other people's shoes. I can't imagine wearing someone else's shoes.

On my way to the bathroom I noticed the red light blinking on Yvonne's answering machine. Three blinks. Three calls. I'm not the kind of person that would listen in to someone else's calls. Besides, I was afraid I'd erase the messages. I don't know how long I stood there watching that blinking light. It reminded me of the confessionals at Holy Cross Church. A red light beamed out from above the wooden box when the person inside was on the kneeler. Once they stood up the light went off and the next person could enter. Whoever was inside was usually so nervous they'd shift around on their knees, fidgeting, half standing, thinking it was time to go, and all this time the red light would be blinking crazily on and off, everyone outside the box getting more and more nervous. I used to keep letting other kids get in front of me as I approached the head of the line, even though it only made the anticipation worse.

I was feeling panicky. I dialed the number for the time, to check my watch. I dialed Mark at the gallery but hung up when I heard Glenda's voice. I dialed Eric.

I knew he wouldn't answer. His voice on the tape is an attempt to sound soothing. "Tell me where I can reach you," it ends. I was going to hang up but at the beep I started talking.

"Eric. Hi. It's Theresa. Spera. I . . . well . . . I can't be reached." *Hi Eric. I'm standing here naked in Yvonne's apartment.*

I hung up. I watched the blinking light dying to know if there was a message from Mark, but I couldn't listen. I thought about Brian. I pictured him holding me, talking to me. For a brief minute I considered bringing him to Yvonne's. To fuck him in the same bed my husband was fucking Yvonne. It was then it hit me that Mark and Yvonne could have been using our loft. I don't know why I'd never thought of it before. We live only a couple of blocks from the gallery and if he had to dash out for an hour what could be more convenient? We'd made love in the unfinished back room when the gallery first opened. They could be fucking in the gallery.

There was a bottle of vodka on the kitchen counter. I poured a glass but couldn't drink it. I thought of adding it to the water in the refrigerator or her contact lens solution, but I wasn't that far gone. I poured it back into the bottle. I guess I really don't want to hurt her. I don't know, maybe just a little.

I took a shower and put on Yvonne's clothes. They felt
good. The way well-cared-for clothes feel. They looked good
on me too. It was almost amazing the way they fit. It's funny
Mark would choose someone almost exactly my size. Who
looks like me. Who also teaches English. Not funny, really.
It's bizarre. Like that Ionesco play where the two strangers
get around to talking about where they each lived. Both
lived on the same block. At the same address. They were
neighbors. The same apartment, too. How extraordinary.
Could they live together and not know it? What's your
name? one of them asks. Bobby Martin. Mine too. They
were both Bobby Martin. I always have a student who
objects to it all. It doesn't make sense.

Yvonne doesn't look exactly like me. But if you described
us both physically you might use a lot of the same terms.

I dabbed her Opium at my neck and shoulders and stomach. A little more than I usually wear. In high school my
best friend Helene gave me a vial of patchouli. She said it
didn't matter what I looked like as long as I was wearing
patchouli. It was irresistible, she said. Scent was important.
Ancient Sumerian prostitutes put their own sex juice—
that's what she called it—behind their ears to attract men.
Something like that.

I stood on a chair looking at myself in the mirror. I love
the way you can stare at something for a long time and make
it break down. I first discovered this looking at my mother.
It amazed me how at first she'd look so familiar—more
familiar than anything. I'd stare and stare, like I was caught
on her, unable to look away. Little by little her face would

distort, the way your own face does when you're looking at yourself reflected in someone's sunglasses. As I stared harder the eyes would move and seem at angles to one another. Her mouth would twist, disintegrate. Then she wouldn't look like my mother at all until I shut my eyes hard and refocused. I practiced making her disintegrate and come back together. It was happening now. At first I looked like myself. Then my face got blurry. I felt almost dizzy. I tried to imagine Yvonne's face there instead of mine. It didn't work. Not like it does in the movies. Like Bibi Andersson and Liv Ullmann in *Persona*. I tried to let my wavy hair straighten. My dark eyes lighten. My olive skin get that whitish look Yvonne's has. I still looked like myself. But I didn't feel like myself. I felt like nobody. I half expected my image to disappear from the mirror.

The phone rang. I jumped from the chair and stood still as though the voice could discover me. Her doctor's office reminding her about an appointment.

I stuffed the dry-cleaning wrap in my bag. I looked around to make sure I wasn't leaving anything behind. But I didn't dry out the shower. It would dry by the time she got home.

It would be scary to walk into your bathroom and see the mirrors fogged and the shower curtains all wet when no one had been there all day.

Brian's apartment was a mess. Books open and facedown on the floor. Lots of them. Teacups everywhere—even in the bathroom. Papers, newspapers. Postcards and photographs tacked every which way on the walls. He lives on 6th Street above an Indian restaurant so there's that sweaty smell of cumin and curry throughout the apartment, a smell I've never liked much until now.

He didn't need to stoop but his ceilings are low and it seemed like he was stooping. There's something cavelike about the apartment. Close. There are no clocks. I like that.

"Tangled Up in Blue" played out of a small black tape player that was spotted with the same orange paint that's on his jacket sleeve.

"*Blood on the Tracks*," I said. "I haven't heard this in years."

"I love Dylan," he said. "I play him when I'm missing home." He nudged a few books aside with his foot. Picked up a teacup and put it on the table. "I play him all the time actually."

I was noticing how pale his eyelashes are. How young it makes him look. I didn't want him to be missing home. I wanted him only to be thinking about being here with me. I'm starting to feel this kind of longing for him—to hold him and touch him and take care of him.

"I sang in a rock band," I said. "This was our name. Tangled Up in Blue."

"Wow," he said, "that's pretty wild." I think he was picturing me on stage at CBGB's. I didn't tell him that we basically played on the Catholic high school dance scene. Strictly Bishop MacDonald.

Dylan was singing the part about her showing him the Italian poet from the fifteenth century. Brian and I stared at one another. We must have stood there through the whole song. It was hot and I'd taken off Yvonne's scarf and my sweater during "Simple Twist of Fate."

"Do you always wear black?" he asked.

"I'm Italian," I said.

We both shifted around a little. He seemed too tall for the room. Like he was cramped in there.

"Why don't you sit?" he said. He cleared off some newspapers and books to make space on a chair.

I almost made a joke about Spiritual Housecleaning but I was nervous and afraid it wouldn't come off.

"Would you like some tea?" he asked. "Water?"

"Water's good," I said.

He went to the kitchen. It was almost a relief to be in there alone.

Yeats lay open on the floor. And Rimbaud, Rilke, Neruda. The same editions as mine. Yvonne's book collection is pretty paltry. Beside her bed where you'd expect to find stacks of books—on the nighttable, on the floor—I'd seen only a copy of the *Norton Anthology of Poetry* and a murder mystery. The small wooden bookcase in the living room contains some good fiction and poetry but has room for three glass paperweights. And a framed painting of a dog. A dog, for God's sake. I hate dogs. I'd pulled out her copy of *Ariel*. Sylvia Plath seemed appropriate to the occasion. No notes in the margins. No underlinings. The book looked a lot less ragged than my own copy. She hadn't even written her name in the front.

Brian stood beside me holding a glass. I couldn't think of

a thing to say. I reached for his hair and stroked it. I pulled his head toward me and kissed him. His lips were soft at first, his tongue a little tentative. Then his mouth moved hard on mine.

I don't think either of us had known what would happen and I guess I was pushing the direction. The way you almost unconsciously move the planchette over a Ouija board. Dylan helped. I rocked with Brian. Moved into the beat.

"If you see her, say hello, she might be in Tangiers," I sang softly to him as we moved with one another. I thought how now he'd always think of me whenever he heard this tape. It still makes me think of a guy I worked with at a bookstore in Penn Station. "Listen," he'd said, as he put the needle back to the beginning, "I can't deal with virgins. Come back when you lose it, okay? I mean it. Send me a note or something." I was to hear variations of that line until I was twenty-four and finally managed to get rid of it in a small hotel in Paris by the Seine.

Brian ran his hands down my back and over my behind. Up my thigh and under Yvonne's skirt. I'd thought I'd have to bring him out. The way Mark had done for me. Undress him slowly, tie his wrists easily with Yvonne's scarf, whisper poems in Italian as I tongued his neck and licked down the length of his body. Pulled his stories out of him. His secrets. Uncovered everything about him. But he seemed to be doing fine on his own.

"Look at me," he said. He held my chin and, with his thumb, wiped off the Scarlet Memory I'd put on at Yvonne's and reapplied in the cab. "I like you so much better without it."

I could tell then he'd be a good lover. His body felt warm next to mine. We fell to the couch. The tape switched to the other side. My first affair. We'd have our own veritable Innisfree.

· 5 ·

$\mathcal{E}$ric tapped his oxblood shoe on the rug. We'd been sitting in silence for ten minutes. Actually, I was lying on the couch.

"Theresa," he said, "if you don't move forward, you *don't* just stay in place. You start slipping back. Regressing."

I was thinking about how much money I was losing each minute I didn't talk. I looked up at Eric's big black-and-white wall clock. I thought of the clock over the bar at the Time Cafe. The way it moves backward, around and around, the whole time you're there. The whole time you're there that clock is speeding backward. I stared at Eric's clock and saw its hands crossing counterclockwise, the hour beginning again, then the day, yesterday, the year. I curled on the couch. I saw me and Brian standing in the Hall of Evolution—right by the apes—the first time we held hands. Before anything had started.

I felt small. A child. A baby. My body got that dense feeling I get sometimes. Like a shape in space. I was buzzing, fuzzy. I could feel myself beginning to unravel. The hair on my arms standing out, thickening, my torso yielding to gravity, bending forward. Hair all over me. A lumpen, cumbersome body. I felt myself slipping backward through the

entire process of evolution. All shuddering blood and fur. I
slipped farther and farther back until I was a fish skittering
through water. A quick phosphorescence on a wave. Then
the mud and I was part of the ooze, seeping into the silty
mush, a leafy thing washed in a bog. Eric's shoe shot past
my line of sight like a salmon slipping upstream. I wanted
to sleep. I wanted Eric to lie on top of me and hold me. Stop
me. Rock me to sleep.

"Theresa," he said, "I want you to try to talk to me."

And I want you to fuck me. I didn't say it. I didn't even
want it really.

Brian and I had not become lovers. By the time Dylan
was singing "You're a Big Girl Now," around again on continuous play, we'd somehow skirted it all. One minute we
were on his couch, kissing, touching, working off each
other's clothes. The next I was sobbing in his arms and overcome by nausea. At least I hadn't thrown up.

He was great about it. In half an hour I told him everything. Well, some of it. Yvonne. Mark. The affair. Pastina,
lipstick, Opium. The green scarf, the Korean woman, the
red plastic alarm clock and all those shoes. In half an hour I
explained about the Three Stooges, Aunt Anita, and the
figure skaters. Tristan and Al-Anon. It all came out in a
jumble and I know he really didn't get what I was talking
about.

He held me and talked to me.

"Theresa," he said. "Do you mind if I call you Theresa?
It's a beautiful name."

"Only my shrink calls me Theresa," I said.

"My name's not Theresa," I said now to Eric.

"Excuse me?"

"I said my name's not Theresa."

"All right. What is your name?"

I could tell he thought I was going to start playing games. I wondered how much I could push him before he'd start to yell at me. Hit me. I don't think therapists are allowed to yell at their patients. Certainly not hit them.

"Terry," I said. "My name is Terry. Everyone calls me Terry. Not Theresa. I don't know why I told you my name was Theresa."

Eric didn't say anything. I could hear him breathing, but now I couldn't even see his shoes. My eyes were closed. I heard the two of us breathing. *Breakthrough*, I could hear him thinking. Maybe he'd come over and hug me.

"What else do you want to tell me?" he asked.

The guy is absolutely dispassionate.

"I've been going to Al-Anon meetings," I said.

This is true. I've gone back. Not to St. Barnabas. I didn't feel I could go back there. I'm going to a church on Waverly Place. I like it better there. The people. Mostly gay men and women. People like me. Downtown people. I've begun talking, too. The place is comforting. As a kind of superstition I always wear Yvonne's skirt and blouse to the meetings. I've admitted I'm a co-dependent, though to tell the truth I'm still not quite sure what that means. When I hear it defined it sounds pretty much like anybody. But I even like that.

"Do you like the meetings?" Eric asked.

"Yeah."

"And what do you call yourself there?" he asked. I'm pretty sure he was joking. Trying to be lighthearted.

"Well, that's the thing," I said. "I say I'm Yvonne."

There was a silence.

"What else do you say?"

I've been introducing myself as Yvonne. Sharing at meetings that I'm having an affair with the husband of a woman I like very much. A close friend. That I found myself trying to look like her and act like her. That I really do look like her. When I write this down it sounds pretty crazy. And I guess I've been feeling crazy. I'm continually afraid I'll run into Sarah at a meeting. I haven't told her any of this. And she's my best friend.

"Terry," Eric said. The first time he said my real name.

"Eric, I'm scared."

"It's okay. It's okay to be scared. It's good you're talking."

"Yeah, I guess," I said, but I didn't feel good. I'd begun to drop by Yvonne's after almost every session and I was going today. "I don't want to leave," I said.

"It's okay. Call me if you need to talk," he said. "And thank you."

"For what?"

"For trusting me with your name."

It wasn't a hug. But it was something.

· 6 ·

*M*ark was staring out over the Arts and Leisure section of the *Times*. I wasn't sure if he was staring at me or just in a daze. Tony curled on his lap, padding his paws against Mark's jeans. I was sprawled on the rug beside Chico, planning Monday's class.

Maybe it was the Al-Anon meetings, but I had started to feel back on track a little. I practiced detaching, like they said in the meetings. I kept trying to see myself as separate from other people. I had taken several pictures of me and Mark and scissored them in half. I wrote my name and Mark's name on a large piece of paper, then I ripped it in half and put the two halves in different places. I did visualizations of my mother in a sealed box hurtling through the universe away from me. I'm learning to separate.

Brian is in both of my classes now, auditing one, just, I think, to be with me. It helps me get to class. And I think I've been helping him too. We spent three days at Angelika seeing every film on the marquee. There's still this longing between us, but after that time in his apartment we've kept things pretty tame. I was reading his poems, encouraging him to write. He was encouraging me to confront Mark. But I wasn't ready. Actually, I was avoiding Mark. I was almost afraid he'd do something to give it away.

Mark put the paper down and held Tony, stroking his fur. He picked him up and kissed him on the nose. He was looking at me.

Ask him, I kept thinking. I'd had a dream the night before about this guy Mr. Italiano, and I thought it might have been a sign. I mean why would I dream about Mr. Italiano? When the gallery opened, Mark and David had two silent partners. One of them—Mr. Italiano we called him, they weren't supposed to reveal his name—owned this beautiful de Kooning he wanted to get rid of *very* privately. The trouble was, Mr. Italiano had a huge insurance policy out on the painting which stipulated that the de Kooning had to stay in his apartment. So Mark had his keys. He had to bring people all the way up to East 67th Street to see the painting. But when he sold it, it covered the gallery expenses for months.

In the dream, Mark had his arm around Mr. Italiano. I thought the dream might be telling me that Yvonne was a silent partner. Still, why wouldn't *Mark* have told me? Maybe Yvonne has a secret painting, too, though all I've seen is that hideous dog—which doesn't look very valuable. Maybe it's illegal, maybe the painting was a gift. And maybe she's having an affair with Mark.

That's the thing about dreams. Maybe it was warning me that Yvonne is the kind of silent partner I should worry about.

"Are you in a Dylan phase or something?" Mark asked

I'd been playing *Blood on the Tracks* for two hours. And reciting the Serenity Prayer to myself.

"I guess." I picked Chico up and pulled him to me.

"I think I prefer Maria Callas," he said. He picked up the Week in Review. "Can we switch? I'm in the mood for a little shrieking and moaning." I'd had on *Norma* all week.

I didn't answer. When I stood to stretch Mark reached his foot across and through my legs and pulled me toward him.

"Cut it out. I'm working."

"What is going *on* with you?"

"What do you mean?"

He stared at me.

"What?" I asked.

He just kept staring.

"*What?*"

"I'm just looking at you," he said. "Take it easy." He leaned back in the chair. "Tonight's the last night of the Three Stooges festival at Film Forum. Want to go?"

"Uh-uh." I shook my head. I'd already gone with Brian.

"How's your stomach?" he asked.

"Okay," I said.

"Are you premenstrual or something?"

"I don't think so." I'd skipped my last period. I always do when I'm upset. So I wasn't sure where in the cycle I was.

"How come you're so quiet?"

I shrugged. "I've been writing," I said.

It was true. Brian had encouraged me to write. I've always kept a journal. Notes, dreams, day-to-day stuff. But last week I wrote a poem. It's more direct than the stuff I wrote in college, but it needs work. It's called "Position of Prayer." I just have the beginning.

> I should have known
> the way you loved
> to fuck me in the ass
> that I would end
> up on my knees,
> if only from exhaustion.
> It's all behind me now.
> I have always knelt
> to the wrong gods.

That's as far as I got. I wrote a lot more, but this is what I could salvage. It's not Yeats, but it's a beginning.

In the middle of "Idiot Wind" I grabbed a small bronze maquette from the bookcase. It was shaped like a weapon or fertility symbol and was made by one of Mark's sculptors. I held it to my mouth and sang with Dylan. It's a song I sang with the band. I always loved to sing when I was angry, jerking back and forth into the mike, into the audience, sounding more angry than I'd ever let myself sound in real life. Even though it was only a small Brooklyn band I've never felt the way I used to feel up there on stage. When you could be someone else, or maybe just a cooler, stronger version of yourself, that music coming through you.

I leaned into Mark, into the Week in Review. I sang. "*I can't feel you anymore. I can't even touch the books you read.*"

"What is *with* you?" He slammed the paper down.

I turned up the volume and kept singing. Louder and louder. The blast from the speaker knocked several rocks off the top of the bookcase. Tony and Chico jumped from the chair and raced out of the room. Mark grabbed my shoulders and started to shake me. Dylan kept going. *"You'll never know the hurt I've suffered nor the pain I rise above."*

Mark held me against the wall. This wasn't the way I'd wanted it to come up. I wasn't prepared, hadn't figured out what I'd say, what I'd ask. On Sunday, for God's sake. I pushed away.

"I know about Yvonne," I said.

He looked positively stunned.

"I know who she is."

"What are you talking about?" He was looking at me the way you watch your opponent about to slam back a tennis ball.

"Oh, come on, Mark. Don't act like an asshole on top of everything."

"Terry, you'd better tell me *exactly* what you mean."

"Oh, *exactly*. I'll tell you *exactly* what I mean. Yvonne Adams. I know everything. I know you're fucking her. *Exactly.*"

"What the *hell* are you talking about? She's a client. She's looked at some work. She has something I'm interested in."

"I can see that."

"A painting, Terry."

I thought of that dog. I'd have to check it.

The phone rang and the machine clicked on but I couldn't hear who was talking. A voice rambled leisurely.

"I'm telling you," Mark said. He stood there looking at me, hands in his hair, elbows out, like someone about to be frisked by a cop. "Wait a minute," he said, "I refuse to be a part of this conversation. I don't believe I'm even discussing this. Even if I *were* fucking Yvonne—*which* I am not—it would have *nothing* to do with you. Do you hear me? *Nothing.*"

The answering machine beeped for the end of the message.

"Are you nuts? Are you kidding? It has *everything* to do with me. I'm your wife. *I'm your wife.*"

"Do you hear yourself? Do you hear what you sound like? Jesus. You sound *just* like your mother."

Dylan was blasting. Mark ripped the needle off the album.

"We went through this five years ago," he said. "I *told* you I didn't believe in marriage. I told you I would *never* allow myself to be in this position. Questioned and cross-examined."

I leaned against the wall. He was right. He hadn't wanted to get married. Kept talking about Nietzsche and Foucault, limits and freedom, good and evil. I'd thought he'd get over it. I mean, it sounds great, but who really believes that stuff?

"I won't be married to someone who's fucking someone else," I said.

"And I won't be manipulated by you. I will *not* allow you to dominate me the way your mother keeps your poor bastard of a father shackled to the bathtub listening to opera. What's more, *you* don't want me to." He turned quickly and knocked over a stack of CDs. "Why the *fuck* do you think you're with me? How long would you have stayed with me if I'd let you lead me around by the nose?"

"Say it," I said. "Just *say* it, goddammit. *Say* you're fucking her."

"I'm not talking to you until you calm down."

"*Fuck* you. *Fuck* you, Mark." I grabbed the maquette and threw it across the room, just missing the Bakelite clock David gave us as a wedding present.

Mark grabbed my hair, yanked me around, and slapped me. I remember the fast scratching sounds of the cats running across the floor. All I could think of was that woman in the pink dress from St. Barnabas Church.

"Jesus," he said. He stood looking at me. I think he was more shocked than I was. "Listen, I'm going out for a half an hour." He took a step toward me. "I'm sorry I hit you. Terry, Jesus, I'm sorry. But when I come back we have to talk."

I didn't say anything. I heard the door shut. I scooped Tony up and held him so tight he started wriggling and scratching to get down.

I tried to calm down. I put Dylan back on, picked up the CDs, did some breathing exercises. I said the Serenity Prayer. Over and over. It occurred to me we hadn't made love. We always make love after we fight. But we'd never fought like that. Except for when we were deciding whether to get married.

I *had* forced him into it. He kept saying he wouldn't love me any less if we just continued living together. He just didn't like the idea of marriage. Didn't like what it did to people. I started thinking that maybe he was right. Whose marriage really looks good when it comes down to it? No one's. I was thinking about how much I love Mark. Love to come home to him, be with him. Go to movies and talk. I've never talked to anyone the way I talk to Mark, never had so much fun. I was thinking how I should be adult about it all. Maybe it was true. You could have a brief affair and it wouldn't mean anything. What harm would it have done if I'd been able to make love to Brian? I could still do it now. It wasn't bad or good. Mark's always gotten on me for that.

"Everything with you is either good or bad," he says. "You're not a child, for God's sake. Life is complicated." Or he teases me. "Good little Catholic girl. Obedient to the bone."

"Remember your Nietzsche," he wrote on his wedding card to me.

I felt calmer and ready to talk. Love was bigger than I was making it out to be. Love was about the long haul. I poured a glass of wine but didn't drink it. I took Dylan off the turntable.

Mark came in exactly a half hour later.

I went over first and put my arms around him. He was tentative, then he yielded.

"Terry, we have to talk," he said. He held me. Kissed my hair. I leaned into him.

"Look, I'm sorry I got all crazy," I said. I rubbed my head along his chest. "It's okay. Just tell me the truth and I'll stop asking."

He dropped his arms and fell into the chair on top of Chico, who hissed and darted out.

"I said I am not going to discuss this."

"You just said we have to talk."

"I *refuse* to talk about Yvonne."

"Just answer this, then. Have you gone to dinner with her?"

"I've had dinner with her."

"Do you like her? I mean, are you attracted to her?"

"Terry."

"Just answer me."

"God*dammit* you're starting again. Yes. I like her. She's cute. She's a little lonely. She reminds me of my sister."

"That's sick."

"Jesus Christ. Aside from *any* of this, *if* I wanted to get involved in a purely sexual relationship, and I am *not* saying I do, I am certainly not going to talk to you about it."

"Oh. And your relationship with your sister is purely sexual?"

"You're not being rational. You're not listening to me."

The keys. I wanted to ask about the keys. Let him try to explain the keys. But then I'd have to explain how I knew about them.

"I just want to know what's going on."

"Terry, you're my wife, *not* my jailer."

"I'm going to bed," I said.

"Fine."

"Fine. *Fuck* you. Fine. I hate you. Your stupid ideas. I hate Foucault. And Nietzsche. I hate Nietzsche."

Mark suddenly laughed. The way he laughs when I've surprised him. He shook his head. I turned to walk to the other end of the loft. He pulled at my shoulder.

"Cut it out."

"Come here," he said. He pulled me toward him and rocked me. "Tree, Tree, Tree," he whispered into my neck. He kissed me. "I think maybe the girl needs a brushup. Yeah, I think she needs a refresher course in Nietzsche."

I yanked away. "Don't touch me," I think I said.

He pushed me forward onto the couch.

"Get on your knees," he said.

I tried to pull away. He put his arm around my waist and lifted me up until I was kneeling. He pushed my head toward the couch. Yanked down my jeans.

"Come on, baby. Time to say your prayers. I think you forgot to say your prayers tonight."

Obey God, Go to Church, Read the Bible. I could see the pencil scrawl on Dean & DeLuca's bathroom wall. The penis with eyes. I felt sick.

Mark must have noticed something because I think he turned me around. I remember him saying how clammy I felt. And then we were in the bathroom. I was puking my guts out. Retching and choking.

Mark held me. Washed my head with a cold cloth. Held my wrists under cold running water. He brought me onto the bed and then held me and rocked me for what seemed like half the night. It was getting darker and darker. Quieter.

Tony and Chico humped up around us. Chico kept pushing his cold nose into my hair and face.

The room seemed so still. Mark and I rocked together on our bed.

"Treas," he said after a long time. "Honey, do you think you might be pregnant?"

· 7 ·

I was.

I was. I could just feel it. I had to be.

I read a book that explained how sometimes you can still get your period after conception. That morning sickness is not always confined to the morning. That some women don't have many signs, and the signs vary. Some women, it said, develop a heightened sense of smell. Well that's for sure.

I can't say I was happy. The thought of growing bigger horrified me. Though the book said to eat well and often, I began to starve myself. I had visions of the wormy thing eating me alive. Syphoning my minerals and living off me. Which is pretty much the way it is. Another person inside getting a free ride.

I still had to see a doctor to make sure. Mark kept bugging me. My real terror was that it might be twins. I felt like I was carrying around my replacement, offering it all the comforts. How long before it made my clothes tight, my walk tired? I looked at my breasts. The thought of them filling with milk made me sick. I thought if I stopped eating the thing would starve and die. Disintegrate. I even stopped eating pastina.

I've started lighting candles to St. Jude. The thing is, I can't figure out what to pray for. It doesn't seem right to pray for the fetus to die. And I can't exactly pray for Yvonne to get hit by a car. It's not right. So I just pray to be happy and calm. For peace of mind. *Thy will be done*, I say, like they say to do in the Al-Anon meetings. *Thy will be done.* Then I light the candles. But I feel nervous leaving it up to St. Jude to decide what to do.

"Honey, you should eat something," Sarah said. We were at Dean & DeLuca. She took a huge bite out of a mozzarella-and-sundried tomato sandwich and held out the other half.

"Here. Have some of this," she said, her mouth full.

"I'm not hungry," I said.

"Oh God, *that* brings back memories."

In the years we lived together—our dieting years—I was always better at it. I could just about starve myself to lose weight. "It's because you're Catholic," Sarah used to say. "You're big on suffering." I could go an entire day on coffee and some carrots, and swear I wasn't hungry, while Sarah often gave up, indulged in a pint of diet ice cream, and never really lost weight.

"You have to start eating. Does Mark know what you're doing?"

"No. I tell him I eat before he comes home. Because of the fetus." I still couldn't call it a baby.

"What about your shrink?"

"No."

"Terry, I'm worried about you."

Fasting, I used to call it. Or *atoning*, if I'd eaten what I regarded as too much the day before.

"I don't know what kind of weird religious trip you're on," Sarah used to say. "You Catholics scare me."

There *had* been some kind of sacramental feel to it all. The ritual. The purity. Even when I peed it was clear. I've always wanted to feel untainted. Pure as bone. Clean and untouched. Ever since I was a kid. But no matter how much weight I lost I could still see my hips, breasts. I was never really anorexic, just a little extreme. It was just something I did from time to time.

Sarah said the food I ate looked like Communion wafers. And it's true, I like white food—white bread, yogurt, apples. White chicken as long as it doesn't have that chicken smell. Really, though, I just loved that feeling of being empty. Hollow. Waking up to feel my ribs, my hipbones jutting out like the lip of a bowl. Even now, my stomach only feels flat when it's concave. I've lost four more pounds. Yvonne's skirt is getting too loose to wear. But the fetus will change that.

"I don't know, Sarah. You know, I don't know if I want this thing."

"Then you have to decide soon. But Terry," she said, ever practical, "you should at least do a pregnancy test. Just to make sure."

Dean & DeLuca was unusually empty. A young child sat on the floor peeling a piece of flattened gum from the tile. Its mother talked away to her companion, oblivious. At another table an enormous pregnant woman leaned back in her chair with that vague look pregnant women get. Like a bloated odalisque. Half of Soho seemed to be pregnant.

"Yeah," I said.

I knew I was being a drag.

"Want to come up to Yvonne's with me?" I'd finally told her I knew where Yvonne lived, though I hadn't actually said I was going *inside* Yvonne's apartment.

"Terry, don't go up there."

"Okay," I said, to agree with something. But I knew I would go.

I started carrying saltines around in case I got nauseous. I brought little waxed paper packages to class, but didn't explain why I suddenly had to eat crackers during my lectures. Except to Brian. When I told him he held his hand to my stomach to see if he could feel any vibrations.

"You could name it Curly whether it's a boy or a girl," he said.

That depressed me. Everything depressed me. Early Christmas decorations. Mark bugging me to see the doctor. Yvonne's.

The last time I went up there things went wrong from the beginning. I was crossing Broadway when I heard someone call Yvonne's name. When I looked around for her I saw a young woman walking toward me smiling. She looked familiar but I couldn't place her. One of my students, I thought at first, though that doesn't even make sense.

"I haven't seen you in the rooms," she said.

Al-Anon.

"No," I said. "No, I haven't been to any meetings."

"Are you all right?" she asked. "Are you at least making phone calls?"

I must have looked pretty bad.

"I'm pregnant," I said.

She looked concerned. "Your friend's husband?" she asked.

I felt like I was beginning to unravel. I said something about not knowing and things working out. I promised to call and got away from her as quickly as I could.

Christmas decorations were hanging everywhere. Dirty fringe garlands and stars. A Salvation Army Santa waved a bell. The Al-Anon woman had thrown me and I forgot to stop at the Korean place before heading to Yvonne's.

When I got there the key wouldn't fit and I started thinking Yvonne was onto me. That she'd changed the locks. Then I noticed the number on the door. 4C. I'd gotten off on the wrong floor. It was a long wait for the elevator to go up and down and back up again and I was afraid someone would see me pacing the hall.

Once inside the apartment I didn't even want to be there. I sat on the couch. I checked the painting of the dog. There wasn't even a signature. So much for that. I went into the bedroom. She'd replaced the battery in her clock. I didn't take anything. I didn't open a drawer. I went back to the living room by the bookcase. *I know everything* I wrote inside the front cover of *Ariel*. Then I left.

Thinking about it now, I guess it makes sense what I did next. I didn't even leave a note for Mark. Let him worry and imagine, just like I'd had to do. On the ferry I regretted it. I decided to leave a curt message on the machine when I got to Staten Island. Just say I needed to think and I'd be back soon. Not tell him where I was, though. Let him worry.

I stood on the upper deck and watched Manhattan get smaller and smaller, the seagulls dropping up and down on their columns of air. The only thing I could see through the fog.

I was trying to listen to myself, hear what I should do. "It's a little voice inside you," Sister Dominica used to say, "telling you what to do. It's your soul, your conscience," she said, "whispering to you." But it always feels like there are so many voices inside me, whispering so many different things. "Sometimes the Devil will whisper to you," Sister Dominica said. "He'll try to trick you. He'll make himself sound like an angel, and you must pray to know the difference." Now what was I supposed to do with that?

When we docked, I found a phone in the terminal, left a message for Mark, and took a cab to Mount Loyola, a Jesuit retreat house I went to once in high school. They hold retreats there every weekend—I know because I'm on their mailing list. I remember the atmosphere as being somewhat punishing, but it's cheap and quiet and always open.

I didn't say a word to the driver as he navigated us through the fog. I was thinking about Yeats. *Love has pitched his mansion in the place of excrement.* Everything felt like shit. I wanted to be somewhere safe and clean. My stomach felt sick. I couldn't eat anything but the saltines and I'd forgotten to take them.

When I arrived, a middle-aged woman with stringy gray hair and a pair of rosary beads around her neck greeted me and filled out a card with my information. I wrote her a check for the weekend.

"Name?" she asked, tugging at the rosary beads.

I just stood there.

"Dearie," she said, "what is your name?" Her yellow cardigan was covered with lint balls and turned up at the wrists.

"Theresa," I said. "Theresa Spera." I was so scared *Yvonne* would leap out of my mouth. "Yes. It's Theresa."

She looked at me like I was a little strange. Then she smiled sympathetically. "Running from your husband?" she asked.

"Yes," I said. It felt important and dramatic.

"Parish?"

"What?"

"What parish are you from?" She had on this terrible shade of mauve lipstick traced over the thinnest lips I've ever seen.

"They don't have parishes in Manhattan," I said. I hadn't heard the word in years.

"Oh, you're funny," she said. "'Course they do."

She took the rest of the details and filled in the card with a stubby pencil. I gave her the wrong phone number and address. It wasn't necessary, but it added to the drama.

She brought me to my room and left me there. "You sleep here Friday and Saturday," she said. "Departure time is one-thirty Sunday." She tugged at the rosary. "Oh," she said, "here's a schedule of events. I almost forget. Have a peaceful stay."

I took the yellow paper.

"Mass is at five-thirty. Right before dinner," she said. "Would you like to help bring up the gifts?"

"Gifts?"

"The bread and wine," she said. "Carry it to the altar."

"No," I said. "No. I'll just watch. I'm a little ill."

"It's okay, dearie. Dinner is at six-thirty, right after Mass," she said. The lipstick caught in little creases at the corners of her mouth. "There's a silent table if you don't want to talk."

"Thanks. Oh," I said, "where's the phone? Is there a pay phone here?"

"No, dearie." She shook her head. "Well, there's one in the office for emergencies. But only for emergencies."

She closed the door. I sat on the bed, which was hard and narrow and pushed against the wall. The plastic mattress was thin as a magazine. The rest of the room consisted of a small writing table, a Bible, a lamp, and a list of instructions tacked to the door. A crucifix hung over the bed.

The room was cold. Really cold. There was only one thin blanket and it smelled like wet wool, so I kept on my jeans and sweater and lay down under it with my leather jacket on top for extra warmth. When I looked up that crucifix was staring down at me, the bronze loincloth a little out of proportion to the thin bent legs. I stood on the bed, pulled it off the wall, and stuck it in the top drawer of the writing table. I'd forgotten my alarm clock so I tacked my wristwatch to the wall by the lamp. Then I got back in bed.

I woke to a bell.

"Mass," I heard women whispering through the hall. I was freezing. Someone knocked gently on my door, whispered "Mass," and passed by. I got up and put on another sweater and went downstairs.

The chapel was all angles and bright colors. Felt banners proclaiming *Love* and *Peace*. It looked like an Al-Anon meeting. Two priests in dark clothes walked down the center aisle after we were seated. I sat in the back row and watched. One—Father Dugan, I was to find out later—was a trim, severe-looking Irish priest with very prominent lips. He walked silently down the aisle, looking neither right nor left. Straight out of Joyce. Old style. The other, Father John, smiled and extended his hands to women he'd obviously seen before. He looked almost jovial, winking and waving. Two tall, plain women without a hint of makeup walked behind them carrying what appeared to be the gifts.

Mass went by in a blur. I hadn't been to Mass, except for Anita's funeral, in years. The prayers had changed. The language. It was bad enough when they went from Latin to English when I was six—one of the first linguistic blows of my childhood—but these new prayers were truly without resonance. They might have been instructions for the use of a blender.

I cried once when Father Dugan talked about atoning for our sins and begging for forgiveness. Our souls suffocating in filth and mire. He read a poem he called "The Hound of Heaven," which I'd never heard. I imagined he was looking at me as he read it. *I fled him down the nights and down the days*, it began. Something like that. I hate dogs, but the metaphor seemed to work. On one hearing though, I couldn't tell if it was about a man stalking God, or God stalking the man.

I wanted to talk to Father Dugan. I wanted to purge. To strip myself bare, beg for forgiveness. Release myself from all the sin and deceit and fear.

I watched him through dinner. I elected to sit at the silent table, and was seated beside one of the thin, tall women who'd carried the gifts. There was a young, very pretty woman with red hair to my left who smiled at me whenever our eyes met. She looked about twenty-eight and I wondered what she could have done to make her feel she had to come to a place like this.

Father Dugan sat at a regular table but did not seem to join in the conversation. The two priests were the only men in a room of about thirty women. Except for the busboys and cook.

"Not eating?" the busboy asked in a loud voice. Then he grinned and put his finger to his lips.

I was fasting. Not that I could have eaten anyway. The center table was filled with stacks of greasy hamburgers, canned peas, and some pasty-looking mashed potatoes. Two huge aluminum bowls of sliced white bread and pats of gray butter. It made me sick to look at it. I didn't know if it was that food or the fetus, but I was feeling pretty bad.

I sipped ice water, but after looking at the food table, even the water tasted greasy. I was starving and nauseous at the same time.

After dinner I wanted to go to my room, but a mandatory orientation was set for 8:00 and I am, as Mark points out, profoundly obedient.

Father Dugan was the one I went for. The other, Father Johnny he called himself, turned out to be a cheery, red-faced, New Age type who chortled on about forgiveness and the love of Jesus. Everything you do can be forgiven and God loves you. Sister Judy, who was leading the structured group retreat, was wearing baggy, stone-washed jeans and a white Save-the-Earth T-shirt. She taught Jungian therapy at St. John's University. She was into women and thought the Virgin Mary was a feminist.

I was desperate to talk to Father Dugan. To ask him about the poem. He announced he would lead the unstructured, silent retreats, in which experienced retreatants would confer with him privately and not attend the group activities. I chose him even though I'd never done a real retreat. There was only one other silent retreatant. A tiny nun who looked about eighty.

Father Dugan told me to meet him at 5:45 before Mass next morning. I didn't have an alarm clock and was afraid I'd oversleep, but I needn't have worried. The banging gongs and bells that go off at five could have woken the comatose.

The red-haired woman—Chrissy her name was—seemed to have attached herself to me. We were clearly the youngest in the group. She asked if I'd like to see a film in the lounge that night on the subject of Medrugorgie—I think that's what she called it—a village in Yugoslavia where Catholics the world over were making pilgrimages to see the Virgin.

I couldn't imagine anyone would be going to Yugoslavia right now and I told her that. I told her it wasn't even called Yugoslavia anymore, but she said it was film footage of an appearance in 1989. I explained I was seeing Father Dugan early in the morning and really needed to sleep.

She looked a little uncertain. She leaned toward me, hesitated. "He's kind of a creep, you know," she said.

"You know him?"

"He's mean," she said. She had a sterling angel pinned to her collar.

"I don't know," I said. "He seems pretty intelligent."

"He's *mean*." She smiled. "But good luck."

I couldn't sleep that night. It's funny, but I didn't think at all about Mark, or the fact that I'd just disappeared. I didn't think about Yvonne or Sarah. Even Brian. I thought about the fetus, but only because it was making me so nauseous. I tried to pray but I felt stupid. I couldn't even say the Serenity Prayer. The room was cold, even under the blanket with all my clothes on.

I was awake most of the night. I'd look like a wreck in the morning, I knew that. I planned what to wear. I wanted to look penitent, but not demure. Attractive, but not obvious. I'd pull my hair back in a bun and wear discreet makeup. No lipstick.

I thought about Father Dugan's being mean. There *was* something ferocious about him. That steel-colored hair. Those lips. I unzipped my jeans and lifted my sweater. I fingered my clit and imagined him questioning me, scolding me. I imagined him listing the things I'd done wrong, telling me severely that I needed to be punished. I couldn't come. I couldn't come and I couldn't sleep.

I got up to check my wristwatch. Four o'clock. The window looked out onto the grounds, which were winter bare with patches of snow. I imagined Father Dugan out there walking in the trees past my window. I went back to bed and tried to continue the fantasy. I couldn't come. I couldn't sleep. I couldn't pray. And I couldn't get warm. When the bells started ringing I was overwrought and tired and in a panic about what to wear.

I felt chilled through. Damp. The way you feel when you've slept in your clothes. In the bathroom each of the seven shower stalls was already filled. No one looked at anyone else's body. No one rubbed oils into their skin. Not like at the gym where part of the pleasure is watching other women dress. Smelling their different scents. It was freezing and we showered and dressed quickly.

The visit with Father Dugan was brief and disappointing. We discussed poetry. Yeats he didn't read. Hopkins he said was a little too passionate and rash and it marred the poems. I agreed with him though I disagree. What I love is that passion. He gave me his copy of "The Hound of Heaven," saying Francis Thompson was devout and one of the best religious poets he knew. I asked him about Herbert, but he kept going back to Thompson, an inferior poet, I realized even then.

Father Dugan said I should walk about the grounds, saying the Act of Contrition, meditating on my soul. Perhaps I could do the Stations of the Cross outside by the grotto. When I was leaving he asked my name.

"Theresa, Father. Theresa Spera."

"Then your name means 'hope,'" he said. "From the Latin, *spero, sperare*."

"Yes, Father, I know," I said. I tried to pull the hair back into my bun, which was coming loose. I'd learned that in fifth grade. When I'd told my mother, she'd laughed. "That's a joke," she said. "That's a real laugh. Hope. Hope for the hopeless." And then she started to cry.

"We must always have hope, my child."

This all felt vaguely stupid. Despite my fantasies, I felt a fool calling this man "Father" and even worse when he called me his child.

"Thank you, Father," I said. "I believe that."

I really said it.

"You're named for Saint Theresa," he said.

"Yes, Father." I hoped he wasn't going to start in on Spiritual Housecleaning and my Interior Castle.

But he just nodded and went back to his book.

I started worrying about Mark and the fetus. It was too cold to go outside and though I thought it would be effective to be cold and suffering and walking the grounds all day, I couldn't get myself out the door. Sarah would say I was losing my touch.

I laid in bed under the blanket and copied out "The Hound of Heaven" into my journal. I looked at versions of my own poem on the previous pages, but it didn't seem right to work on it there. I walked around the halls, sat in the chapel, went to the lounge and bought a pair of wooden rosary beads in the bookstore. I tried to meditate on my soul, but I've never been able to picture the soul. I've always imagined it as shaped like one of those big cans of cured ham with the metal key they used to display in the windows of butcher shops. Except it was white, with black spots representing my sins. Whenever I try to think of the soul I see that can of cured ham with its metal key, sitting inside me, covered with blotches, and I can't get any further.

At about 2:30 I ran into Chrissy, and went with her to Rosary Recitation. At least it killed an hour. I was starting to give up on the private retreat and went with Chrissy to the next group activity, called "The Rite/Right of Penance."

Sister Judy talked about the spirit of forgiveness and led us through a meditation in which we all closed our eyes and imagined descending a series of stairs. We saw our names written on a large door down a long, dark hallway. The door turned out to be a Bible, and we were invited to walk into the pages and find ourselves. When she finished the meditation she put on a recording of a Beethoven quartet which seemed particularly grim. I opened my eyes to get a tissue and I saw that everyone around me was crying. I have to say, it was a pretty depressing place.

When it was over we all shared our thoughts and experiences of the meditation and after that everyone starting hugging and kissing. A lot of the women were using Al-Anon lingo, saying things like *you are only as sick as your secrets*. I was feeling pretty sick. I hugged Chrissy, but it was more for some kind of human contact than anything. I realized I hadn't been touched in over a day. Chrissy smiled through her teary face and kissed me solemnly. Then we all did this kind of anointing ritual, dipping our fingers in bowls of water and blessing one another.

Father John came in to speak about forgiveness. Father Dugan stood to the side. I could tell he was a little put off by it all. Then the priests left and we did some more rituals with the water and anointing oils. Sister Judy said we were each encouraged to go to confession. *Reconciliation*, she called it. *The sacrament of reconciliation*. They'd changed the name. She said we could arrange a private appointment with one of the priests.

"For example," she said, "just go knock on, say, Father Johnny's door, and talk to him. Just tell him everything. He's a good guy." When she mentioned Father John, it seemed she'd given me a rather pointed look. But I already knew who I was going to see.

I arranged an appointment for 4:30, and waited out the half hour in my room. I was actually looking forward to it. I've always loved the idea of confession. The fact that you could sit in a dark box and tell someone who couldn't see you, sometimes a complete stanger, a voice in a dark box, all the worst things about yourself and come out feeling pure and clean. Whole. The thing is, I never did. From the time I was seven and made my first confession, I never did. I'd listen to that whispering voice absolve me and I never felt pure, which made me think that there was something wrong with me—or something I wasn't telling. And of course there *were* things I didn't say, things that would take too long to explain, things I wasn't sure *were* sins, but felt wrong—like the way I clumped the pillow between my legs and rocked on my bed thinking about Lassie and Timmy, whispering "Timmy, Timmy." It didn't fit under any of the Commandments. And so I always left confession thinking there was something other people felt that I was supposed to feel. Some people are fundamentally bad, Sister Dominica used to say. And I just figured I was one of them. That's when I started pretending I felt pure. I'd come home smiling and sit quietly at dinner pretending I was at prayer.

I wanted to tell Father Dugan everything. About Mark and Yvonne, Brian and the fetus. How I felt like I was disappearing. Everything. I thought if I could say it all, all the things I couldn't tell Eric, I would get it out of me. I would be blessed and forgiven. Washed clean. I didn't think it would be wise, though, to tell him I'd been considering an abortion.

When I knocked at his door there was no answer. I waited a minute or two and knocked again. I knocked pretty softly, so maybe he didn't hear me. I pushed the door open. Father Dugan was sitting in a swivel chair, back to me, facing the window. There was no confessional box. It hit me then that I was supposed to sit in that room and look at him and tell him everything. Without the partition screen. I couldn't see how that made it any different from therapy. I thought maybe he'd keep his back turned and I would just stand there talking. I'd always knelt in confession, begun with the formal *Bless me, Father, for I have sinned.*

"Come in. Come *in*," he said and swiveled around to face me.

I must have looked terrified. The way Mark says I look whenever I see a dog. He says I look like a trauma victim.

"Sit *down*," he said. He was definitely not welcoming.

"I'm not quite sure what to do, Father," I said, moving into the folding chair opposite him. It was metal and cold through my jeans. I was about to start the *Bless me, Father*, when he asked when I'd made my last confession. This guy did not talk in terms of reconciliation.

I considered lying. "It's been twenty-one years, Father," I said. He looked disgusted. It was hardly the rejoicing welcome given the prodigal son. It was then I noticed his teeth. Perfect teeth. Evenly spaced. The kind of teeth you can floss easily, without getting the floss all stuck.

"I stopped going. I mean . . ."

I couldn't think of what to say. Everything I'd thought of telling him went out of my head and the only thing I could think of was his perfect teeth and that I wanted to have an abortion. I tensed myself up so I wouldn't blurt it out.

"I'm so hungry, Father," I said. I still don't know why I said that. How I let it slip through.

"What is troubling you, my child? What have you done?"

What have you done?

My hands came up around my neck. Yvonne's scarf.

"I have stolen, Father." At least that was a normal sin. Sixth Commandment. No, Seventh. I think the Sixth is about adultery.

"What have you stolen?"

"This scarf, Father."

"Anything else?"

"Some clothes."

"Are you needy?"

Well, yes, I wanted to say.

"No, Father, I am not."

"What else have you stolen?"

"Stockings, Father."

He was really having a hard time with that one. His hand
went toward his lips, which were strangely full and sensual.
I'll bet anything he likes his teeth better than those lips.

"Anything *else?*" he asked.

I don't know what made me tell him.

"And condoms, Father."

"Excuse me?"

"Condoms, they're . . ."

But I realized he knew what they were.

"Are you married, child?" He was looking at my hands.

"Yes, Father."

And then it all came out. I told him about Yvonne and
Mark, the affair, the fetus.

"Have you committed adultery?"

I thought of Brian. I didn't answer.

"Do you know what mortal sin is?"

"Yes, Father."

"Tell me what it is."

I couldn't remember if adultery was a mortal sin. I knew
murder was, and missing Mass, but adultery they'd always
skipped over in school.

"*A grievous offense, sufficient reflection, and full consent of the will*," I recited. Third grade. Memory has always been one of my strong suits.

I think he almost smiled.

"Have you committed adultery?"

I knew that a sin was committed once you thought about it. I'd sinned in thought and word if not all the way in deed.

"I didn't sleep with him, Father." As soon as I said it, it was as though I'd screamed *fuck* in the room. All sorts of pictures came into my mind. Then I was thinking it was crazy that lying on Brian's couch holding him was a sin but being shoved over a table ledge and fucked up the ass was not, as long as it was your husband. Or maybe it was a sin. If you liked it. I can't say I'd really liked it. But I can't say I didn't.

"*What* you are saying"—he bit off each word and seemed to spit them at me—"is that you are thoroughly without integrity."

"Yes, Father." *You are not my father you fucking asshole*, is what I really wanted to say. "Yes, Father."

His face stayed the same. He looked still and calm, but when I think now of his face I remember it as all twisted up.

Moe, I'd bet anything Moe is his favorite Stooge.

I couldn't even cry. I thought if I cried he'd feel sorry for me and be a little more gentle. This was just cruel.

"You are cruel," I said. I can't believe I said it. "You are cruel and mean and I refuse to be manipulated by you." I stood up. The last part made me think of Mark. What he'd said to me. I wanted Mark. I wanted to get out of this place. There was another whole night to get through and I just wanted to get home.

"Sit *down*," he said.

I sat down.

"You are to go into the chapel and get on your knees. You are to say the rosary—the full rosary—seven times before dinner. Each time asking Our Lord for forgiveness. Do you hear me?"

"Yes, Father." My voice sounded little, like it was a seam of air seeping out of my mouth. I don't remember how I got out of there.

I got to my room and closed the door. There was no lock so I pushed the desk against it. *You are thoroughly without integrity.* I put on my Walkman and blasted *Blood on the Tracks* until I couldn't think anymore. It was dark outside. The bell started ringing for Mass. I heard the footsteps build as women walked quickly down the hall. I hadn't eaten anything except an apple in two days and I was beginning to feel dizzy. The footsteps died down. When I was here in high school, my friend Helene had snuck into my room during the night. "Let's get out of this creepy joint," she'd said, as we lay under the covers, both doused in patchouli oil.

I threw my journal and books into a pile. I took my watch off the wall and put it back on my wrist. I stuffed everything into my leather bag and put on all the clothes I had. I kept the Walkman blasting. *What's good is bad what's bad is good*, Dylan was singing. I stood by the door holding all my stuff. I waited until it was quiet, then I moved the desk and left the room. I didn't pass one person in the hallway but I could hear the dull petitions and responses coming from the chapel. I got to the front door and though it was bolted I let myself out onto the grounds.

It was dark. A dog was barking somewhere nearby. It might even have been two dogs. *Dear God, don't let the dogs be loose*, I prayed. I walked toward where I heard cars on the road. Even with my terrible sense of direction it didn't take long to find my way off the grounds and out to the road. I still heard the dogs. I prayed and prayed they wouldn't be loose.

Several cars went by. There are no cabs on Staten Island. I stuck out my thumb. Puffs of air leapt out of my mouth as I breathed hard to stay warm. Within five minutes I had a ride. Before I got in the car, I threw the rosary beads into a clump of bushes.

"Merry Christmas," the driver said, looking at me. He was young. Italian it looked like.

"What?" I took off my Walkman.

"It's pretty cold to be out walking," he said.

"Yeah," I said.

"Where you going?"

"Ferry," I said.

"You live in the city?"

I nodded.

"Listen," he said. "I'll drive you to the city. I got no plans. I got nothing to do. Just riding around, you know, thinking. You know how it is."

There was a heart-shaped plastic picture frame hanging from the rearview mirror. A young woman's face smiled out of the photograph.

"My girlfriend," he said. "Debbie. She's working tonight. We're gonna get married." He grinned. "You married?"

"Yeah," I said.

"You wouldn't catch me letting my wife walk around on a cold night like this."

I laughed.

We drove past a McDonald's. "Listen," he said, "mind if I stop for a quick burger?"

I shook my head.

"Want something?"

"No," I said. He was getting out of the car. "Wait. Could you ask them for a plain roll? One that hasn't been near any meat. And coffee. Could you get me a coffee?"

He smiled. "Sure," he said. "Debbie's like that. Always on a diet."

I handed him some money.

"Get outta here," he said. "It's a Christmas present."

I lay back against the headrest and waited. The heat was beginning to reach my hands and feet. He came back with the coffee and roll. I could smell his hamburger, but it was okay. The coffee was hot and good.

The night was clear. There were a lot of stars. We ate. We drove. He talked about Debbie. Inside an hour I was back on Spring Street at the loft.

· 8 ·

$\mathcal{I}$ canceled my session with Eric this morning and went straight to Yvonne's, a little earlier than usual. I couldn't wait to get there. I don't know how I knew, but I knew she wouldn't be home. I'm starting to think we have some kind of connection. Nothing mystical, just that she must wonder about me, feel some kind of remorse. Wish she could meet me, be my friend.

I can think better at Yvonne's. There's no clutter, no clothes humped over chairs, no knocked-down stacks of books on the floor. No art or postcards or photographs— except for that dog, which I have to say I have an urge to throw out. It's like a blank screen, that place. It helps me to think. And I need to think. There's so much I need to think about: About the fetus. About Yvonne. I can't get calm enough at the loft. I can't even do a headstand in the morning anymore. I keep toppling over. I do them at Yvonne's. Then I have coffee and a raisin bagel I pick up at the Korean vegetable stand on the way. Sarah taught me how to say good morning in Korean so I've struck up a bit of a relationship with the woman at the counter. I told her it's not good to eat ice cream in the morning. Though maybe it cheers her up. Maybe she's pregnant, too.

I eat my bagel and coffee in Yvonne's bedroom, careful to brush the crumbs off the bed. There's still no sign of Mark. Not even a book he might have suggested. She's reading another one of those murder mysteries. I was thinking of pulling out a novel—something good. Maybe she'd like *Crime and Punishment*. I'm in the mood for Dostoevsky and I like the idea of us reading the same book at the same time. I looked for her class notes to see what poems she's teaching, but she must take all of them to school. In folders. Different colors for each class. She's so anal I'm sure she's a Virgo. On Tuesdays the Sunday *Times* is already thrown out. Mark and I let papers and magazines pile up week after week and it takes months to get around to throwing them out. I keep the Book Reviews around for several months and then go through them tearing out all the stuff I want to save. I know it would be a lot easier to do it week by week, but I never get around to it. I keep saying I will but I don't. I'm Sagittarius.

Mark and I haven't brought her up again. She's like a secret we've agreed not to talk about. Last Saturday night when I got home he was frantic. *Really* upset. He'd been at Sarah's and when I got to the loft all there was to greet me was a bunch of messages on the answering machine. My mother: "Mark honey, I still haven't heard from her. I'm *sure* she's fine. You *know* how *dramatic* she gets sometimes. Call me *immediately* when you get in." Sarah: "Mark, you there? I'm worried. Why don't you come over. I made some pasta. We can worry together." Mark: "Treas, if you call in or get in *please* phone me right away. I'm at Sarah's. I love you."

(He'd also left a note on the kitchen table on top of *Blonde on Blonde*.) Glenda and David: "Mark. You okay?" (I could tell they were trying very hard not to say anything funny.) "Call us if you need anything." Eric: "Hello Mark, this is Eric Anderson. I'm sorry, I haven't heard from her. Call me if there's anything I can do." It made me feel good. *Immediately. Worried. Right away.* All those people worrying about me. I have to say I was a little disappointed there was no message from Yvonne.

I didn't call Sarah's. I wanted to see Mark's expression when he walked in. To see the relief. Remorse. When he finally got home he was stunned to see me there. Maybe he'd been thinking I wouldn't come back.

"When did you get home? Didn't you get my messages?"

His first words.

I was revved up after having spent an hour dismantling my altar, throwing out all the religious paraphernalia I've accumulated over the years. Miraculous medals and novena tracts. Rosary beads and retablos and bottles of holy water I've collected at different shrines. Scapulas and holy cards and miniature statues of the Blessed Virgin. I was doing a little Spiritual Housecleaning. I threw out everything but St. Jude and the St. Lucy devotional candle from Italy. And my grandfather's statue of the Infant of Prague. Even though the Infant looks like a teenager in furs making a peace sign, I was thinking about the fetus and I'm too superstitious to throw it out. Besides, it's the only thing I have from my grandfather. I hadn't meant to take it, but once when Carla and I were using it as Barbie's husband I accidentally knocked his head off. Though we fixed it well enough with Elmer's glue and toothpicks, I was too scared to put it back.

"Why didn't you call?" Mark asked. "Where've you been? You look like hell."

Mark saying "hell" reminded me of God, and I'd sworn not to think about God. I went over and leaned into Mark, put my arms around him.

"I love you," I said. "I'm so tired. So hungry."

He made me a bowl of pastina and I drank two glasses of red wine—fuck the fetus. Then I collapsed.

I still haven't told him anything about those two days. But I'm eating again. And I have an appointment for an ultrasound tomorrow. My pregnancy test came out negative, but Dr. Bradford said my pelvis and vagina show definite signs of pregnancy and with my missed period we have to be sure. I've lost nine pounds since the last time I was there. That surprised me.

"You look pathetic," Mark said last night as I was getting undressed. "Where are your tits?" He nudged me around with his foot, felt my ribs, my behind. "Your ass is disappearing. You're getting skinny." Then he pulled me on top of him and kissed me. "My crazy pregnant wife," he said. "Those hormones are making you a little nuts, you know."

Well, maybe they are making me crazy, but I don't *look* any smaller. I've checked myself in all our mirrors—and Yvonne's. Yvonne's clothes have begun to hang on me, though. This morning I brought them all back. The black skirt and blouse I wore on my first date with Brian. Everything but the scarf and stockings. I had the skirt and blouse dry-cleaned, but when I got there I balled them up and shoved them in the back of the closet behind the shoe-boxes. I like committing secret acts of messiness in her apartment. She needs it. The way babies need to ingest a lit-tle dirt to make sure they don't develop too weak an immune system. I threw one of the cookies back there with them too. Let her get ants.

I went through her lingerie drawer and found a pair of black lace panties. I did my yoga in them. I laid across her bed and ate my bagel and coffee in them. It's strange to sit in someone else's apartment in your underwear. *Their* under-wear. I slipped my copy of *Blood on the Tracks* into the cheap tape player on her nightstand and thought about Brian. I've seen him every day since I got back and he's the only one I've told about the retreat house.

"Fuckin' *Jesuits?*" he asked. It was a relief to talk to a Catholic and not have to explain.

"You went to the fuckin' *Jesuits?*"

I love the way he says the word. *Fuckin'*. With a sharp *f* and a kind of a grunt.

"What did they do? Beat you with a stick? Throw you on the floor and make you lick the fuckin' hosts off the tiles?" Brian had gone to a Jesuit school in Ireland, so he knows all about them.

I laid across Yvonne's bed thinking of Brian shoving me to the floor. Falling on top of me. Pulling my hair as he pushed up my skirt and came hard inside me. I turned over on my stomach and pressed against the spread. Pushed two fingers up against my clit, wedged a throw pillow between my legs, my head grinding into the rough chenille. Dylan was singing "Tangled Up in Blue." Brian was holding my breasts, slamming against me, yanking my hips up as his cock moved quickly in and out. *Come, goddammit*, he was saying. When it occurred to me that Brian would never be this kind of lover, I flipped it around and pictured myself humped over him, shoving my fingers up his ass as he moved down on them and pushed back away from the pain. *I'm just going to hurt you a little*, I whispered beside his head, holding him, rocking him. *Come on, baby*. I rolled him back over, mounted him, mouthed down on his cock and sucked. It was the third time I came this morning. Maybe pregnancy makes you horny.

Dylan's voice was getting weaker and I popped the battery out of Yvonne's red plastic alarm clock and switched it with the one in the tape player. It reminded me of the first time.

Eric made me pay for my missed sessions. He insisted it wasn't meant as punishment, that I knew what the rules were and if he'd felt there was a substantial reason I'd missed he'd bend the rules a little.

"*Love has pitched his mansion in the place of excrement*," I said.

"Terry, I can't force you to talk to me."

Try, I wanted to say. I liked the idea of him forcing me to talk. Strapping me to the couch and injecting me with truth serum. I've always been fascinated by the idea of truth serum. That something could make you say things you didn't want to say, say things you didn't even know you knew. I don't even know if there is such a thing.

I was on the couch. Eric thinks it will help me open up. There's so much I haven't told him, I get confused just trying to keep track of what I *can* say. For the longest time I just laid there watching little bits of plaster drift from a crack in the ceiling. *What you are saying is that you are thoroughly without integrity.* I was thinking about Father Dugan and "The Hound of Heaven." About Yeats and things falling apart. I felt like I was falling apart.

"Do you want to talk about where you were last weekend?" Eric asked.

I did. I wanted to talk. I wanted to tell Eric everything. Just like I'd wanted to talk to Father Dugan. But I didn't know where to start.

"I hate Christmas," I said, just to say something.

He crossed his legs. He was wearing the black shoes. "What do you hate about it?" he asked.

We were like two gears that wouldn't get in sync.

I rolled over onto my side away from him, my face pressed to the back of the couch. I wonder what he'd do if I started to masturbate right in front of him. Mark's the only person who's ever seen me masturbate. He made me show him.

"You touch *what?*" he asked once, teasing. "Come on, let's get a little specific."

I was lying on his couch. It was early on, when we'd first become lovers. I remember Miles Davis in the background. Miles Davis was always in the background. Mark loves Miles Davis.

"Come on, I want to see you do it."

In some ways it's the most shocking thing he's ever asked

me to do. By myself. With him watching. It took a couple of hours, quite a lot of red wine, and a little pot before I could even make a gesture.

"You lay on your stomach?" he asked.

"Sometimes on my back."

"Show me."

But I couldn't. Not that time.

"What are you thinking about?" Eric asked.

I started humming Dylan's "Memphis Blues Again." I'd been playing *Blonde on Blonde* incessantly and realized the other day that the line I've always heard as *to be stuck inside a mobile* actually said nothing of the sort. All these years I've been hearing it wrong. I was high the first time I heard it. I'd imagined myself hanging in a gray vapor, blowing around on a piece of string, separate and alone, dangling from a wire hanger for all the world to see.

"Terry . . ."

I'd dreamed about it again and again, for a long time. Blowing in a vapor on a mobile. Blowing in the wind.

I rolled onto my back.

"Mobiles," I said.

"Mobiles?"

"Yes, mobiles."

Neither of us said anything for a minute.

"The kind you hang over a baby's crib?" he asked.

I was staring at the ceiling. The peeled patch looked like an enormous breast. I closed my eyes.

Baby. I turned toward him. I started to cry. I started sobbing so hard I couldn't stop.

Eric looked pleased, as though he'd been waiting for this moment all his life.

"Go ahead," he said. He leaned forward. "That's good. Cry all you want to."

As if I could have stopped.

He pushed the tissues toward me and I thought I'd scream. Everything felt dead. Like I was stuck out in a fog all alone. More alone that I'd ever been. I felt scared to be that alone. There was no one I was sure of. Nothing. Not Mark. Not Eric. Not Brian. I'd seen Brian flirting with one of my other students in class the day before.

Eric leaned toward me, his chin resting on the tips of his fingers. I could feel his eyes going over me, waiting.

I couldn't breathe. I tried to breathe, but I started choking. I made myself cough harder and more violently but Eric didn't come over. He wouldn't touch me.

I wanted to kill him.

"The baby," I said. "The baby."

He leaned all the way forward in his chair, those praying hands moving toward me.

"Did you have an ultrasound?"

I had. I'd done everything they said to do. Followed every direction.

"Did you drink your gallon of water?" the technician had asked.

"Good girl," she said when I answered.

"You told me to," I said.

It seems I was one of a very small minority that actually paid attention to the directions.

"I'm Catholic," I said. "Obedient to the bone." Mark's words.

The technician laughed. "Madre de Dios," she said. "Me too." She had a smile button and a tag that said "María."

"You think you can show me my soul on that thing?" I teased.

María laughed. She laid me down, pulled up my gown, and placed her hand on my stomach. The clear cream she smeared across my abdomen had a babyish smell. I watched the TV monitor as she flipped on the machine. I tried not to move. I had to pee so badly I was afraid it would start to leak out of me. My stomach puffed up like that made me look pregnant. My belly rounder than I'd ever seen it. I thought of the baby curled up in there. My baby. Mine and Mark's. How it could be six weeks old by now. How I would take care of it. Bond with it. How it would think I was the most important person in the world. It. *Her*, maybe. I could find out if it was a boy or a girl if I wanted. Maybe there were two of them. Twins. My cousin Nora had had twins and said how amazing it was to see them both on the screen curled around one another. To know they were hers. Her babies. She saw the little penises form, the babies move and kick and punch against one another. There's a good chance I would have twins. I know that. A very good chance. I looked at the screen.

"That's your uterus," María said. "What do you see?"

The baby looked like a cloud of gas. Bubbles and vapors and a gray blotch hanging in the center. I couldn't remember what size it was supposed to be by now, but I guessed the gray blotch was it. My baby.

"There's only one," I said, relieved.

"None," she said. "Nada. There's nothing in there. That's the water you're seeing." They hadn't told me not to drink carbonated. "And your ovaries."

"There's no baby?"

All around me, tacked to the walls, were foggy gray-and-white photos, X-rays of the insides of women. In the glary fluorescent light María's smile button kept ricocheting this weird grimace.

"No baby." She leaned toward me. "Are you relieved?" she asked.

I couldn't stop looking at that button. "I'm not pregnant?"

"You're not pregnant."

"Are you sure?"

She started to laugh.

"I'm not pregnant," I said to Eric. "There's no baby. No baby. I think I killed it. I think I starved it to death."

"Terry, there'd have been a dead fetus in there," Eric said.

That struck me as a rather callous thing to say.

I stared at him.

"Are you disappointed?"

Disappointed.

"*Please* hold me," I said.

He didn't say anything though I heard a change in his breathing. I wonder if he was sitting there thinking of himself as a prism.

"I can't hold you," he said, "but I think it's very important for us to talk about why you want to be held."

"Why can't you just hold me?"

"And what is your fantasy about that?"

"Don't you love me?"

"*Who* is it you're talking to?"

I still can't believe I let that one go by without a good crack.

We just sat there.

"I don't know," I said finally, "I don't know who I'm talking to. I don't know who you are."

I got up, wrote him a check, and left. Ten minutes early.

That afternoon he left a message at the loft saying I'd written out the check to myself.

· 9 ·

J feel so empty without the baby. I'm continually hungry. Nothing fills me up. Yesterday I ate three-quarters of a raisin bagel as I walked down Bleecker Street. In the middle of the day. Then I had half of a banana, the better part of a vanilla yogurt, and a peanut-butter-and-jelly sandwich when I got home. I was still hungry but by dinner I was afraid to eat anything else so I just sat with Mark while he ate. I even picked at the sautéed zucchini on his plate. If this keeps up I'm going to look like Anita Ekberg before the month is out. *What's wrong with that?* I can hear my mother ask. Anita Ekberg is my father's idea of the perfect woman, a standard my mother comes pretty close to meeting.

Last night I dreamed I was sucking Brian's cock, spitting the come into a brandy snifter. When I woke up I was starving and furious with Mark. I felt his arms around me and pushed them away, yanked some of the blankets over to my side. I hate it when he hoards the blankets. I was thinking about what I could eat for breakfast. He kissed my neck, my back, his cock hard against me. I pushed away from him but I started to get excited. I climbed on top and straddled his hips.

"You're wet," he mumbled.

I was thinking about Brian. How much I wanted to touch him, hold him. For long, indefinite periods of time. My mouth all over him, my hands. I wanted to lick him, suck him, tongue his nipples. Brian's nipples are smoother than Mark's. His whole body is smoother. Paler. He's more a boy somehow, though he's only eight years younger than Mark. I wanted to feel him between my legs, to ride him, rock him.

He knows.

"Maybe that wouldn't be good for you right now," he said the other day. We were in the adjunct's office. "You've been so upset."

"Don't you want me?"

"Terry, it's not that." He closed the door, put his arm around me, and kissed me, his tongue kind of tentative and exploring. I held to it with my mouth. It was almost enough.

I explained that maybe for a while I just needed him to hold me with sexual intent. He's the first man I've ever tried to get into bed and it's harder than I thought. He always has some kind of excuse and it always has to do with me, but I think he's just protecting himself. I've studied language, so why it took me so long to realize "I'd really love to" is a long day's haul from "I will" I still can't figure out. I guess it's bad to want something too much. It somehow leaves the other person out of it. Mark used to quote this line from Nietzsche—something about in the end one loves only one's desire and not what is desired. I hate it when he says stuff like that. Mark, I mean. I had the quote lettered onto a T-shirt for his thirty-third birthday. Above the quote I had the guy put a picture of Moe. I have to find that.

Mark slapped me on the ass. "Where'd you go?" he asked. He held my hips and circled me over him, lifted me up and down his cock. Our pubic hair is almost identical in color and texture. It's hard to tell us apart. Once I braided us together. "Now you have to marry me," I said. "Now we're inseparable."

I didn't want to look at Mark, think about him. I looked at the framed picture of Curly above the nighttable. He looked so innocent, so sweet. I can't imagine that Curly ever hurt a woman. Had an affair and then lied about it. Made her think she was pregnant when she wasn't.

The other day Mark said he thought I blamed him for suggesting it. I said it wasn't true, but it is. He said didn't I think he'd have feelings about it, too. That I wasn't the only one who was disappointed. Disappointed. The same word Eric used.

Mark came. I barely felt him. I pushed away and got up before I came myself. The first time I ever did that. He didn't say anything. I felt a little crazy inside. *My pelvis in a welter*, I thought in the bathroom, brushing my teeth. I liked the sound of it. *Pelvis in a welter*. I knew I'd be nuts all day if I didn't come, but I was going to Yvonne's in a couple of hours.

I saw her. I saw Yvonne. At first I didn't realize it was her. I'd been thinking about her so much that when I was looking right at her I must have thought she was in my mind. She looked different from the way she looks when she's teaching. In the first place, she was naked. We were both naked. We were in the locker room at the NYU gym. I've been swimming for an hour a day instead of my usual half hour, to make up for the extra calories I'm taking in. I do some c.v. for twenty minutes—bike or Stairmaster—then I swim.

I don't know what Yvonne was doing there. I've been going to that gym for five years and I've never seen her. I don't think she's an alum though I'm going to check her credentials in the Columbia bulletin. Anyway, the strange thing is that she was right there, naked—except for these big greenish earrings—talking to this blond woman I've talked to a number of times. Once the blond woman had asked if she could smell the bottle of Neutrogena sesame oil I was using and I let her try some. It was strange to think of her knowing Yvonne. Talking to her as though they were friends.

"That's the guy you went out with once last year, right?" Yvonne said. "The one who doesn't eat meat."

I'd really only seen her lecture on Yeats, so it was odd to hear her talking about such everyday stuff—to think of her conversing with someone I knew. Although when you think of it, why should it seem odder than her fucking my husband? Her voice sounded different from the way it did in class or on the telephone. It was a little voice. A little squeaky voice. Well, not squeaky, really, but I couldn't believe Mark would go for that little voice. The high pitch.

Mark says I have a deep voice for a relatively short woman. He says he loves my voice.

"Is he going with you?" the blond woman was asking Yvonne.

I was at the end of the aisle by the mirror and my locker. I leaned back out of view. Yvonne, as far as I know, had never seen me, but I didn't want to take any chances. Just in case someone had pointed me out to her at that opening in October. Mark, or even Glenda, that bitch. Besides, if she's been to the loft or the gallery she might have seen a picture of me.

"No. No, he can't," Yvonne said.

The thought that she was probably talking about Mark made me get that shaky, hypoglycemic feeling. I leaned against the locker. She could, I thought, as easily be talking about a dog. I wanted her to talk about Mark. And I wanted desperately for her not to. It's conceivable, I thought, that she could even mention me. I was scared. I was thrilled. I wanted to hear my name cross her tongue. I wanted to hear her talk about me. Wonder about me. Express shame, remorse, curiosity, jealousy. The dreams I'd had of her rushed back to me, our Opium smell. I stole her bottle of Opium last week. It felt like a mythic thing to do. Something Medea would do.

I was listening hard, but I was in such an erotic panic, watching her move, watching the body my husband had made love to, had maybe only fucked, had maybe made love to and fucked, that I could barely hear. She turned to her locker. Her body was still wet and a little red from the shower. So was mine. I tipped my bottle of Neutrogena sesame oil and began to rub it into my skin, watching her all the time. It was exam time so the locker room was relatively empty. We were just about the only women in the place, though I heard voices from a few rows down, the hiss of the showers going.

I was rubbing oil into the same leg over and over. The panel of light above me had gone out and I had to move down a row to use the mirror. If I'd gone to the nearest mirror I would have been within a few feet of them and I didn't trust myself.

Dear God, keep me calm, I whispered. Then I remembered I'd sworn not to say "God" anymore. I moved back.

Yvonne has a beautiful body. Her skin is nearly the same color as Brian's, which strikes me as funny. She's pale, with little moles here and there. Her breasts are small, her nipples not very prominent, but they're inviting. Her belly's flat. She almost looks like a girl except for those earrings she wears, which are too big for her. They look like garbage can lids with streamers hanging from them. When you're under five-foot-five large earrings like that tend to make you look like a Christmas tree. She had one foot up on the wood bench and I looked up her legs into her cunt. She rubbed baby oil (I made a note to check Mark for that smell) along her calf and blocked the view but I waited. Her pubic hair isn't as curly as mine and lays flat against her mons. I thought of Mark fucking that body. Thought of his hands holding her ass (she has a nice ass), his tongue slithering through that pubic hair into the folds of her. I wonder what she tastes like. I know women taste different from one another, just like men do.

Sarah always says so. So does Mark. I've only once had my mouth to a woman's vagina and it was too fast and scary to remember much of anything. I remember thinking it was like a cat licking itself, it was all so familiar.

Yvonne was so close to me I could have smelled her if I was blind and had so trained my sense of smell. I memorized her body as I dressed, catching snatches of conversation. I mean I heard everything they were saying, but they were talking in snatches the way women do when they're getting dressed, checking the mirror, tracing an eyelid, turning to see how they look from different angles. I liked watching Yvonne watch herself in the mirror. For a moment I believed I could have enjoyed watching her fuck my husband.

As I reached for my clothes I realized I was holding her panties and I almost laughed. I wondered if she would notice. Part of me wanted to put them on and walk over to her and ask a simple question, say about the hours the gym would be open during Christmas break. At the last minute I chickened out. I thought she might recognize the panties. I've lain on her bed in them, seduced my husband in them, taught my classes. Each night I rinse them and hang them in the kitchen window to dry and wait for Mark to notice. It's like hanging out a flag.

I fingered styling gel through my wet hair and waited for it to dry. Yvonne leaned into her mirror, patting eye cream below her eyes. A Lancôme sample. I recognized the tube.

"I'll only be gone five days," she was saying. She closed her eyes and sprayed her face with toner. "I leave next Thursday."

Gone. I moved a little closer. I willed the blond woman to ask her questions, show some interest. *Pump* her.

"I've never been to St. Croix," the woman said.

Yvonne said something, but someone in the next aisle turned on a blow-dryer so I missed it.

St Croix. So she'd be gone. That's probably why her name wasn't on the guest list for the gallery Christmas party I saw on Glenda's desk. I wanted to know if anyone would be staying at her place but it didn't come up. It'll be easy enough to find out.

"You coming tomorrow?" Yvonne asked.

"Same time."

"Okay. I'll meet you. I have a week to get in shape."

She looked in pretty good shape to me. I watched her get into the pantyhose I remembered were Donna Karan. She pulled on a teal green cashmere sweater I'd considered stealing but hadn't, a black wool skirt I didn't recognize. Every edge was tucked, every piece in place. Not a string loose. I could guess her workout clothes were the same. If I had to bet, I'd guess she did the bikes or Stairmaster. That she had new white sneakers, sweats impeccably laundered and pressed. Not a ragged edge on the T-shirt. I figured I could meet them the next day and see for myself.

"Are you staying downtown?" the blond woman asked, slamming her locker shut.

I couldn't hear what Yvonne said. It hit me then that she was only a few blocks from the gallery. How could she be this close and not drop in? I swore to myself, swore to God, I would not follow her. I didn't think I could take it. Besides, I still hadn't put my clothes on and they were ready to leave.

But I checked Mark later for the scent of baby oil.

The next day I got there a couple of hours early just to watch. I didn't know how long they worked out and I wanted time with them. I figured I'd stay the whole day at the gym if I had to, to see them change, figure out her routine, watch her shower and dress. And I needed to get in at least twenty minutes on the bike and an hour of swimming.

I'd forgotten to eat lunch, which I saw as a good sign. I'd brought several of my students' papers with me to read. It was the end of the semester, I had a backlog of papers I needed to read, and I was ready for a break. I have to admit I've been falling off. Winging it. Thank God I've memorized as many poems as I have because I've stopped preparing lectures.

They came at 2:00, not long after I got there. Yvonne was in jeans with the same cashmere sweater. I guess that's one of the staples. Maggie is the other woman's name. When they arrived I was straddling the bench, reading a student paper on love and betrayal in Yeats's poems. It's interesting how many of them have chosen to write on themes of betrayal, loss, and the beloved.

Yvonne lifted her blouse, unhooked her bra—one of those white lacy kinds that hooks in the front. I've seen it in her drawer. She slid her pants down over her hips and I could see her doing it for Mark. Mark loves to watch women undress. "Take off your clothes," he used to say to me in perfect imitation of Daniel Day-Lewis in *The Unbearable Lightness of Being*. I've seen that movie three times. I love the way Tomas watches women, but my favorite part is when Tereza and

Sabina are naked together. When Tereza is photographing Sabina, then Sabina Tereza. How Sabina seduces Tereza into her own nakedness. I love the way Tomas becomes almost secondary. An afterthought.

"Take off your clothes," I imagined myself saying to Yvonne. I'd tried it on Brian the other night, but he'd resisted, saying, yet again, he thought I was too upset. I hate men sometimes.

"Take off your clothes," I whispered. "Take off your clothes."

Yvonne is a methodical undresser. I could bet she takes her clothes off in the same order every time. Maybe everyone does.

"Do you think I look fat?" she asked Maggie, stepping up onto the bench—not three yards down from where I sat—and looking in the mirror. She turned to look at herself from behind. She frowned. It almost made me love her.

Maggie let out a puff of breath for answer. "Right," she said. "Enormous." She didn't understand.

No, you look good, I wanted to say, you look beautiful.

I stretched my legs out and leaned my chest down on my knees. I was afraid to keep looking. I wanted to be naked with her again. I wanted to talk to her. I wanted to tell her I was Mark's wife just to see how she'd react, to see the way her expression would change. I pulled off my clothes and threw them in the locker. I almost did it too, almost went over, but I got scared. I was afraid I'd blow it. I was looking at the slight impression the zipper of her jeans had left along her abdomen when I noticed Maggie looking at me.

It wasn't a shocked look. No, it's pretty common for women to watch each other's bodies in the locker room. Even to comment on them if the situation's right.

"Hi," Maggie said, nodding.

"How're you doing?" I asked. I tried to sound casual. "We have the place pretty much to ourselves, huh?"

"Yeah," Maggie said. "I love end of the semester."

"Do you teach here?" I asked.

She pulled on her sweats. Yvonne was doing the same. Navy blue shorts. White T-shirt. Clean and pressed. Impossibly white sneakers.

"No," she said, "alumni."

"Me too," I said. I wanted to get in the fact that I taught here, too. Draw Yvonne into the conversation. Impress her.

"I just joined," Yvonne said. "I teach at Columbia and can work out there for nothing but I like being downtown these days."

Sure you do, sweetie, I thought, and tried to keep my face natural.

"What do you do? Bicycle?" I asked. 'Course she did. Probably reads one of those murder mysteries while she's at it.

The whole encounter makes me shake now, but I truly started to feel almost ordinary as I talked to her.

"Those are pretty big earrings," I said. "Do you work out with those on? It looks pretty dangerous."

"I always forget," she said, and took them out.

"You look really familiar," I said. "Do you live down here?"

"Uh-uh," she said, tying her laces tighter. She did it carefully, didn't yank and choke.

"Huh," I said. It's what people say when they feel like they have to say something but have nothing to say.

We said a bit of this and that and then they were gone. I'd managed to find out how long they spent on the bikes and made sure I got down in time to meet them again.

"Looks like we're on the same schedule," I said. I shook the water out of my hair. I'd been swimming for only half an hour, but figured I'd make the rest up later.

And then we were both naked. Maggie was in the shower. I usually don't talk much to the women around me at the gym. Once you're on someone's schedule and you begin to talk you're almost obligated to talk to them every time. I hate that. Even when I'm using the same mirror as another woman I usually just smile and stay focused on putting on my mascara. But Yvonne was different, and I had the feeling I wouldn't be seeing a lot of her. She didn't seem the sort who would come like clockwork. We were both in front of the same mirror. Yvonne had her back to me and was applying lipstick to her lower lip. Scarlet Memory. She held her bottom lip stretched across her teeth and traced the familiar color without one false move. She was an expert.

"I figured out where I know you from," I said. It was out of my mouth before I could think. Even then I knew I could easily backpedal, say something about the MLA conference, or simply be mistaken.

We were standing by the mirror. She looked at my reflection as she pressed the bottom and top lip together to spread the color. She smiled. There were still tiny drops of water down her back and her hair was in a towel. I leaned into the mirror and traced eyeliner across my left eye.

"I remember you from Daisy Lewis's opening."

She looked like she was trying to remember the name.

"Oh," she said, "at Holder."

"Yeah," I said.

"Is Daisy a friend of yours?"

She was brushing her mascara on. After the lipstick. I thought most women put on their lipstick last.

"Not really. My husband owns the gallery."

Just like that. I said it. Like I was saying that my eyes are brown or that tomorrow is Thursday. She held the mascara wand in front of her eyelashes. I hadn't noticed before that there were goosebumps along her arms and back, but now I could see the light bumps along her shoulder. She has pretty shoulders.

"I don't know why, but I remember seeing you there. Isn't that funny?"

Now I think this is what I said, because I got so excited talking to her that I can't really remember exactly. I was standing next to her, looking at her face in the mirror, about to reach into my locker and put on her panties.

"God, you must have a great memory," she said. Pretty cool. I could barely detect a quiver. As a dramatic touch, I pulled the Scarlet Memory out of my bag. I must have been nervous because I had to keep wiping the excess off from under my lip.

"I do," I said. "I used to think it was just for words—you know, poems, stories—I've memorized half of Yeats"—she looked surprised—"but more and more I realize it's for faces, streets. I guess I have a good eye. I take things in. Mark always says so. And I have to say I was bored by the work, so I spent the night talking people up and looking at the crowd. I remember you."

Right. A face for what had only been a name. Yvonne. Yvonne laughing. Smiling up into Mark's face with that unmistakable look of rapt adoration. The way she giggled and held on to his arm as she reached down to fix the strap on her shoe. Mark bopping her over the head with a rolled stack of announcements. And me right there, on the other side of the room, watching.

"The work wasn't very interesting, was it?" Yvonne said. "Typical minimalist stuff."

"Yeah. Not my favorite thing the gallery has put up. I think it looked better on the slides." I wondered if we were just going to talk about art.

"You know, I teach Yeats," she said.

"Really," I said. "Where?"

I have masturbated on this woman's bed. Worn her clothes. Written in her books.

"Oh, of course. Columbia. You said before. My short-term memory lags sometimes," I laughed. "I teach Yeats, too."

She really is hard to read. Good WASP upbringing. Do not betray your thoughts. We had a pleasant little exchange about teaching and Yeats, the new collection of letters to Maud Gonne. That kind of thing.

"You really love Yeats," she said at one point. I had a feeling the moment was important, but then Maggie wandered back.

Yvonne and I were almost dry by then but still naked. Maggie was dripping. A tampon string hung between her legs. She pulled out the Neutrogena.

"I put it on when I'm wet," she said. "Just like you said." Something I remembered from my sister Carla's compulsive magazine reading and tidbits of beauty advice.

"What's your name?" Yvonne asked.

"Tereza," I said. I wonder if this is becoming pathological.

"Oh," Yvonne said. "I'm Yvonne and this is Maggie."

We all smiled. Maggie began to put on her makeup. Yvonne and I towel-dried our hair. I'd chosen a locker nearer to the ones they'd used the day before, gambling on the fact that most people gravitate to the same spot day after day. Do something twice and it's a habit. That's how I am, anyway.

We talked about end of term, student plagiarism, the art world. It was almost bizarre. In the spaces where we weren't talking I hummed and sang. Some country song about cheating hearts and stolen lovers. It made me feel like a director creating a scene. Then we'd talk some more. Nothing unusual, but something felt strange to me and for a while I couldn't put my finger on it. Then I realized what it was. Yvonne and I were flirting with one another. Maggie was busy dressing and Yvonne and I were completely focused on one another. Her attention was drawn. I don't

think it was my imagination. She was curious. She was looking at me, comparing. I wonder if she sees the similarities.
I'd noticed in the mirror that we are almost exactly the same
height. I was glad I wasn't wearing any more of her clothes.

I wrung out my bathing suit over the tiles and looped the
straps around the combination lock.

"I wish I could swim," she said abruptly.

I began to pull on black tights and my boots. I felt shy in
front of her, wearing her underwear, so I tried to dress
quickly. My winter coat had half fallen out of the locker
onto the floor. I shoved it back in with my foot.

"You can't go to St. Croix and not go in the water," I said,
zipping my skirt. "That's crazy." Neither of us noticed that
she'd never mentioned her trip to me.

"Could I learn in a week?" she asked in a flirtatious kind
of way. Her left hip was pushed slightly forward, her head
tilted.

"I could teach you," I said. It occurs to me this is tanta-
mount to Medea telling Jason's new wife she'd take her
shopping for a new brocade robe. "But not in a week."

She stood looking at me as if she were afraid to turn
around and dress. Shy all of a sudden. Both of us shy and
ashamed. Exposed, but not knowing how exposed. There's a
light down on her arms, no rings on her fingers, which she
held at an angle on her narrow but shapely hips.

"You have a good body for swimming," I said. Then I
noticed a faint bruise at the very top of her thigh, near her
pelvis. Like a thumbprint.

Leave a mark on me, I used to say to Mark while we were

fucking. *Leave a mark. I want to see you on me.* We developed
a game in which he'd mark me—the mark of Mark, he
called it—somewhere different each time. Nothing obvious
or brutal. Nothing that hurt really. Or just a little. Enough
for me to feel him there. Later I'd have to remember where
it was. Then I began to mark him, leave my impression—a
toothmark, a sucked spot on his neck. Terry the Terror, he
called me. Marking my terror-tree. He's always played with
my name like that. When I get scared he says I'm terri-fied.
Sometimes he calls me Terrible Terry. Well, it's possible
he'll find out just how terrible I can be.

I jumped up, bent over and began brushing my hair. I
don't know if it was the rush of blood to my brain or what,
but I felt really funny—like I was going to pass out. I sat on
the bench.

"Are you all right?" Yvonne asked.

"Dizzy," I said. "I feel terrible all of a sudden."

"Push your head down," she said. She bent my head to
my knees.

The hiss of showers and occasional laughter and voices
sounded through the locker room. I felt like I was under
water. Yvonne's cool hand on my neck, her fingers gently
rubbing the tense cords. Water drops from our wet bodies
spotted the floor. Her bare foot, a callus on the third toe. A
shaving nick just below her knee. I could smell her baby oil,
my Opium.

"Maybe you need to eat something," she was saying.
"When was the last time you ate?"

· 1 0 ·

$\mathcal{I}$t might seem odd or dangerous telling Yvonne I'm Mark's wife. That she'd report back to him, that he'd tell her—if he hadn't already—that I'd accused him of having an affair with her. But I know Mark. Mark keeps things separate. When I picture Mark's mind it's like a series of little boxes, rooms without doors. Like accordion files lined up in a file cabinet. Mark doesn't mix. He doesn't mix drinks. He doesn't mix styles. He doesn't mix friends. If he's playing Coltrane he gets—*uneasy* is the only word for it—if, when it's over, I put on an opera or the soundtrack from *The Sound of Music*, even the Beatles. I mean it's not necessarily the music he objects to, just the combination.

Just like he refused to talk to me about Yvonne, I know he would not have mentioned me to her. I mean beyond the fact that he was married. He would *never* have told her of our argument about her, I know that much. We were married two years before I found out he'd been to the emergency room with his old girlfriend, Isabelle—on the same night we saw *Casablanca* at Theater 80—and never mentioned it. I don't even remember now why it was he finally told me. If she knew Mark, Yvonne would probably never mention meeting me. She'd already know which room was hers, which file. Even if she brought it up Mark wouldn't say any-thing. To me or to her. And I don't particularly care if he *does* find out I spoke to her.

In fact, I wouldn't be surprised if she preferred me to Mark. I'm much more passionate and emotional. Yvonne would like that.

Yvonne. Yvonne. Yvonne. I can't stop thinking about her. When I'm not thinking about Yvonne I'm thinking about Brian. It occurs to me I'm becoming obsessive. Eric says I have to learn to separate, to see myself apart from everyone else. Which is funny because the other night I dreamt that our accountant showed me Xeroxes of Lisa and Carla and asked which twin was the original. Which had the soul. I said Lisa was born first, so Carla must be the replica. "Yvonne," he said. And then Yvonne was there. I told Mark about the dream—leaving out the part about Yvonne.

"You should write it down," he said. "Maybe you could make a poem out of it."

I think he's annoyed that I still haven't shown him my poems. He said I was probably just worried about the Christmas party and all the different people who would be there.

"That's your thing," I said. "That's about you. Lucky a lot of people have already left town, huh?"

But I was glad Yvonne would be out of town for the party. I was reading our horoscopes. Hers—I read Virgo for her—said she'd be at her most radiant in the coming days and would be a smashing success in matters of love. I was glad she was in St. Croix and hoped she'd meet someone. I did a visualization in which I imagined her in passionate embrace with two native men in long dreadlocks. I surrounded them with a beautiful pink bubble and sent it floating up into the universe, as far away from New York as possible. Even if she didn't meet anyone, I didn't want her radiating up here.

Then I checked mine. I'm a sucker for horoscopes—the idea that there's some large system to rely on, an order and reason for what happens. Even though Sarah once got me a freelance job in which I revised them. Rewrote them actually. I remember thinking how many lives I affected by deleting a line about not making a job switch. Just because the copy was too long. Or changing Libra because it sounded too much like Pisces. Mark had said not to worry, it didn't matter. Mark doesn't believe in horoscopes. Neither do I, really, but you learn to cover your bases.

The entry for Sagittarius said to be clear on what you want and you would get it. I wrote what I wanted in the most precise language possible: *To get rid of Yvonne. To get Mark back.*

I met Sarah at Dean & DeLuca.

"Honey, I think you're going a little overboard with this," she said. She shook cinnamon into her cappuccino.

Overboard. I flashed on myself in Yvonne's clothes, in Yvonne's apartment. For a minute I couldn't believe what I've been doing. It scared me. It's like I have two lives. I wanted to tell her about Yvonne's. Now that she was away I'd been there every day. She has a tiny cactus I was taking care of. I knew I should tell Sarah. It always makes me feel better to talk to her, gets some of the anxiety outside of me. Sarah's different. When she feels bad she holes up in her apartment, watches videos, and won't talk at all.

"I mean, you used to be a lot more fun, you know." She took a forkful of the gingerbread we were sharing and pushed the plate over to me. She said, anyway, the best way to get rid of something is to put it out of your mind. That's what's she did with Karen. I reminded her that she'd been the one to put it *in* my mind.

"Yes, but Terry, I just mentioned it. I didn't say I had proof. I didn't say it was a fact. Listen," she said, chewing, "what woman goes to St. Thomas in the middle of a torrid affair?"

"St. Croix," I said.

But it was something I hadn't thought of. I sliced off a sliver of gingerbread and put it on my napkin. A man at the next table stuck his cigarette in a giant potted palm that was between us. I gave him a dirty look but he didn't notice.

"Honey, what proof do you have?"

"You *told* me," I said.

"I said she gave him her keys. You just took it and ran."

She had no idea how far I'd run. *Tell her*, I kept thinking. Give her Yvonne's keys. I had the keys in my bag.

"Why would he have her keys?"

Sarah broke off another piece of gingerbread and stuck it in her mouth. She stirred her cappuccino.

"You have *my* keys," she said.

I ate the gingerbread. It's true. We've had her keys ever since she locked herself out one night and had to sleep at the loft. We have Glenda's keys, too. Glenda's always losing her keys and she likes to keep a set at the gallery. Glenda says Mark's a good person to give your keys to. He's the most responsible person she knows.

"Maybe she doesn't know a lot of people," Sarah said. "Maybe it's some kind of business thing. *Ask Mark.*"

I thought about it. The keys are in the gallery, not in his wallet where he used to keep mine. I used to love watching him slip my keys into his wallet after he let himself in. I'd never know when he was about to show up. Maybe there was an explanation. Maybe it *was* a business thing.

But I wasn't convinced. I thought about Mark saying he'd learned from Proust how to tell if your lover was having an affair. I considered starting the books. But it's seven volumes. And I don't have time.

"Terry, let it go. Let Yvonne go for now. She's out of town anyway. Try to just be in the moment."

Sarah's starting to sound a little too Buddhist for me, but I decided to try. I got rid of Yvonne. I just stopped thinking about her. I made a vow not to go back to Yvonne's. I think I was drowning that cactus, anyway.

I wrote my objective: Get Mark back. I figured I could start at the party.

The worst moment of the party was when Glenda and David wheeled out a surprise birthday cake for me. Glenda was wearing a belted plastic garbage bag and these huge earrings made out of bunches of grapes, the kind my mother keeps in a bowl on the kitchen table. Women with big earrings like that scare me. Anyway, Glenda had this sneery grin and was leaning into David who was wheeling what looked like a gurney with a big cake on top. The deejay was playing a jazz samba. Imitation art masterpieces hung throughout the gallery. That afternoon, David had recounted the plots of about fifty movies while we all painted. I did a Klee, Mark did a Picasso, and Glenda did a Magritte—a couple kissing with sheets wrapped around their faces. David just slapped down a rectangle of black paint, called it a Reinhardt, and kept talking.

It was 11:15. I was looking for Mark. I was trying not to think about Yvonne, but the gallery was filled with all the same people who'd been there the first time I'd seen her. Moiling crowds of black clothes consuming what seemed like an endless supply of liquor and hors d'oeuvres. Now and then I'd see my father's red Christmas shirt. My mother had on her red-and-green Christmas suit and huge earrings made out of green glass ornaments. The thing is, hers were for real. Hers were not worn with attitude, as a comment— the way Glenda's were. She wore them sincerely. Mark had insisted on inviting my parents. He said that as long as it was going to be a weird mix we might as well go all the way. Besides, he really likes them. Lisa and Carla were there too, and both of them were wandering the crowd trying to pick up a man like Mark. Sarah had given up on the Buddhist stuff and was in the bathroom crying, and I'd promised to scout the room for a gorgeous, unpretentious, sexually aggressive, *and* available woman. And she had to be gay, or at least willing.

That's when I saw Glenda and David advancing upon me

with the gurney. As if that weren't bad enough, the deejay, who was, it turns out, David's friend, put on a record of "Happy Birthday Baby Jesus" that came with the little red record player my parents bought me when I was eight. I'd been drinking red wine, then white, then anything that was handed to me, which is not a good thing for me to do, my tolerance for alcohol being what it is. Anyway, I was thinking what a coincidence it was the deejay had that record, when my parents appeared by my side singing "Happy Birthday Baby Jesus," my father in his forced baritone that gets more operatic after he's had a drink, my mother tilting her head, smiling and flirting up the crowd. Glenda was tossing those grapes this way and that as if to say "isn't that cute," and David—who sported a black Mylar suit and an aluminum foil tie and looked like the guy grinning over the drugstore counter in the Kotex ads they used to run in *Seventeen*—was leaning toward me asking if I'd seen the cake.

The cake: It was a portrait—a replica—of Yeats. All done in this grayish and pinkish icing. What I remember most are the glasses and the tufts of gray hair. With those continuous burn candles glowing in a kind of halo around him. Yeats looked awful as a cake. I couldn't think of a more stupid thing to put on a birthday cake. Yeats. Jesus.

"Oh, isn't that cute," my mother said. "Who is that? He looks like Lionel Barrymore."

"Did you meet them? They're great," someone behind me said. "They're Terry's parents."

"Yeah," someone else said. "Can you believe her sisters? Classic. Straight out of Scorsese."

Others because you did not keep. I tried to smile. I wanted
Sarah. I wished Brian had come. I'd invited him but he said
he didn't think it was proper. Well, it's not proper to have
Yeats made into a birthday cake either.

"Yeats," I said. "It's Yeats." I tried to laugh.

"Why don't you recite one of his poems," Glenda said,
and I could feel the entire room hoping I wouldn't.
Everyone was clapping. Mark appeared by my side and
kissed me. I was thinking that if I started to cry I'd have
mascara under my eyes for the rest of the night. And a salt
blur on my lenses. I was thinking how this is the first year
I mind getting older. I mean I guess I look pretty young.
People my age always ask why I don't have any wrinkles.
I've never even *thought* about wrinkles. But at the gym the
other day I'd noticed a tiny crease under my left eye, the way
the mascara had caught under there.

"Do you like it?" Mark asked. I wondered if he'd gotten
the idea from Yvonne.

"It's great," I said. "Yeats. What made you think of it?"

"It was him or Curly," Mark said. He put his arm around
me.

"Yeah," I said, "or Medea."

I took an asparagus tip dipped in balsamic vinegar from
a passing tray and bit into it. The woman holding the tray
was dressed as Richard Serra's *Tilted Arc.* I don't know if it
was the costume or the vinegar but I started to choke. The
candles were still glowing around Yeats's head. Burning
down. *The broken wall, the burning roof and tower. And
Agamemnon dead.*

"It's Brian's birthday, too," I said between coughs.

Mark had just shoved a sundried tomato topped with mozzarella and basil into his mouth. He gave me a funny look.

"Honey, how much wine have you had?"

That was it. I started choking really hard. Mark pounded me on the back. Glenda thrust a plastic cup of wine at me. My parents' red-and-green outfits seemed to be poking through various textures of black cloth. Crowds of it. Everything began to blur and I didn't care about anything except getting to Sarah in the bathroom. Somehow I managed to blow out the candles. It did occur to me that nobody had sung "Happy Birthday" to *me*. Glenda was slicing and everyone was getting a piece of Yeats's face.

"Excuse me," I said, and pushed through the crowd.

". . . then George Segal—he's King Rat—and James Fox become buddies, even though Fox is this upper-class British officer." David was leaning toward my sister Carla, looking down her blouse. The two brothers cut out of the same cloth. I made a note to warn Carla. For a minute I even felt bad for Glenda.

On the way to the bathroom I maneuvered to avoid this pretentious performance artist whose name I can never remember, and came face-to-face with a small dark-haired woman who had a desperate, hunted look about her. It took a few seconds to realize I was looking in the mirror. I stood there staring. Another woman appeared beside me.

"*Hi*," she said. She seemed surprised. Even pleased.

"Hi," I muttered. I walked away.

"Yvonne, right?" An English accent.

I'm never good at recognizing people out of context but I knew that voice. She was from Al-Anon. Elly. She also goes to OA, AA, NA, and CODA, but she's got a great sense of humor and she's one of the few people who can make fun of the meetings. Once, during a particularly demonstrative "share," she leaned over, raised her eyebrows, and, in that clipped British voice said, "Some people shouldn't lose their inhibitions. There's a reason we have them." I liked her immediately.

"Elly," I said. "Hi." She looked so composed. Her black wool suit fit perfectly and she had on these tiny gold earrings. Tasteful. I grabbed her arm. It might have been the wine. Maybe the cake. "Elly," I said, "don't say anything. Don't say my name. And don't, *please don't*, ask me any questions. Now help me get to the bathroom."

A woman walked by and shoved a plate in front of me. "Chicken saté?" she asked, pointing to the skewered blobs of meat. I almost pushed her.

"Sorry," Elly said. She steered me to the bathroom. "Ssh," she was saying, "ssh, it's okay. It's okay."

"Terry?" Sarah sat on a papier-mâché wastebasket that was shaped like an erect penis.

"Sarah, Elly. Elly, Sarah," I said.

"Terry, what happened?" Sarah asked. She was looking at Elly, trying, I think, to figure out if I'd procured her as a potential partner.

"You mean Yvonne, don't you?" Elly said.

"*What?*" Sarah asked.

"I said *no* questions," I shouted.

"Okay, okay," Elly said.

"Lock the door," I said to Sarah. I looked at my reflection in a metallic electrical strip that ran along the wall. I found a Q-tip to wipe the mascara from under my eyes. In the stark fluorescent light I saw exactly how bad Yvonne's Scarlet Memory looked on me. It had looked fine at the loft. I rubbed it off and washed my face. I put my head under the faucet and doused my hair. Then I think we all just sat there quietly, me scrunching my hair dry, Elly leaning against the door, Sarah propped on the penis trying to transition from her misery to mine.

Elly and Sarah took to each other instantly. Sarah's a sucker for an accent.

"My name's not Yvonne," I said to Elly.

"Well, no need to break your anonymity," she said, smiling.

It was *that* easy.

Sarah caught on pretty quickly.

And then we were all laughing. Someone banged on the door but that only made us laugh harder. Sarah realized what she was balanced on and laughed so hard she rolled off the penis onto the floor. I picked it up, dumped the contents onto the floor, and shoved it head first into the toilet. Elly leaned against the door laughing. I realize now she was the only one of us not over their alcohol limit. She hadn't drunk anything. She was just laughing.

"This dress is Yvonne's," I said, but neither of them heard.

Maybe it was saying Yvonne's name. Maybe it was David

leaning over Carla, or that stupid cake, but I remembered
the first time Sarah had pointed her out. The opening. The
same crowd. How nervous Sarah had been. Tentative and
conflicted. *Maybe I shouldn't have said anything*, she had said.
Yvonne holding Mark's arm, smiling up into his face. Mark
bopping her with those rolled announcements.

She gave him her keys. I saw them. At the gallery.

"Terry?" Sarah was standing beside me.

"*Why* did you tell me?" I moaned.

Sometime around midnight whoever was left ended up on
the dance floor. I'd gotten the deejay to play some old Stones
and we were dancing hard. Me and Sarah and Elly. I knew
they were with me but could sense Sarah investigating Elly,
Elly flirting back, and even in my misery I wanted to leave
them a little time alone.

I danced with anyone who asked. Anyone who just happened to be jerking along next to me. Men, women. I
danced with my father, who got a little winded during
"Satisfaction." I danced with my mother, who was having
the time of her life, laughing and flirting and generally
playing up to the crowd. And I danced with Richard.

Richard is pure sex and moves like he's part of you.
Maybe I'm imagining it was even better than it was because
I know Mark was off to the side, watching. I've always loved
to dance with Mark watching. And I know he's always wondered about me and Richard.

I leaned into Richard, held to him, pushed and knocked
into his body. Richard dances expressively. Doesn't hold to

moves the way people who don't really dance do. Richard knows dancing is whatever you do. What Mark taught me about sex. We leaned and twisted and knocked to the music. We flew. The way you can fly only with someone you've never actually slept with. All that pent-up desire spilling into the small radius your bodies make. When "Out of Time" came on we were fused. A slow and snaky two-step with entwined legs and crotch kissing. I sang with the lyrics. *"Baby, baby, baby,"* I sang and caught Mark's eye. *"You are left out."* I sang. *"My poor unfaithful baby."* Richard's arm caught around my waist, my arms hung down, and we swayed and sunk pelvis to pelvis down toward the floor and up, the pressure holding us together. I love Mark's eyes on me when I'm with someone else. I love watching the territorial come up in him. I knew then that if I were to have an affair with Brian he would not abide it. No. Not at all. He would not.

And I was going to do it. I was going to have an affair with Brian. I was going to get Mark back.

After everyone was gone Mark and I fucked on the gallery floor—harder than we've fucked in the two months since I've known about Yvonne.

· 1 1 ·

The other day I read something Yeats said about the ethical impulse always breaking the ethical law.

That afternoon I finally got Brian into bed.

It was different from what I'd expected—what with everything that had led to it. Friendship. Desire. Whatever. When we were finally lying together, Brian inside me, gently moving in and out, me holding him, sweaty against him in the way I'd so often imagined, it almost felt less real than it had in my head. When you're alone, imagining, you can bring all your concentration to bear on what he feels like beneath you, inside you, above you. When he's there you get diverted thinking about what he's thinking, how he's responding, what he's feeling, wanting, what your body feels like to him. You monitor and modulate his arousal. Your arousal. All that stuff. It's much more complicated. In some respects, the other person always gets in the way.

Brian's a quiet lover. Not like Mark. Mark fucks emphatically. Talking talking talking. Ordering me around. Bend. Kneel. Lift. Suck. I climb and move all over him. I feel like I'm a part of something. I couldn't tell if it was me coming or him coming when I finally started to

come and despite what people say about it—about knowing when it happens—I still often confuse our bodies at
that moment. What's moving, spasming, contracting.
Which one of us.

With Brian it's different. I mean it's lovely, but I'm as
quiet as he is while we're fucking. It's almost like I'm afraid
to disturb him. Afraid to say anything to break his concentration. The way they say you should never wake a sleep-
walker. His sounds of appreciation and excitement are low
and deep and genuine. But quiet, which is strange for someone so talkative and generally boisterous. It's like being in
church, a library.

He keeps his eyes closed and I feel like I want to bang
him against the bed to crack him open. *Let me in*, I remember saying when we were making love, and I know he had
no idea what I meant. He's a puzzle. It surprises me because
I feel so connected to him, attached. When my mouth closes over his cock it feels *right* in there. I feel I could touch
every part of him. Reach inside him. But it's harder than I
thought it would be. Harder to get inside.

I was thinking I'd have to train him, bring him out. The
way Mark did for me. But it's not the same thing.

"It seems like you want to be dominated," he said after
we made love again the next afternoon. He said it in a dis-
interested sort of way. Anthropologically. It was funny, him
spelling it out like that. We were on his floor. He ran his
hand down my back, pushed away a copy of *Les Fleurs du
Mal* he'd been reading to me.

"I'm not like that, Terry," he said.

"It's okay. I'll teach you." I climbed back on top of him, but there was a gulf I couldn't cross.

Wear your black silk dress. Nothing underneath. And those black heels. And be here in fifteen minutes, Mark used to say over the phone. It would be midwinter, freezing.

Nothing underneath, do you understand? No stockings. Nothing.

I remember squirming out of my pantyhose in the back seat of a cab, nervously eyeing the driver in the rearview mirror to see if he was watching. I remember thinking he'd probably seen worse. Once I even left the stockings behind. I was so turned on I think I might have done it on purpose.

When I'd get to Mark's he'd pick me up at the door and fuck me with my dress and shoes on. For hours. At some point the dress would come off but I'd never remember when.

I wonder if he does this with Yvonne.

"It's *freezing* out there," Brian said when I suggested the thing about the dress.

"Just *tell* me," I said. "Tell me what to do. *Force* me to do something."

"Get me a glass of water," he said, and we both laughed.

Brian's the first Catholic man I've ever made love to. I can feel the guilts and hesitations, the conflicts inside him. Like they're my own. And I can't help but feel he disapproves. We fuck, then barely mention what we've done. It's like we're trying to do it without actually acknowledging what we're doing. I think he keeps his eyes closed so he doesn't have to register it's me. His teacher. A married woman. I can't even say we are lovers. We can't take the liberties lovers can.

I'd wondered if he could handle me—I even asked him—but now I'm beginning to think that it's me that won't be able to handle him. I can't break into him.

"Tell me your fantasies?" I said. Brian just laughed.

I have to accept the fact that maybe he doesn't have any.

"There are things I haven't been telling you," I said to Eric, "but I can't remember what they are."

I was back in the chair. I was sick of that couch. I hadn't told Eric about sleeping with Brian. I hadn't been to Yvonne's since I'd vowed not to—not even once—but I still felt like I needed to tell him.

Eric leaned back. On the wall behind him was a new painting of a sailboat. A bad painting, though probably he doesn't think so. The boat—*hangs* is the only word for it—in the middle of a swirl of greenish-blue that has white icing-like ripples smudged at intervals. It seems stranded, unmoored. A lost soul.

"Just say everything that comes into your mind," he said, "and don't worry about repeating yourself."

I thought of long strands of cutout paper dolls. I could see whole rows of me repeating, joined at the hands and shoulders.

"Nice painting," I said. "It makes me think of A *Portrait of Jenny*."

It didn't. It wasn't moody or atmospheric in the least. It

was moodless. Without weather. Like a magazine ad plunked down on a piece of construction paper.

"The film?"

"What?"

"*A Portrait of Jenny*."

I couldn't help laughing. I was looking around the room for something to talk about. My eyes scanned the book-shelves. *Discipline and Punish* stuck out at eye level. Foucault.

"I had a dream," I said.

He nodded.

"I dreamed you and Father Dugan—I told you about him, right?"

He nodded again.

"Anyway, you and he kept changing into one another. He—you—were wearing a priest's collar and those oxblood shoes you have. 'I want you to tell me everything,' he kept saying."

"And what did you tell me?"

"I don't remember."

Eric just sat there waiting, his chin balanced on the tips of his fingers.

"He tied my hands and feet with rosary beads," I said after a while. I was making it up. "And spanked me."

"So you feel safe when you're tied down?"

"I don't know."

The clock said 12:30. The hands a solid line dividing the face in half.

"Why do you feel you need to be punished?"

He was trying everything. I felt almost sorry for him. But I was also feeling sorry for myself. *Help me*, I wanted to scream.

"Do you think I'm bad?" I asked him. It was out of my mouth before I could stop it. I remembered Yeats and breaking the ethical law, but it seems to me I don't know anything about ethics. Everything feels all helter-skelter inside me. Haphazard.

"What do you mean 'bad'?"

"Do you think I'm ugly?"

The night before I'd stood for the longest time in front of the mirror. Mark was on the bed writing catalog copy for the gallery. I'd been trying on clothes, checking to see if I'd gained any weight, waiting to see if Mark would notice anything different about me.

"What do you think I look like?" I asked Mark.

"A lot better than this shit I'm supposed to be showing."

He said it without looking up.

"Do you think I'm ugly?"

"Oh Christ, not again."

For someone who is Jewish, Mark says *Jesus* and *Christ* a lot.

"Treas, I love the way you look. You know that." He put his notes down and came up behind me. He hugged me, kissed my hair, my ear, closed his hands over my breasts, then slid my shirt down. I looked at the two of us in the mirror. Adulterers.

"But don't you sometimes look at me across the table and think, Jesus, she looks hideous?"

"Well, you do get that Karl Malden look from time to time." I've noticed that Mark's gotten really cautious whenever we enter any potentially serious conversation.

"Come on, you know what I mean. I mean don't you look at yourself sometimes and see something completely different from what you'd expected? What you're used to seeing. I mean, *look* at me. Do I look the same as I did yesterday? I think I looked completely different yesterday."

Mark just shook his head and held me. We looked at each other in the mirror. He crossed his eyes and made a face that used to make me laugh. I had assumed he'd know in a second I was having an affair. So much for Proust.

I looked back at the mirror. Sometimes I think if I look long enough I'll see myself the way other people do. I read somewhere that no two people see precisely the same thing. Like the color green is slightly different to each person. Even if someone says *teal* green everyone will point to the same thing. What *they* see as teal green. But what they're each seeing is something different. So what really *is* teal green? I think Judy Davis is beautiful and Mark thinks she's just okay. I wish I could see what he's seeing. But that's about taste. I'm talking about what you see. It's always bothered me that there are parts of me that other people will always be able to see better than I can. Like if I turn around to see myself from behind, I'll always be seeing a slightly twisted version of myself. Or take the back of your head. How many people really know what the back of their *ears* looks like? But a stranger sitting behind you at a concert might spend the entire time watching them. Know them

better than you'll ever know them. See how they give you
away.

So why couldn't Mark see I was having an affair?

"Do you think I look like Yvonne?"

Mark dropped his hands and just looked at me.

The phone rang.

Neither of us moved.

And I could tell he was still seeing her.

"Do *you* think you're ugly?" Eric asked. It was 12:40. Ten
minutes to go. Eric fingered his tie. He hardly ever wears a
tie. It makes him look like a serious child.

"Who do you think thinks you're ugly?" He was trying
everything.

"I want to know what *you* think," I said. "I want to know
what you are seeing when you see me. I want to know what
you hear when I talk to you. *Damn* it, I want to know what
you think of me. I mean, do you ever think of me when I'm
not here? Do I ever occur to you while you're watching a
movie, or sitting at home with your wife? And what do you
think of when you think of me? How do you picture me?
What am I wearing? Have you ever wondered what I look
like naked? I mean, do you really want to *know* me?"

"Terry, what do *you* want?"

He always turns things around.

"I want you to know me," I said.

"Yes," he said, "I think you want to be known. I think
you want someone to know you very well. The way you
think your mother knew you when you were a child."

I almost laughed. *I know you like a book. I know you inside out. You can fool your friends but you can't fool me.* My mother knew everything. Eric was looking very earnest and intent. Maybe it was the tie.

"And I think you are conflicted about that as well. You say you want me to know you, but look how long it took you just to tell me your name."

He just sat there, waiting for it to sink in or waiting for me to say something. I wanted to help him. To say something revealing just to show him I was willing. But I couldn't think of anything to say.

"They want to be tied down by someone they trust so that they can go over what they imagine is an edge, while someone is watching them, holding them. In control. To experience themselves as whole and complete in front of another person."

I think this was the most sentences he'd ever strung together at the same time. But it made sense. I've always loved being tied down by Mark, the way he whispers *now you need to be punished.* How I knew he would never really hurt me. That no matter what happened he'd be there.

Eric leaned toward me. That hanging boat behind him looked so stupid and lost. I guess that's what that phrase means—*at sea.*

"At the same time you want someone to establish boundaries for you. To punish you if you cross them. To decide for you what is good and what is bad."

He kept changing person. From *you* to *they* to *you* again. He was gesturing with his hands, carving lines and circles in the air in front of him. I think he was nervous.

"But Terry, that's what you're here for. You need to learn to establish these things for yourself. You're not a child. It's up to you to decide what you want to be obedient to."

He droned on and on, his voice making a buzzing sound inside me. I was thinking of Mark and Proust and being spanked. I got this feeling I get sometimes. I felt dense, like a shape in space. Like a Goodyear blimp. I felt a familiar swell and movement inside. A gush of blood. My period. The first time since October. Eric's chair is white and I was afraid of leaking.

"Terry . . ."

I was wondering if I should stand up.

"I have to go," I said.

"Have I upset you?"

I think it's an expensive chair. Have any other women ever leaked in the middle of therapy? I sat on my hands. I couldn't remember what he'd been talking about. I knew he'd said something important. That I should write it down.

After my session I stopped for tampons at the Korean vegetable stand. Then I headed to Yvonne's. It was snowing lightly, which made the street seem clean and old-fashioned. A young guy selling Christmas trees on Broadway and 103rd had a tape recorder playing Joan Baez's version of "O Holy Night" in French. "Cantique de Noel." I have that album. I've played it a million times. But I never imagined anyone else had it. I stopped by the trees. The snow, the pine smell, the pure voice, the guy's wool cap and mittens, his slightly out-of-this-century face, I don't know, they lifted me. I looked up and let the snow fall on my tongue without once thinking about acid rain. I felt I could rise above, surmount and survive, anything. Mark and Yvonne. Brian. Yeats cakes and Glenda's earrings. I thought of Midnight Mass and candles, my grandfather's Christmas cookies. *Your spirit,* I heard Sister St. Rita saying. *Your pure and holy spirit resides in Jesus. Rides,* I used to think she was saying. I used to picture myself riding in Jesus' arms. I'd been a child seduced by the idea of the holy and always at Christmas vestiges of it come over me. I felt the way sinners must feel at the moment of conversion. The way Jimmy Stewart must have felt when that little man came over and he knew, somewhere, it was an angel. The way that angel wouldn't let him despair. I thought, I even said it to myself, *I am made of stronger stuff than this.* Cliché, I know, but that's what I thought. I touched the branch of the fullest tree, breathed in the fragrance. *J'vous en desperance* Joan Baez was singing, or what I've always sung along with her, faking it. I don't know whether she's singing about hope or despair. *Jesus Christ help me,* I prayed. *Let this lift. Make my spirit clean.* I recited the Serenity Prayer. The Our Father. I don't know how long I was standing there but suddenly I realized that Joan Baez had yielded to "Jingle Bells" and I was holding a handful of pine needles, dropping them onto the snow-dusted sidewalk.

"You like this one?" the man asked. Up close his face lost some of that old-fashioned look.

"It's beautiful," I said, "but my husband is Jewish. We never have a tree."

The guy shrugged. He pulled the tree I'd been fondling and rolled it against the others on the stand. Then maybe he felt bad.

"Here," he said. He smiled and handed me a short bough. "It'll be our secret. Merry Christmas."

"Merry Christmas," I said.

Something about the exchange made me feel pathetic. I crossed Broadway to Yvonne's. Redemption is never as easy and atmospheric as it is in the movies.

I slept at Yvonne's. I slept all afternoon. I'd pulled aside the curtains slightly so I could see the snow falling. I hung the bough in the window. I undid the covers and blankets and lay down on her bed. I had that heavy, drowsy, menstrual feeling, my belly swollen and tender. I wanted to sleep. I'll say one thing: that room is neat. No distracting paraphernalia. You could almost forget you have a history in a room like that. It felt good to be back. I closed my eyes and imagined myself held. Yvonne's bed is big and soft and the sheets felt clean. No doubt she changed them before she left. I let myself sink into her bed. I let myself be held. The thing is, I couldn't figure out who was holding me. Not Mark. I didn't want to think about Mark. Not Brian. He was too vague and separate. Not Eric or Father Dugan or my mother. I imagined myself embraced by huge, strong, furry white arms. Feathery arms. Like a big muscular bird. I imagined myself held by the universe. I rocked gently. I hummed "O Holy Night." And then I started saying my name. Over and over. *Terry. Terry. Terry. It's okay, honey. It's okay, Terry. Ssh.*

Ssh. You are going to be all right, honey. It's okay. It's okay. I felt like I was inside myself. Holding myself. *You're enough*, I said. *You are enough.* I crooned and whispered. Like I was cradling myself with my voice. I rocked and rocked.

I woke to the phone. For a second I thought it was the doorbell. The room was dark and I was pretty groggy. Four times it rang—time enough for me to realize what it was and where I was. The machine clicked on and I counted the seconds for Yvonne's outgoing message. She hadn't changed it to say she was out of town.

"You look pretty hot in that bikini," the voice was saying. I can't remember what else. The voice. Mark's voice. It was unmistakable. I can't remember what else he said though I played that message over and over, backward and forward, in a daze. *You look pretty hot in that bikini.* Harmless words, really. Any friend could have said them. *I* could have said them and I hardly know her. My husband's voice coming like a ghost over the phone machine. Like a sneaking, unfaithful ghost. Spraying through the room like a shot of come. *You look pretty hot in that bikini.* There were no endearments. No *honeys* or *loves* or *babys*. I remember that. But Mark's not stupid. You don't leave incriminating messages on your lover's machine.

The red incoming light was blinking like crazy. Calls that had piled up over the week. I thought of the confession box. Father Dugan. *You are totally lacking in integrity.* I thought of Yeats and the ethical impulse always breaking the ethical law. I thought of Jesus and Nietzsche and the Serenity Prayer. And I erased every message on that tape.

Then I laid down on Yvonne's bed and imagined her plane exploding, sending that bikini shooting out over every part of the universe. I couldn't even surround it with a beautiful pink bubble because every time I tried to picture it the bubble turned into a hellish moil of boiling red fire.

· 1 2 ·

$\mathcal{I}$ see myself pacing Yvonne's little apartment. I see myself staring into her mirror. I see myself hiding her copy of *Crime and Punishment* in the oven, going through her kitchen cabinets, standing before her open refrigerator. That's what I remember most. The plastic container of slivered almonds, the frozen chicken breast, the end slices of an old bag of bread. Baking soda. A bottle of blackberry preserves. Half a jar of that Paul Newman dressing. Two containers of Dannon plain nonfat yogurt, dated December 17. My birthday.

How dare she.

I pulled jars and containers out of that refrigerator and stacked them on the counter. I piled a layer of slivered almonds on a piece of bread, spread some blackberry preserves across it, folded it, and ate it. The almonds were cold and crunchy and dry. The bread was stale. I chewed, staring ahead at the wall. I washed the food down with a swallow of bottled water. Then I made another. I spread the jam, not bothering to catch the crumbs, though I did wash the knife. It was a sharp knife. I tried to eat a handful of dried oatmeal, but it wouldn't go down. I dipped an old carrot in the Paul Newman dressing and ate that. I remember thinking how

Yvonne could have walked in and found me like that. I see myself knowing I should stop, knowing Yvonne could walk in at any moment. But I couldn't stop.

There was nothing for her to eat when she got home. She'd probably be starving unless she'd eaten on the plane. But I doubt she eats airplane food. Maybe she'd pocketed a packet of cashews or one of those wedges of processed cheese. I always do, even though I end up throwing it out. Anyway I couldn't worry about her. I was starving.

You look pretty hot in that bikini. I kept hearing it. The way you keep hearing an annoying voiceover in a movie.

I checked Yvonne's closet, pulled out a knee-length black leather coat. It was from the back of the closet and she'd probably never miss it. I almost switched it for something she'd be more apt to wear, but I really did like this coat. I put it on, stuffed my own jacket into a canvas bag I found on her top shelf, made the bed, and checked the bedroom for signs of me. On the way out I took a swallow of old red wine she'd left on the counter. It was only later I remembered I'd left the bough in the window.

I missed the first appearance of the Beatles on *Ed Sullivan*. I missed Jack Ruby shooting Lee Harvey Oswald live on TV. I missed the moment when the *Challenger* exploded into that incredible martini glass. I've seen clips of these events again and again, but there's something about seeing a thing before you know it will be an important part of history. Your history. When you're taken unawares. Even a thing like the Beatles. I have gone over that particular Sunday

again and again and I just can't remember how it is possible
I missed the *Ed Sullivan Show* that night. And no matter
how exciting the clips are, no matter how many times I see
them, I still know it has already happened. I'm not seeing it
for the first time. It's part of history.

So I see myself going through Yvonne's apartment. I
think I can remember every moment, but I can't really
remember doing it for the first time. It all feels like something I watched after the fact. I write it down and on paper
it feels more real than it did when it actually happened.

The snow had stopped. It was cold and everything had that
tinge white socks get when you wash all your clothes
together. The wind had overturned a garbage can and
banana peels and coffee grinds and wadded paper littered
the sidewalk. It must have rained because the streets were
puddled and slushy and the water seeped through my suede
boots. I stopped by a dirty-looking Dunkin' Donuts to get
a coffee and on impulse bought a powdered sugar doughnut
that looked as dirty as the snow. I tore a corner off the coffee lid, sipped the coffee, and ate the doughnut as I walked
down Broadway trying to balance the coffee, my own bag,
and Yvonne's canvas bag. I looked inside the Korean vegetable stand to see if that woman was there. She wasn't. Just
the old guy. The sneaker vendor had added a stash of
umbrellas and plastic juice containers and red-and-green
striped scarves. He was reading a copy of the *Post*. The head-
line said HOLIDAY HORROR!, but I couldn't see the photograph. I passed by, then went back to the Korean place to

buy a banana. I was starving and thought it might fill me. It was five o'clock and I couldn't imagine getting on a subway. I didn't want to take a cab. I thought of taking the bus, but after calculating how many calories I'd consumed in the last half hour I decided to walk down to Soho. It was only a matter of a hundred and fifteen blocks. I was warm enough except for my feet which were soaked. And I wasn't in a hurry to get to the loft.

You look pretty hot in that bikini.

I avoided the corner where the guy was still selling Christmas trees. At Broadway and 95th, by the marquee for Symphony Space, I stopped to call Sarah. A couple was arguing about whether to walk or take a bus—the woman yelling, the man calmly telling her it was not a big deal, not to get all worked up, and if it meant that much to her they could walk. So what they'd be late. I couldn't hear the rest and then I saw them get on a bus.

I got Sarah's machine. I remembered she'd said she was meeting Elly for coffee. Four hours is a pretty long coffee. I slammed the phone down without leaving a message. I don't like Sarah moving in on my territory. Without me there, anyway. I called Brian and there was no answer. It infuriates me that he doesn't have a machine. It's just obstinance. I stuffed a bunch of quarters into the pocket of Yvonne's coat. Then I called Yvonne, got her machine, and hung up. I did it six times so the light would be blinking when she got home.

You look pretty hot in that bikini. I kept hearing it as I walked downtown. I pictured confronting Mark and

Yvonne in her apartment. Just standing there waiting calmly for them to explain. For Mark to start going on about
Nietzsche. And I'd just stand there, quiet and controlled.

The streets went by in a blur. It seemed like everyone was
shouting at one another. A young kid grabbed an orange
from an outdoor fruitstand and ran away laughing as the
owner screamed down the street after him. A woman
slapped a crying child again and again outside the window
of Tower Video, in front of a huge poster of *It's a Wonderful
Life*. A man and woman stood by the Regency, the woman
cried, sobbed really, touching the arm of the man's jacket as
he looked past her with no discernible expression. *That*
made me cry.

When I got to Columbus Circle, I was crying so hard I could
barely see. I leaned against the scaffolding around the entrance
to the subway and tried to calm down. Then I doubled over,
holding my stomach, sobbing. I felt a hand on my back.

"Hey, you okay?"

I felt arms lifting me up. A young man put his hands on
my shoulders and pressed me gently to tilt my head.

"*Hey*," he said again, "you okay?"

He was black, about nineteen. He had a blue striped cap
pulled over his ears. He looked so concerned, so sympathetic,
I wanted to lean into him and rest. I wanted him to hold me.

"Come on, girl, talk to me. Something happen to you?"

I shook my head, but couldn't stop crying.

"You're gonna get hit by a car you walk around like that."
He'd slid his headphones off his ears. They dangled around
his neck. I could hear the buzzing music, the rap beat.

"Hey. How you gonna get home doubled down and dragging there like a old dog?"

"Yeah," I said, trying to sound normal, "I was wondering how I was going to get across that street."

It was a huge intersection. You couldn't tell exactly which way the light was flashing or when to walk. I always hate crossing there. I rested Yvonne's canvas bag beside a garbage can.

"Tell you what," he said. "We'll cross together. I'll skate you across." He hooked his arm through mine and picked up the canvas bag.

"Thanks," I said. Sometimes only a stranger can make you feel better.

He looked at me with a big grin. I think he was trying to cheer me up.

"I'm okay," I said. "I guess I just need to walk."

"Walk?" he said. "It's cold as fuck out here. How far you walking?"

"Soho," I said.

He shook his head back and forth, slowly. "Another crazy white girl," he said. "Girl, why don't you take a cab? That's a pretty nice coat you got there, so I *know* you could spring for a cab."

"I stole this coat," I said. Then I started to laugh.

He shook his head again. The halo of music buzzing out of the headphones and cold fog puffing out of his mouth when he talked made him seem like some kind of angel.

"Do you ever go ice skating?" I asked.

"Shit, you *are* crazy."

"I'm serious," I said. It had just occurred to me I could stop by Rockefeller Center. It was just a few blocks down. I could skate for a while and maybe it would make me feel better. The lit-up tree. All those people. At any rate it would burn off a few more calories.

The guy just looked at me. "Crazy white girl," he said.

"My husband's having an affair," I said.

"Shit," he said. "That all? Wha'chou goin' on for? Nobody dead, right?"

He had a point. I could feel myself starting to calm down. Looking at it from a larger perspective.

"I was in her apartment," I said.

He squinted at me. "Shit," he said. "You didn't kill her, did you?"

I laughed, but it started me thinking. Normal people kill. Crimes of passion. Girls who kill their fathers after school, women who bludgeon their husbands. People like me. Who knows what you're capable of. I remembered Brian telling me he'd done something. In Ireland. Something he couldn't tell me. Something terrible. And I knew that whatever it was I'd try to understand it because of how I feel about Brian. But it's possible he did something really awful. It's possible I could do something really awful. One drink too many. Mark saying the wrong thing at the right time. I thought I should curtail my drinking for a while. Not drink anything at all. You can't be too careful. Then I thought about Sleeping Beauty, how her parents tried to avoid the prophecy that she'd be pricked to death. Outlawed spindles, needles, any sharp objects. But she was caught by an antique sewing spindle she just happened to find in an attic somewhere. It was fate. She couldn't avoid it. Maybe I was fated to kill Mark.

"Hey," he said again, "you didn't kill her, right?"

"No," I said. "I didn't kill her."

"So cool it. It's Christmas. It's a beautiful night. You're young, beautiful. And you haven't killed anybody. So screw 'em."

He offered me a cigarette. I shook my head.

"What's your name?"

"Terry."

"Terry what?"

"Terry Spera."

"Italian?"

"Uh-huh."

"Well, Terry Spera, you're Catholic, right?"

I nodded.

"Well," he said, "I'm Chris. You can call me St. Chris 'cause I helped you cross that big street."

I laughed. He laughed. He danced around a little to the buzz his earphones were making. Put his hand on my shoulder.

"Wha'chou got in this sack?" he asked, holding out Yvonne's canvas bag.

"My jacket," I said.

"You took hers?"

"Yeah," I said.

"Shit," he said. "My grandmother's Santería. She could tell you what to do with that shit. But you're crazy enough. You better stay away from that shit."

It hadn't occurred to me to cast a spell on Yvonne.

"You gonna be okay?" he asked.

"Yeah, I'm okay," I said. "Sure you don't want to go for a skate?"

He did a comic imitation of a figure skater, waved, and danced off. Like he was some kind of angel that appeared at a crucial moment. Mark says I'm always looking for signs and I guess it's true. It's hard enough living without feeling bad for expecting there to be guideposts here and there.

I liked the idea of going to Rockefeller Center. It seemed like a cheerful thing to do. A holiday thing. I didn't stop to consider that it would be filled with people—couples, lovers, families. Children with their parents. Nobody out there alone. Just by themselves. It was only about 6:30 but it looked like midnight. I went downstairs to rent skates, but the line was long and my feet were freezing so I walked back up.

I hadn't been in a pair of ice skates in over eight years. And only four times in my whole life. When I was eleven the people next door had moved and left assorted pairs of skates and my parents had taken the three of us to Wollman Rink—one of the few times they ventured into the city. I loved it. The music, the crowds, the smell of winter, and the lit-up buildings overlooking Central Park. Something, excitement maybe—I almost threw up from the excitement—propelled me around the ice. When I let go of the rail and tested my skates (I was wearing three pairs of socks because the skates were too big) it was like I'd been skating all my life. It was like flying. It seemed everyone was admiring me—the line I made as I handled each curve. Every face was smiling at me. I was a combination of Audrey Hepburn and Marlo Thomas. Even the buttons on my coat seemed beautiful. It's one of those memories that's surrounded by a kind of glow, one you return to again and again, not really knowing what made you think of it. A feeling of pure joy and belonging in the world. No fear. No dread. No worry about school the next day or going to hell or being caught by your mother in a lie. Just light and color, the smells of cold air and women's perfume and hot chocolate and steamy fat pretzels. The world dazzling and beautiful around you. Maybe there are only a few moments like this in your whole life. "Movie moments" I call them. It's funny how the times you feel the most real in your life it feels like you're in a movie. I read an article in the Science Times about how memory works, and why you remember certain things in certain ways, but I can't really remember what it said. Anyway, it took a while before I saw Carla and Lisa clinging to the rail right beside two boys fist-fighting on the ice, and my mother ordering me back to the café enclosure. "You've had enough now," she said as I sobbed and begged to stay. Even now, given the distortions of memory, I think I couldn't have had more than a few minutes of skating. "You only think of yourself," my mother said and slapped me when I wouldn't stop crying. In front of all those people. Then we all sat inside, damp and uncomfortable and drinking hot chocolate. And Carla threw up in the slush.

I tied my scarf around Yvonne's coat collar, pulled my beret down over my ears, and wriggled my toes and fingers to get warm. I held my hands under my armpits. "Silver

Bells" was playing on a scratchy recording and the skaters whirled and spun and fell and showed off. There was every kind of skater—but they were all together. . . . *in the air there's a feeling of Christmas. Children laughing, people passing, meeting smile after smile* . . . I saw a young girl in a red skating skirt wobbling yet clearly delighted with herself and I thought of her having one of those experiences she'd always remember. A movie moment.

I walked around and around the perimeter of the rink. Banging into people. Stepping around wheelchairs. I knocked over a little child by accident and tried to help him stand. When his mother bent to lift him I noticed someone had stickered her fur coat with an orange circle that read *If you think this looks good on you, you should see how it looked on its original owner.* A Muzak version of "MacArthur Park" started playing. Hardly a Christmas song. *Someone left the cake out in the rain* . . . I remember every word of it, every intonation. Why should I remember that song and forget whole pieces of novels I've read?

I was walking around the rink, piecing together the words to "MacArthur Park" and trying to remember how we remember and suddenly I was overcome with nausea. I felt hopeless. Like my life was over. I remembered Carla throwing up by the hot chocolate counter and tried to find a bathroom, but the place was so crowded I couldn't move through fast enough. I just wanted to get out of there. I just wanted to get home.

I didn't go home that night. I called Brian from a pay phone in front of St. Patrick's Cathedral and waited for him to ask me over. To tell me to stay put and he'd be right there to pick me up.

"Terry, what's wrong? You sound funny," he said. "Come on, talk to me. Where are you?"

I could still hear Christmas songs from the skating rink. *Have yourself a merry little Christmas* . . . A Pakistani pretzel vender dropped a handful of hot chestnuts across the slush and two children started throwing them at one another. A man with no jacket and bags rubber-banded around his feet came up to me for money. I must have looked a sight: head against the phone dial, freezing, wiping my nose with my glove.

"Change," he said.

I wanted to kill him. I leaned into the pay phone. I looked for some change. I thought of Sarah seeing this homeless woman sprawled on the sidewalk with a paper cup and a dog, and thinking, "You think you have it bad. My girlfriend just left me." The man gave up and moved on. When I found some quarters I stretched the phone cord as far as I could to follow him, but he was already too far away.

"Change . . . change," he kept repeating, as though it were some kind of divine warning.

"Terry, get in a cab and come over," Brian said.

I wasn't too far gone to notice that Mark would have done it a little sexier.

"Are you sure you want me to?" I asked. I tried not to sound too needy.

"Just get in a cab. Come on now."

I must have looked pretty desperate because it took a while for a cab to stop.

Heading downtown I watched each block pass, bringing me closer to Brian. Fifth Avenue was jammed with tourists and shoppers and I blessed the cab driver who had on a Haitian station and spared me any more Christmas music. I didn't want to hear anything vaguely recognizable. Not even English. The deejay yammered on in French and that was fine with me.

"Would you like me to change the station?" the driver asked.

"No," I said. "C'est bonne."

"Tu parle français?"

"Oui," I said. Though I don't.

I took out my journal and tried to write a poem about skating as a kid but I couldn't get the feeling right and ended up writing a lot of rhyming jibberish. A limerick about Yvonne and the Sorbonne.

· 1 3 ·

$\mathcal{E}$ ric's office was cold. He'd called to say the boiler had broken and did I want to cancel. My first reaction was that he was lying and just needed an extra day to Christmas-shop, buy some lingerie for his wife, a new mobile for the boy. I suggested meeting in his apartment and after the silence told him I'd be at his office regular time.

I was wearing Yvonne's leather coat, lying on the couch under a huge blanket. Eric had on a heavy alpaca sweater under his wool jacket and looked sportier than usual. I hadn't brought him a Christmas present and I was beginning to regret it. I thought I should have brought a book or some music. A silk scarf. Then I thought of his wife giving him an expensive sweater, helping his little son make a gift for him, and I was glad I hadn't brought him anything. I laughed to myself.

"Is something funny?" Eric asked. A puff of air formed when he spoke. The room was that cold.

"Yeah," I said and watched my own breath take form in front of me. The boat hanging behind him looked like it was sitting on his head like an angel on top of a tree.

"Christmas," I said.

Eric didn't say anything.

"What do you think your son is going to give you for Christmas?"

"What do *you* think he is going to give me?"

"He told me not to tell," I said.

It wasn't even funny. Everything I said sounded weird. I couldn't even be funny anymore. I pulled the blanket closer and kept talking so he wouldn't think *I* had thought it was funny.

"Maybe he'll make you a finger painting so you can get rid of that awful boat."

"You don't like that painting?"

I ignored it. Maybe he had painted it himself. In which case I hope he's a better shrink than he is a painter or I'll end up like that boat—stuck in the middle of a setting that has nothing to do with me.

"You know," I said, "in second grade I made my father a tie-clip and cuff link holder out of an old tunafish can covered with black and white felt."

It's true. Miss Hudson had slit the can and bent two edges back so it looked like a jacket, collar, and tie. Lisa and Carla had made the same thing in their class so my father ended up with three of them.

Eric didn't say anything.

"But you don't wear cuff links, do you?"

"Terry, isn't there something you wanted to bring up?"

I didn't say anything.

"About the other night?"

"It was wonderful," I said, and regretted it immediately. Eric stared at me like he could wait forever.

I was beginning to think *he* was crazy. I wanted to tell him about hearing Mark's message, but then I'd have to tell him about going to Yvonne's. Maybe he already knew. Maybe that's what he meant.

I pulled the covers up and around me and brought my knees up to my chest. The clock was making a buzzing sound that was louder than usual. It felt funny to be all wrapped up in a blanket looking at Eric sitting in his chair. The fact that it was the week before Christmas and there was no heat gave the room an unusual feeling of intimacy. Like we were really supposed to be sharing cups of hot chocolate and talking like old friends around a fire. Or like he was visiting me in a hospital, that he would see how cold I was, come over to the couch, and tuck me in tighter. When he handed me the blanket I'd almost asked him to cover me. I had the strangest urge to call him "Daddy."

"What was your favorite song when you were a kid?" I asked him.

"What was *your* favorite song?" he asked.

Predictable.

"What was *your* favorite song?" I sounded like an ornery five-year-old.

Eric didn't say anything.

"What was *your* favorite song?" I said again in a mimicky voice.

"Terry, I think you are angry at me."

I wanted to push his face into the wall clock.

"MacArthur Park," I said.

Eric just sat there, legs crossed at the ankle, arms wrapped around himself. He must have been cold but he didn't even shiver. I wonder if he was upset I hadn't just canceled.

"Do you want to hear a poem I wrote?"

He said nothing. I propped up on my elbow and stared at him. *"There once was a girl named Yvonne / Who studied French at the Sorbonne / She struck her instructor / Who bucked when he fucked her / Until she would scream 'bonne, c'est bonne.'"*

"Terry, I want to talk about the other night."

Not even a comment about the poem. No sense of humor. Eric is starting to sound like Mark.

"Terry I want to talk about last night," Mark said after I'd spent the night at Brian's. I got home late yesterday and didn't say a word about where I'd been.

"Where were you?" He was standing on a ladder, changing a bulb in one of the fixtures that had been out for a couple of days. "I don't want to have to wonder whether you're going to be here on any given night."

I looked up at him standing on top of that ladder thinking he was so great. I didn't even hold the ladder to steady it, the way I always do. He screwed in the light and climbed down.

"Terry, I want to know where you were last night," he said. He tossed the old bulb into the trash can.

"I don't feel like talking about it, okay?"

"No. Not okay. You don't just disappear without any explanation and then come home no questions asked."

"Oh," I said, "and do you think Foucault answered his wife's questions?"

"Foucault wasn't married."

"Maybe you don't want to be married."

"Terry, I am tired of playing games," he said. He really said that. "And stop doing that."

I'd been chipping pieces of paint off the wall as I talked. The chipped area looked like a giant loofah mitt.

"I feel like I don't have anything," I said now to Eric. "Nothing is mine. Mark owns the loft and pays most of the maintenance and I feel like a poor relation. Or a guest. Everything in there is his. Paintings, sculptures, furniture. Pots, plants. Espresso machines. Even the bed. Everything except the books. The books are mine. And most of the CDs."

"Why are you bringing this up now?" Eric asked.

"I was just thinking about it."

"I think there's something you are really afraid to talk about."

I lay back down and pulled the covers up higher.

"Okay. What else don't you feel is completely yours?"

"Have you forgotten the minor fact that my husband is having an affair?"

"No. But who else?"

"Well, I don't like it that Sarah and Elly are starting to be friends." I figured I might as well be cooperative.

"Terry, what about me? I think you are very angry about having to share me with my family. And I think you are very upset about the other night at Rockefeller Center."

"*What* are you talking about?"

I hadn't even mentioned Rockefeller Center. And I know he's not psychic.

"You don't remember?"

"*What?*"

"Seeing me."

"Seeing *you?*"

Eric leaned forward. The boat looked so forlorn and alone, hanging there in that water. Nowhere to go.

I sat up, pulled the blanket around me, and held myself. Eric was staring at me pretty intently, both oxblood shoes positioned squarely on the floor, leaning forward as though he were about to run the marathon. And then he told me. It seems I walked right into him and his wife and child by the rink at Rockefeller Center. Stared right at them. Walked right past.

"I didn't see you," I said.

"You *did* see me. Us. Maybe you didn't *consciously* see us, but you *did* see us."

I couldn't believe it. I tried to remember. I pictured myself walking around the rink. Now that I think about it, maybe it's why I felt so nauseous and hopeless and alone all of a sudden. But it's hard to believe you could see something and not see something. That some part of you could register it and the rest of you remain unconscious. Like it completely bypassed part of your brain. It's absolutely scary.

"Did you feel that you couldn't speak to me outside this room?"

"Eric, I didn't see you."

"You did see me. You obviously could not handle seeing me with my family . . ."

"I hate when you say that. I can't *handle* it."

"You're angry at me."

"I am not angry."

"You *are* angry."

When I play back the session it sounds like two second-graders fighting in a schoolyard.

"Terry, we are going to have to stop."

I looked at the clock. We'd gone over two minutes. Eric was standing stiff and erect, like a statue of a mayor in a small town park.

"I think this has been an important session," he said.

I folded the blanket and stuck it on his couch. He looked bulkier with that sweater under his jacket. I wanted to hug him, feel his chest next to mine. For a second I thought he'd lean over and hug me for Christmas.

"Well," I said. I didn't want to leave. "Have a nice Christmas."

"You too," he said.

"My best to your family. I don't believe I've ever met them."

He smiled.

When I thought about it later it seemed like the kind of smile someone who liked you would smile.

I made a note to send him a Christmas card. To him and his family. But I didn't.

· 1 4 ·

I didn't go to Yvonne's after my session. I didn't want to be alone. Anywhere. I called Brian and asked if I could go over there and though he said yes pretty readily, there was a slight hesitation in his voice. I heard it. He teases me whenever I accuse him of being tired of me. "You're nuts," he says. "I love having you here." But still, I don't know, sometimes I can sense his relief when I leave.

A crowd of people waited along the platform at the 96th Street station. I leaned over the edge but the long curve of tunnel looked unpromising. An impeccably dressed man walked by me carrying a shopping bag with *OBSESSION* lettered on the side. I took it as a sign. A warning. I've become obsessed. Sarah tells me. Elly tells me. I have the distinct impression they've discussed me over coffee, used me to woo and flirt with one another. But it's true. I've become obsessed. About Yvonne. About Brian.

I can't stop thinking of Brian. Where is he at any given moment? How much does he care about me? Want me around? I think it's because he gives so little away. He's circumspect. Says things like *I'll always hold you in high esteem.* Now what would he mean by something like that? I try to remember every word he says. Songs he's hummed, lyrics from tapes he's given me. Who was he thinking of when he heard that song? What kind of message was he sending when he recorded it for me? Or did he simply like the chord changes and ignore the words? Sometimes I feel like I've missed or forgotten something important—some small response or comment that would give me what I need to figure it out. Does Brian like me as much as Mark likes Yvonne? I monitor his words and gestures the way you go over a body looking for ticks.

The man with the *OBSESSION* bag stood a few feet away. The subway showed no sign of coming, no promising string of lights along the tunnel wall, but the man just stood there. Not once did he lean over the platform to check for the train. It makes me think that we could evolve into a completely expressionless species that exhibits no thoughts or feelings, but carries placards to indicate our states of being. *Obsessed. Depressed. Elated. Suicidal. Guilty.* I wish Brian would carry a sign. Or Mark. What would Mark's sign say? *Not Guilty.* Because he doesn't think he's doing anything wrong.

The lights flashed then brightened on the tunnel wall and when the subway screeched in I followed the obsessed guy. I sat next to him. Maybe Sarah is right. I need to figure out how to be enough. Figure out why all of a sudden I need Brian to love me. It keeps coming down to that. Does he love me? If he says he loves me one day why do I need him to say it the next? How could it change in one day? Sometimes while we're making love it *feels* like he loves me, but it could be just the indications of love, and not real love. Sarah says what I call love is more like obsession. That I don't believe someone loves me unless they're obsessed with me. "I really care about you, Terry, but I think you want me to lose my balance," Brian said the other night. Can a man hold and caress and kiss and fuck a woman in *like?* Of course. Men can hold and kiss and caress and fuck in hatred. Or disinterest. So why not in like or enjoyment? And why would that be so bad? Why do I need him to love me? We're friends. I keep telling myself that. He likes being with me. Likes to talk to me. Maybe that's how it is with Mark and Yvonne. Maybe he just likes her a lot. But if he does I'm sure she's trying her damnedest to pin him down to love. To cross that bridge from like to love. Then again, maybe there is no bridge. Maybe all likes do not have the potential to become loves. And maybe you like some people more who you like than you actually like the people you love.

You look pretty hot in that bikini. What a stupid thing to say. But it definitely sounded like he liked her. The train jerked and I realized I'd been staring into a poster of a very tan woman in an orange-flowered bikini. *Why not spend a weekend on St. Croix?* the poster read. Maybe Yvonne would have a great tan.

The guy beside me sat, bag in hand, not moving or looking in any direction, not even reading. I'll bet if he saw his shrink on the street he'd notice him immediately and strike up a pleasant and decorous conversation.

Between 72nd and 66th the intercar door slammed and a tall, bearded guy came through with a packet of *Streetnews* tucked under his arm.

"I no longer have to panhandle or beg," he shouted in a whiny monotone. "I am regaining my dignity."

I want to regain my dignity. To stop feeling so desperate. Get my balance back.

The obsessed guy beside me shifted. I wondered if he were going to buy a copy of *Streetnews* and whether I should too. Then the door opened and slammed again and a short fat black woman in a striped wool hat lurched into the car.

"People, I'm hungry," she said. "It's not easy, people. I have no home. I have no job, people . . ."

Now *that's* desperate, *that's* a tragedy, I thought. Not to have a home, a job. I'm just having a hard time, that's all. Things will work out. Then I looked back at that woman in the orange-flowered bikini and I couldn't imagine how.

A man walked down the aisle dropping those deaf alphabet hand signal cards with rabbit's feet and requests for money attached to them on everyone's lap and it started to feel like a traveling Al-Anon meeting. I thought that maybe I should stand up and start talking about Yvonne.

". . . people let me tell you, I'm not living in a house like yours. I am sleeping on a *train*, people. I am barely surviving."

I've always wondered how God figures out in what order to help people. Whose prayers he listens to first. Sometimes it feels like he's not listening to anyone. Like nobody's listening to anyone.

The *Streetnews* guy stood against the wall as though he didn't know whether to continue or leave. From the other end of the train an old Chinese man approached with beep-

ers and baby nipples on long strings and cordless phones
and toy tops—all of them spinning and beeping simultane-
ously.

". . . I am barely surviving, people. Please, people.
I worked at the World Trade Center . . . Have a heart, people . . ."

I pulled out a dollar for the woman and the Chinese guy
raced over to me holding out a beeping top. I tried to ignore
him but I couldn't get the woman's attention. I shoved the
dollar back in my pocket.

When I got to Brian's, "If I Fell" was playing on Mark's old
turntable, which I'd brought over there. I'd given him my
prize Beatles single—"If I Fell" / "And I Love Her"—for his
birthday. It was hard to part with but I like to give him
things. I have the feeling he hasn't been given enough.
Hasn't been cared about enough.

"'allo there, luv," Brian said and pulled me toward him.

I hugged him. Pressed into him. The softness of his lips
doesn't surprise me anymore. It's getting familiar. The song
started working on me, making me sad, but I think Brian's
begun to anticipate me. He reached back, flipped to the
guitar wood-block opening of "And I Love Her." He pulled
me close and we began a slow circling cross between a cha-
cha and a waltz. 1-2, 1-2-3. It's one of my all-time favorite
songs but I never realized it was a cha-cha. We circled, Brian
holding me, me kissing his neck, occasionally tripping over
a book or pile of papers.

I love it when he feels close to me. When he's right there.

Brian. Not the monster I make up in my mind who is resisting me, pulling away. I love it when he stays with me, touching me, kissing me, when I can't feel his body pulling away, gently, like he's waiting for the right time to disentangle. He says it's my imagination, but I can feel things like that—an impatience, a caution. How nervous he's gotten since pleasure turned into need.

It was only two days since I'd spent the night and I was getting the feeling it hadn't been a good idea. I had wanted to tell him about hearing Mark on Yvonne's answering machine but then I'd have to tell him about going to her apartment. Anyway, what you can tell people changes when you go from friend to lover.

"Things are a little crazy," I said as we danced. "With Mark and everything."

"What happened the other night?" he asked. "What did your husband say when you got home?" Somewhere along the line Brian stopped using Mark's name.

"Oh, you know, 'Where?,' 'Who?,' blah-blah-blah." I was smoothing his T-shirt over his chest, rubbing his nipples. "It's funny," I said, "I'm scared of him finding out about you—and I know all about him and Yvonne."

The truth is I still have the tiniest bit of doubt. There's still the possibility I've misunderstood something. That I jumped to conclusions. I keep thinking about *Romeo and Juliet*. Things aren't always what they seem. And I don't want Mark to know about Brian in case it's *not* true about him and Yvonne. In case it's nothing. Just a flirtation. The reason *Romeo and Juliet* is such a tragedy is that everything is so unnecessary. All those deaths. And we know it all the time and can't prevent it. I always use it with my students to explain dramatic irony. It's the same with Othello. He believes Desdemona is guilty. Because she seems to be. He *wants* her to be. He believes everything about the handkerchief. Immediately. So I try to cover my bases—in case I'm wrong.

"So what did you think of my paper?" Brian asked. In some ways Brian is just like Mark.

"It was great," I said. I still feel a little awkward about being his teacher and lover. "I love the part about Yeats's exploration of aging in the Crazy Jane poems."

In fact Brian's was one of the few papers I could actually read with attention.

Brian kissed me, pulled me over to the couch. A candle burned inside the top of a Chianti bottle. I hadn't seen him light it. With the Beatles in the background and that Indian restaurant smell it all seemed impossibly sixties.

"So," he said, "now for my reward."

He pulled me on top of him, rolled up my T-shirt, and started licking my tits. I hadn't expected to, but now I just wanted to fuck all afternoon and not think about anything. About Yvonne. About Mark. About seeing things I didn't know I was seeing and whether Brian loved me.

I opened my eyes while he was kissing me and saw one of those cheap Chinatown alarm clocks on his shelf. He must have just bought it. He'd never had a clock before.

He tongued my ear, tugged at the lobe.

"Do you love me?" I asked.

His body tensed.

"You don't have to answer," I said before he could say anything. I ran my hand between his legs. "Just fuck me," I said and unbuckled his belt.

It was all pretty fast after that. Brian on top of me. Me on top of him, straddling his hips, sucking his nipples, his fingers rubbing my clit the way I've showed him. I came before he did, quietly, as I've learned to do with him. It's the way I used to come when I was a kid, with Lisa and Carla in the next bed. The way I could rub and squirm, barely moving, come without making a sound. I think it lets both of us pretend we're not really doing this. Maybe two Catholics together is a bad idea.

Brian groaned *oh Jesus* and collapsed onto me. I stroked his head, rubbed his ass, scratched him and pet him and wriggled my finger around his asshole while he leaned into me making low moans and animal sounds.

"And I Love Her" had ended without us noticing and the needle skidded back and forth over the label making that *sst-sst-sst* sound, but neither of us got up to turn it off.

Brian rolled onto his back and spread his arms. He smiled. It made me think of this fresco I saw in Italy of Jesus lying at the bottom of the cross in Mary Magdalen's arms. I rubbed the milky tip of his penis, his belly, scratched the thatch of hair under his arm, and all the time he was sighing and moaning like a dreamy dog. I pulled him over again, and began to rub his ass in small slow circles. His arms reached around me, his lips wet against my neck. An armful of him. That's what I love. The heft of him on me when he's quiet like that. When I can hold him, talk to him. Like I own something in him.

"Mmm," he hummed, "mmm."

And then I started to feel it. Probably even before he did. The way I can feel him thickening to come. The world coming back. Something he had to do. His body began to stiffen, pull back into itself.

"It's getting late," he said.

"*Hold me*," I said, and he wrapped his arm around me and lightly scratched up and down my back. Dutifully, not with delight—the way I touch him. Now we were on a schedule. Now he had to determine how short a time he could decently hold me before he could get up and dress.

I tell myself over and over that I'm too demanding. And before I know it I'm whining. I'm like a train on course and there's no stopping me.

"You're not really holding me," I said, and then he really moved back.

"I am," he insisted. "Terry, ease up. Come here," he said, trying to appease me, but it was too late because I could already feel how annoyed he was. That we're always on my schedule. That I see him when it's good for me, even though it's not always convenient for him. That his time gets all twisted around and he ends up having to cram in schoolwork and freelance jobs. That he's lonely when I can't be around for him and I want him when it's convenient for me.

He didn't say any of this. He never does. He rubbed me and I knew he was trying to see that new clock. And I couldn't stop.

"Don't you want to hold me?" I asked. "I love to hold you. To touch you. It feels good. *God*, I mean I don't want to have to *beg* you."

It all feels justified, legitimate, though when I step back I can see how I overreact.

Then he starts to seem exasperated and I am afraid he is going to say we should end it, so I rub his hair and say, "It's okay, honey, I know you're busy. I know it's hard. I'm sorry," and then we can start to get up.

"I'm sorry, honey," I said.

"Ssh," he whispered, and kissed me. He pulled his jeans toward him, yanked a sock from the ankle of the pants leg. "I didn't know you were coming by, you know. I wouldn't have made plans."

What plans, I wondered. But I didn't ask. I pulled on my clothes, and began, slowly, to check my jewelry, to feel for the bits of silver and gold. Bracelets, earrings, watch. I hate rushing out the minute I have my clothes on. There's something not quite decent about it. To rush from that almost timeless feeling you have when you're making love—when you seem fused to the other person, fused to yourself—to break apart, go back and forth about plans or time or where you might go for dinner. It takes a little time to move from being naked to being dressed. The way you let wine breathe. The way you don't rush up to the coffin to look at the body the minute you enter a funeral parlor. You hang back, talk to the relatives. Console.

"Come on," he said, "walk me to the laundry. I have to drop this stuff off."

Like it's normal to think about laundry right after you make love.

I hadn't planned on going to the gym but I passed by after I left Brian's and before I knew it I was down in the locker room. I'd felt so awful after seeing Eric, and being with Brian hadn't made me feel any better. Nothing was making me feel good. It was getting hard to keep all of myself inside myself and I thought a half hour swim would make me feel more normal before I went home. I needed to get some endorphins going. Besides, the gym is closed the week after Christmas and I'd already missed a few days.

It was only 4:30 so I had time for 20 minutes on the bikes before I swam. I changed, stretched, and went up to the Aerobic Fitness Room.

And there was Yvonne.

She was on a bike, pedaling fast and looking straight ahead. She wasn't reading a magazine or listening to a Walkman or anything. I'd assumed she was one of those people who pedal leisurely for a few minutes, thumbing through a copy of *Self*, but she was engaged, really working out. She looked, not depressed, but more thoughtful than I'd ever seen her look. The way you look when you think no one's looking at you and you're just kind of drifting in your-self, thinking.

She didn't even look tan.

You look pretty hot in that bikini.

It had been only two days since I heard that message, and

I thought maybe Yvonne would look at me and hear those very words. Then I remembered I'd erased them.

She stared ahead, not looking at anything, and pedaling like mad, the way I do, to burn calories and raise your heart rate but not create those big bulgy muscles. She was sweating—that surprised me—but she still looked neat. Like everything fit inside her, like there weren't all these pieces of herself, pieces of other people, spinning around inside her. I wonder what it feels like. To feel like all of yourself fits inside yourself. To feel like just the way your clothes look so perfect and feel so perfect, that all of yourself fits so perfectly inside. It must feel wonderful. Like figure skating with a great partner to the most exquisite music. Just skating and spinning and holding the balance. Except that you're by yourself. You're your own partner. It must feel really great.

But maybe she doesn't feel like that at all.

Yvonne looked up at me. For a minute she looked like she was trying to figure out who I was. Then she nodded. I was right by the Stairmaster and could have gotten on, but the gym was empty and the bike beside her was unoccupied. I adjusted the seat and got on.

We said hello.

She was breathing hard. Her Elapsed Time readout said 5 minutes. She was doing a manual program at level 2. I punched in the same levels. The blinking red lights reminded me of her phone machine.

"How *are* you?" she asked between breaths.

The last time I'd seen her I'd been here at the gym. Leaning against her leg, her fingers on my neck. Looking at that bruise on her thigh. I wondered if she was thinking about that.

"Fine," I said.

She gripped the bars to check her heart rate. 157. A good target rate for someone our age.

I pedaled quickly, watching her readout grid and inside of 2 minutes and 13 calories I matched her rate. We were both at 112 pedal rpms. Me at 2.37 minutes, Yvonne at 7.42.

"Our hearts are in the same place," I said. But I'm not sure she heard.

We pedaled in silence. I was surprised at how I had to struggle to keep up. I didn't have my usual energy. And my rpm kept slipping if I didn't pay attention, but then Brian and I had just made love and you don't have as much energy after sex. Yvonne was really going at it. I was impressed and relieved. I figured if she had just fucked Mark she wouldn't even *be* at the gym. Not with that kind of energy.

"Don't you usually swim?" she asked. She looked straight ahead as she spoke, leaning her body toward me slightly. Her locker key dangled from her wrist.

"This first," I said, already out of breath. I looked at her legs. Those little moles. "How come you're not tan?" *How come you're fucking my husband?*

She said something about sunscreen. The seconds and minutes ticked away on the time/calorie readout and she kept on talking about sunscreen. Like I was Maggie or some casual acquaintance. I didn't want to be talking to her. I wanted to watch her. I wanted to look at the body my husband evidently found so appealing and see what made it so different from mine.

"I shouldn't have gone down alone," she was saying.

My rpm started climbing. I couldn't think of what to say. *Gee, too bad Mark couldn't get away.* Something like that.

Two women jogged side by side on Lifestep and another couple worked the benchpress. Aside from the echo of a pounding basketball the gym was pretty quiet. I could hear Yvonne panting.

"I heard some great reggae," she said after a while.

I hate reggae.

"I love dancing to reggae," she said.

It's like dancing to someone whining and hiccupping. For hours. I can't imagine anything more boring than dancing to reggae. I should have known Yvonne would like reggae. Maybe she bought some of those tapes while she was there. Well, if she thinks Mark's going to like reggae she's in for a big surprise.

I couldn't think of anything to say.

"Meet any nice men?" I asked.

"I wasn't really looking," she said.

There might have been an edge in her voice. I was at 10 minutes, 66 calories, 3.52 miles, 115 rpm.

Of course she wasn't looking. I couldn't figure out why she'd gone down there. She doesn't swim. She didn't get any sun so I know it wasn't to dazzle Mark with a winter tan. Maybe she went for the reggae. Maybe she's a shell collector. Maybe she hadn't even gone to St. Croix, but I don't know why she would have lied about it. I thought I could follow her to the locker room and wait until she took off her clothes. She'd at least have a *faint* tan line. A thin strap across her back, her ass a shade whiter than her thighs. I pictured her ass, the way she bent over the bench to her locker. Mark wriggling his finger up inside her while he talked to her. Mark lying on top of her, kissing her neck, fingering those little moles on her legs. Whispering *I love you* and *you feel really wet*, while she wrapped those legs around him.

Stop pedaling if you feel pain the readout grid said in big warning letters. I'd never noticed it before.

"Yvonne," someone yelled.

I looked up. It was the first time I'd heard anyone call her by her name. It was really strange to hear that, to see one of her friends. Then I realized the woman was looking at me. Someone I'd talked to a couple of times near the showers. She was smiling and wiping her face with a towel. I kept pedaling and looked back at my readout as though I hadn't heard her.

"See you after the holidays," she called.

Yvonne looked like she was trying to place the woman, trying to be polite.

"Have a good one," the woman yelled.

"You too," Yvonne called out, and I opened my mouth and mouthed the words too. I was afraid the woman would take it as a sign of encouragement and come back over. But she didn't.

I don't think Yvonne noticed anything.

My heart was pounding, the bike shifted slightly. I looked at Yvonne's grid. 24.49. I saw her look at mine. I wondered how long she'd keep going. Maybe she was waiting for me. Maybe she was just as curious about me as I was about her. I mean I would be curious about the wife of the man I was having an affair with. I'd want to know everything about her. I hit 20 minutes and kept going. I wasn't going to stop until she did.

We were panting. Sweat dripped off my hair down my chest, my arms. Yvonne was soaked. Her legs gleaming. Her heart rate flashed 164. Maybe she'd have a heart attack. I looked straight ahead and raced to catch up. Through a tangle of weight machines and equipment I saw the two of us in the mirror across the room. Black shorts, white tanks, speeding, our legs in sync. We looked like precision dancers. We looked so much alike that anyone looking at us might have thought we were sisters.

My pedal rpm went to 123, 136, 147—the highest I'd ever gone. I kept waiting for the *Pedal Slower* light to start flashing, but it never did. The mile-per-hour readout was ticking away faster than I'd ever seen it. I was going so fast the bike started rocking and I thought it would tip. At 27.58 the pedal strap popped, my foot slipped out banging against the side of the bike, and I couldn't catch the pedal again. I stopped.

"I've had it," I said. I balanced on the seat with my legs dangling and waited to catch my breath. Then I got off.

"Me too," Yvonne said after a couple of seconds.

We were drenched. Yvonne's face was red. I was spinning. My legs felt like they were still pedaling. We walked over to the mats and dropped down side by side, Yvonne right beside me. I could hear her panting, myself panting, just lying there face up beside one another, our breath in sync. I lay there feeling my heart pump.

And then I smelled her. I mean at first I wasn't sure if it was myself or Yvonne I was smelling, but then I knew it was her. Sweat and Opium. Really sexy. I guess she could have smelled me too. I could feel her listening to me. I could have moved my head over to her and rested it on her chest, let it rise and fall with her.

We lay there quiet and panting. Like we belonged together. Like two enemies side by side on a battlefield.

After a while we stretched. We didn't say anything, we just stretched. I thought of that scene in *Norma* when Adalgisa swears to give up the man she loves, who is actually Norma's secret lover, Pollione. How she vows to beg Pollione to return to Norma. Then Norma and Adalgisa have this beautiful duet where they swear eternal love and friendship. That their loving hearts will beat together for the rest of their lives. Except that Norma is still supposed to end up with Pollione. Maria Callas just rips me apart in that scene.

Yvonne stood up, stretched, and got ready to go. It's funny, but I almost felt hurt—the way I'd felt earlier when Brian checked the time and got up to leave.

"You going to swim?" she asked. She pulled off her sweatband and pushed her hair back. She stood over me, looking down at me. What could she have seen? My stomach rising and falling. My skin all wet and flushed. Mark's wife, is that what she thought? Would she have gone to him to beg him to return to me? Would she have chosen me over him? I looked up at her. She looked really beautiful. I shook my head. I thought I was going to cry.

"I have to go," she said. "I have a date."

I watched her walk out and didn't even follow her to the locker room to check her tan line. I didn't go for a swim. I just lay there breathing.

It was only later that I remembered her saying something about a date. And Mark was going to be home with me. Maybe she was cheating on Mark.

· 15 ·

$\mathcal{I}$ called Sarah as soon as I got home. I was surprised not to get her machine. I started talking right away, trying to tell her everything.

"Honey, I'm sorry, I can't stay on right now," she said. "I've got to run. Listen," she said when I didn't answer, "I'll be around later. Call me later, okay?"

I knew I should say something about being fine, but I couldn't. What could be so urgent that she couldn't spend five minutes on the phone? Elly. I'm sure it's Elly.

"Terry," she said, "there's a seven o'clock meeting at the All Crafts Center on the East Side. You need a meeting. Go," she said, "talk about it. Or just listen. It'll be good for you."

"Yeah," I said, "I'll talk to you later." I hung up. I've never done that to her before. The phone rang immediately, but I lowered the volume so I wouldn't hear who it was.

That's what I hate about Al-Anon people. *Go to a meeting,* they say. *Keep it simple.* Right. Simple for them. *They* don't have to bother talking to you. They hand you over to the group. The fucking committee. I was tired of needing people.

I poured a glass of wine, filled Mark's Mont Blanc with red ink and wrote Brian's name on a piece of paper. I wrote mine on the opposite side, then I wrote Mark's name under Brian's. I added Eric, Glenda, Yvonne, Sarah, and Elly. Just before I tore it up, separating my name from the others, I scribbled Father Dugan's name at the bottom. I put the half with my name under a candle I lit for myself. The other half I tore into strips and dropped them, one by one, out the window onto Spring Street.

"Keep it simple," I said, and tossed Mark's name.

"I will not become attached to persons, places, or things," I said, and dropped Brian.

"Easy does it," I said, and watched Eric float out over the pocketbocks and sweaters in the Spring Street Market.

"You can't buy oranges in a hardware store," I shouted and dumped the rest of the papers. Only Yvonne's I kept. Yvonne's name I burned over the candle I'd lit for myself.

"What are you saying?"

Mark was dangling a bottle of wine, leaning against the brick wall beside one of the few pictures in the loft I actually like. A painting of a puddle done by this Australian woman. "This is how my mind feels sometimes," she'd said to me when Mark bought it. And I know what she meant. I love the way the lines and swirls, the blues and grays and yellows, take you further and further in. You're pulled into the background, and the painting makes you feel like you could just keep being pulled. It reminds me of the ultrasound. Those gray shapes hanging in space. And nothing there.

"Nothing," I said.

Seeing Mark there, leaning against the wall in his leather jacket, made me want to go back to the old days. Before Yvonne and Brian. When things were simple. When I knew Mark loved me. When I knew he'd be there for dinner, or I'd be there for dinner. Before I began going through his datebooks and copying keys, before I began stealing clothes and sneaking into apartments.

Outside a sax player blew a moody version of "Silent Night." I thought of our first Christmas. The framed picture of Curly. My first bottle of Opium. *I always want to smell you on me*, he said. *Always and everywhere.*

I'll always love you, he said. There would be temptations, attractions, but staying together is a decision. He said all that. Now I wonder whether he meant there would be times one of us would succumb. And whether he considered *I* might be the one.

I'll always love you, I'd said to him. And I meant it. I couldn't have imagined anyone else.

I thought of a night years ago, around the time Mark and I were sliding from like into love. We were at the Time Cafe, having dinner. I was going on about a show we'd just seen. *From Our Lips* it was called. I've never seen such awful stuff. A woman who smeared peanut butter all over herself and recited passages of Virginia Woolf. Enormous vaginas made out of putty with objects stuck inside—toy sports cars and eggbeaters, photos of George Bush and Eydie Gorme. I'd just stuck my fork into Mark's arugula salad, telling him about how Virginia Woolf would have hated the show.

When I looked up, Mark was leaning forward, his chin in his hand, smiling at me.

"Do you know what I love about you?" he asked. Just like that, smiling at me, really looking, taking me in, not the way some people do, flitting over you and noticing the whole restaurant at the same time, every potted cactus or snooty waiter.

"What?" I'd asked. It made me feel funny—the way he was looking at me—but loved, really loved.

"You don't remind me of anyone," he said.

It was such a simple thing, I don't know why it thrilled me, but it did.

"You're an original," he said.

Maybe *that's* when I fell in love with him.

I looked at Mark leaning against the wall and I thought about that night, the crazy clock over the bar, its hands spinning around in the wrong direction, and I understood what people mean when they talk about wanting to turn back the clock.

Red and green flashed on the floor, reflected from some Christmas lights across the street. Tony jumped from his post by the heater, curled into the light, a red glow on his blond fur.

I have no evidence Mark's been having an affair. No hard evidence. *I'm* having an affair. Maybe this is all my own doing. My obsessions and jealousies. My imagination. Maybe I've blown it all out of proportion. You see what you want to see. Like Othello. Some part of him wants to believe Desdemona is guilty. He's obsessive and bullheaded and completely lack-

ing in perspective. Why would Mark be having an affair with
Yvonne? Maybe it was a flirtation, maybe he was even tempted. Mark loves to flirt. I mean Yvonne's not even his type.

And she said she had a date.

Mark uncorked the bottle of wine and held the cork
between his fingers. I love his hands. His long fingers.
They're familiar. I can't even picture Brian's hands.

He poured a glass, held it to the light to check the color.
His fingers took on some of the red glow.

"It's freezing out there," he said. I hadn't even noticed. I'd
been so revved up after seeing Yvonne.

I wanted to go over and put his hands under my armpits,
hold him, forget the past few months and just spend the rest
of the night making love. Lying on the floor in the red
lights. Watching the light play across his ass, his long back.
I was about to confess everything: How Sarah had led me to
believe he was having an affair. How I'd blown it out of proportion. I was going to ask him if we could go away for a
while. To Italy or Mexico.

"So you decided to come home," he said. "What an honor."

Mark is so rarely sarcastic I didn't catch the tone.

"Or are you planning to spend the night out? Just home
to pick up a change of clothes."

He held out the wineglass as if to ask if I wanted any,
then just poured me a glass and handed it over.

"Right," he said. "It's Friday. Maybe you're thinking of
taking off for the entire weekend."

I wanted to say *stop. Let's just stop.* I stood there.

"Why not the whole holiday? Why not just take off for

the whole *fucking* two weeks? Wherever the hell it is you go."

Chico walked into the room, blinking and stretching as though he'd just woken up. I picked him up and held him to me. I didn't know what Mark knew and I couldn't think fast enough. Couldn't think how to turn this. And I'd just downed two glasses of wine.

"Mark, stop," I said. Chico jumped out of my arms.

"I am so *sick*," he said, "of this shit. Of your moods. Of these *fucking* acts of aggression." He poured another glass of wine, looked at me and laughed. "What? I'm not supposed to notice my shirts ripped up and used as rags?"

Yesterday morning I'd torn up the Sorbonne T-shirt he used to wear all the time. Used it to polish my boots. I'd been looking for the shirt with the Nietzsche quote and Moe's picture. I was glad now I hadn't been able to find it.

The phone rang. I wondered if Mark thought Yvonne when I thought Brian. Nothing. Then I remembered I'd lowered the volume and leaned over to adjust it.

"I just wanted to see about Christmas. To make sure you're coming," she said. "Everyone's going to make it." My mother.

We stared at the machine as if it were some kind of oracle.

"Are you there?" she continued. There was a pause. She always waits for us to pick up, as if she can't imagine no one being there to take her call. "Well, okay. Call us back."

I remembered what Mark had said about her keeping my father tied to the bathtub. *Shackled*, he said. I should have thrown her name out the window, too.

The phone rang again.

"It's me again."

"Shut *up*," I screamed, and picked up a brick that was holding a row of books along the windowsill. The books slid to the floor. I think I would have smashed that machine. Mark grabbed my arm.

"I forgot to tell you," she went on, "someone called last week from Mount Loyola. I gave them your number."

I must have given them my parents' number by mistake. My mother hung up after asking again whether we were there. It was as if she could see us. Mark looked at me.

"Terry, I don't know what's going on with you anymore. I don't know when all this started, but I can't live like this."

He took off his jacket. He was wearing a black T-shirt and jeans, looking the way he looked years ago, when we first met. I wanted him to call me *Treas*, to push me on the floor and fuck me, to whisper *Tree, Tree*. I thought I could jolt him into it.

"Maybe you need some time away," I said. "I mean do you want to be alone for a while?"

"Yeah," he said, "I do."

Just like that. Like I'd asked him if he wanted spinach for dinner. *Yeah, I do.*

It struck me then that that's exactly what he'd said the day we got married. When the priest asked *Do you take this woman . . .*

Yeah, he'd said, *I do.*

I couldn't talk. I know I said something, but I can't remember what. I should have begged him, promised I'd be different, gotten him down on the couch, opened his jeans, sucked his cock. But I didn't. I don't know what I did. It's funny that when you look back on some of the most crucial moments of your life you can't remember at all what you said or did.

I remember he came over and put his arms around me. Held me.

"I was thinking of staying with a friend for a while. Just for a while. Give us both time to cool out. Maybe I could stay with David and Glenda."

Right. Or maybe Yvonne.

"It's Christmas," I said.

He just held me. I held him. Maybe we kissed.

I don't know how things have gotten to this point. One day you're making love after breakfast, the next you're old and alone and wheeling around in some nursing home.

· 1 6 ·

Last night I slept on the floor between Tony and Chico. Tony curled up under my neck until morning when he started nuzzling me awake to feed him. I'd been dreaming about Yvonne and I thought it was her. I had a headache. The phone was lying beside me off the hook. Sarah had stayed on with me until I fell asleep and I guess I hadn't even woken to hang it up.

Tony pushed against me for breakfast. There was no cat food and no tuna, so I made a couple of bowls of pastina and split it between the three of us. They just sniffed and walked away.

My head still hurts. I want to call Eric but I'm afraid he'd be annoyed. I called his office three times but left no message. I've been sitting here listening to *Tosca*, eating pastina, and trying to remember what happened last night.

I'm pretty sure I left the loft first and I guess Mark decided to stay out. By the time I left I'd had three glasses of wine so I don't remember exactly what happened in what order. What we decided. Maybe he said he wouldn't stay there. Maybe he told me where he was going. I don't remember.

I went to that Al-Anon meeting. That I remember. There didn't seem to be anywhere else to go—and probably anywhere would have been more appealing. I hate going to that part of St. Mark's Place. Any part of St. Mark's Place. Cheap restaurants, incense, and dirty-looking, raggedy-dressed people in lots of clunky jewelry—most of them smoking. Twelve Step has taken over most of the stretch between Second and Third. Alcoholics and drug users, overeaters and undereaters, debtors, sex obsessors, and cross-addicted whiners hanging out drinking Cokes, smoking, eating Twinkies, and encouraging one another up and down the filthy stretch of street.

Anyway, I don't think I even noticed anyone last night—what with the cold and the three glasses of wine. I took a cab there. I gave the driver a five for a three and a quarter fare and got out in front of a shop called Religious Sex.

To get into the meeting room you have to pass through a long tunnel—kind of like a fallopian tube—painted a deep shade of Pepto Bismol pink with black trim. The whole thing seems like a passage into another realm. I think it used to be a famous club for rock bands in the sixties. Someone was smoking at the back of the room. The meeting was crowded. They'd just finished reading the Twelve Steps and they were at that part where they say "We already love you even if we don't know you," or something like that. Something stupid. And is that ever a lie. They're a nasty, self-absorbed bunch. They love *themselves*. That's what.

Anyway I was feeling really bad. This girl in black leather pants pinned up the leg with about twenty-five safety pins said her name was Spike, and that she was obsessed with the wrong guy. That's how she put it. She said she was afraid she was going to "pick up." She started going on and on about how she sabotages herself. How she has these tendencies.

"I mean," she said, using her hands a lot for emphasis, "I mean I *get* on a train and the sign says Boston and I am going to Pittsburgh." She looked at us like we were supposed to get it. "I mean I *know* I am going to Pittsburgh and I see the sign says Boston. But I sit down. And then, when we get to Boston, I say 'Hey, this isn't Pittsburgh.' I mean, the *sign said Boston*. You know what I mean?"

It really was the stupidest thing. I wanted to tell her she should go to *hell* and spare us all. Then some weasly-looking guy with a nose ring started saying that stuff about trying to buy oranges in a hardware store. I was thinking that they should read some real poems if they're that excited about language and analogies. I almost started to laugh. I stood up.

"Yeats," I began, "said that the intellect of man is forced to choose between the perfection of the self and the perfection of the work . . ."

"Hey," this fat girl shouted, "you didn't raise your hand."

". . . and I have to admit I am in the process of perfecting neither." I thought that was pretty good.

"Please," the group leader said. She was a short woman with green hair. "You have to wait to be acknowledged."

"Hey," I returned, "I've sat through about ten of these meetings and rarely said a word. *Now* it's my turn."

I wasn't going to let a woman with green hair tell me what to do.

"She's drunk," someone shouted from the back of the room.

"You're not allowed to come to a meeting drunk."

"No crosstalk," the leader with the green hair was saying.

"My name is Yvonne and I am *not* an alcoholic," I said as though it were the wittiest thing on earth.

The first rule of humor, Mark says, is that it has to be funny. Even last night I knew I wasn't being very funny.

"I need to talk," I said. I was afraid I was going to cry. For some reason I thought of that woman in the tight pink dress from the first meeting I ever went to. Her whining and rubbing her hands up and down her hips and moaning about how her husband beat her. "I *wish* my husband would beat me," I said, as though it logically followed.

People had stopped talking. Everyone was looking at me as though they didn't know what to do. I had the floor.

"My husband is having an affair. Her name is Yvonne," I said. This part is all really clear. I heard someone whisper that maybe I was crazy.

"Isn't *she* Yvonne?" someone else asked.

I started telling them about Norma and Adalgisa, giving them the whole synopsis, explaining about Pollione and Mark. Then this big beefy guy came up behind me and took my arm.

"Come on, honey," he said, "let's get you some air."

"Keep coming back," I yelled into the room on the way out.

Then I remember sitting on top of a school desk, in that pink-and-black fallopian tube, talking to him, telling him about me and Yvonne, never bothering to explain about the names. He kept nodding—I don't know if he was even listening. He gave me a cigarette. I let him light it for me and took a drag. It tasted awful. People were walking in and out. A young kid strummed a guitar, a burning cigarette wedged under the top strings.

"Professor Spera?" A bald young woman hesitated before us at the desk. I couldn't connect who she was. Then I remembered. Most people don't know too many bald women.

I jumped down. An ash from the cigarette dropped onto Yvonne's green scarf.

I could see her in the back of the classroom. She always sits in the back. I tried to think of her name.

"Stacey," she said.

"Stacey," I said. I couldn't think of anything else. The wine was wearing off and I was beginning to realize what I'd just done in there.

"Are you okay?" she asked.

"Jesus," I said. It never occurred to me I might actually know someone in one of those rooms. I wanted to mention that stuff about anonymity, but I don't know her that well. And I didn't want her to think I was scared.

"You were pretty funny," she said.

"Jesus," I said again, "I've been having an awful day."

"Yeah," she said, "me too."

Then we were both quiet. I couldn't tell what she was thinking. I had the feeling she was laughing at me. I hoped to God I hadn't given her a C.

"I liked your paper," I said after a while. I couldn't remember what she wrote but I needed to say something.

She smiled.

Maybe I gave her an A. I hope it was an A.

"Stacey . . ."

A few kids walked in with a blaring radio. The beefy guy told them to turn it down.

"You don't have to worry," Stacey said. "I wasn't sure it was you until you said that thing about Yeats."

"Oh, God," I said. I tried to picture her with hair just to center myself.

"It's funny," she said. "My mom does stuff like that all the time."

Her mom. Now I have to worry about her trying to get back at me for something her mother did when she was eight. I think maybe I gave her a B. Certainly not less than a B minus. I should call NYU and find out.

I started to put on Yvonne's leather coat. With that coat I almost fit in. All I needed were a tattoo and a nose ring. Maybe a swastika.

"Need me to help you find a cab?"

"No," I said, "it's okay. I need to walk."

She kept stalling. Like she was trying to keep me there. The way they say you're supposed to keep an obscene phone caller on the line long enough to trace the call.

"I kind of thought you've been having a rough time," she said. "You've seemed really, well, different toward the end of the semester. Great class, though."

So they'd noticed.

"I kind of like it," she said, "when a teacher seems vulnerable, too."

"Yeah," I said. I was feeling pretty vulnerable.

When I recounted the conversation to Sarah she seemed
to think there was nothing ominous about it, but I don't
know. Sarah didn't see what she looked like.
I waited in front of Religious Sex and tried to figure out
where to go. I kept thinking people were going to stop me.
Ask what I was doing there. I bought a pair of dark glasses
at an outdoor kiosk, and, on impulse, a packet of tattoos.
I put on the glasses. Funny how one person seeing you,
recognizing you, makes you feel so exposed. I've been thinking how I have to be really careful from now on. When
you're not careful you start making stupid mistakes. Like
Raskolnikov. I haven't been careful enough at Yvonne's. I
have to start trusting people less. I thought of calling
Brian—he was only a few blocks away—but I thought he
might not be alone. And I wanted to be strong and composed the next time I saw him.

I walked crosstown to the West Village where it was cleaner, more civilized. I picked up a take-out cappuccino and
walked around drinking it through the sip lid. I went into the
Gap. A schmaltzy version of "Have Yourself a Merry Little
Christmas" was playing and I walked right out. I was tired
but I kept walking deeper into the West Village, past
Waverly and Bank to Jane Street, Mark's old apartment. I
stood outside the building thinking about the way we used to
make love in there, the way I learned how to make love in
there. I walked into the vestibule and looked at the names on
the mailboxes. The names were different but it still smelled
the same—like Sunday dinners at my grandparents' house.
After a while I felt so bad I bought another bottle of wine and

hopped a cab to the loft. Mark hadn't even left a note. I dialed Yvonne's three times and got no answer. It was only 9:00.

Somewhere into the bottle of wine I called Sarah. She told me to breathe and let go, kept saying things like "God is the breath inside the breath." But that just made me feel worse. It depressed me to think of God just being a breath. What kind of help is that? A breath. I told her I thought she must be hyperventilating.

She offered to come over, but we decided to go to sleep on the phone. For company.

· 1 7 ·

$\mathcal{I}$ have one more session before Christmas. I called Eric to schedule an extra one, then I wrote a list of things to talk about just to make sure we cover it all.

THINGS TO TALK TO ERIC ABOUT:
Me and Mark
Me and Brian
Me and Sarah
My mother
Going to Yvonne's (maybe)
Reducing my fee (to $50?)
Stacey
Buying oranges in hardware stores

Eric's going away. He says he told me but I don't remember. He said it's the same as my not remembering seeing him at Rockefeller Center.

"It's not the same," I said. "I *didn't* see you, so I couldn't *remember* seeing you," I continued. "Why can't you consider the fact that you might have forgotten to tell me?"

If things went on this way I knew we would spend the entire session talking about whether I'd forgotten or he'd forgotten.

"I'm scared," I said.

He nodded.

"I mean I feel like someone else is walking around in my body. Like a seam opened and I slipped out of my life. I don't feel like myself."

I'd told him on the phone about Mark moving out so it would be one less thing I had to bring up in the session. So he'd have to think about it beforehand. Mark has been gone for two days, staying, he says, with Glenda and David, though he hasn't been there once when I've called and he always calls me from the gallery. We've talked each day.

"Who do you feel like?" Eric asked. He shifted in his chair and crossed his legs. I wonder if he resented working on his day off.

"Moe," I said.

He didn't say anything.

"I wish you weren't going," I said.

"Are you afraid of something? Afraid something will happen?"

Something. "Could you leave a number?"

"Of course," he said, "I'll leave a number on my service. My colleague Raymond Stone will be available if you need to talk."

Stone. I hated him already.

"Where are you going?"

"Cape Cod." At least he didn't ask why I wanted to know.

"Won't that be too cold for the baby?" I asked. I'd read once about a baby being left outside on Cape Cod and freezing to death. When he didn't say anything I said I was glad he'd gotten the heat fixed, but that I kind of missed lying on the couch under the blanket.

"Why don't you lie down."

It was 12:10. There were only forty minutes left. I laid down where I could keep my eye on the clock.

"Why don't we try this?" he said. He shut the light and the clock disappeared.

I like it when he gets spontaneous. I could see his shoes, but couldn't tell the color in the dim light. I could just about make out the outlines on the painting behind him. I could see the sail, the prow.

"Terry, what are you afraid of?"

"The dark."

"What else?"

"Losing Mark."

"What else?"

I wondered how long I could keep the rhyme going.

"A green shark, an aardvark. Petula Clark."

This was stupid. I tried to remember my list. I liked being in the dark, though, where he couldn't see me. It was like confession, just listening to his voice in the dark. I thought about this thing Sarah always says about integrity being what you do when you think no one is watching.

"It always feels like there's someone watching me," I said.

"Who is watching you?"

"Being alone," I continued, ignoring him. "I'm afraid to be alone." It felt like a contradiction. Then I started thinking how I've always felt like part of me was missing. That

I'm only half of something. My dead twin. I took one of the pillows and held it to me.

"I've been going to Yvonne's," I said.

Eric didn't say anything.

"I said, I've been going to Yvonne's."

"What do you mean?"

"What do I mean? I mean I leave here. I walk up to her apartment. I let myself in." It was exhilarating. "I have her keys. Sometimes I just follow her."

"How long have you been doing this?" He sounded alarmed. I love it when I surprise him. I wish I could have seen his face.

"Since October," I said. "This is her scarf I've been wearing. I burned a hole in it last night."

I could almost hear the gears shifting. Eric trying to figure out what to ask, what to say. I thought about that time I'd walked around his office—the time I snuck around his office and saw that picture of his wife and child on his desk. I always wondered if he knew, if he'd left me in there alone just to test me.

"Terry," he began, "this is very serious."

I wondered if he thought everything else I'd been talking about had been a big joke. I stuck out my tongue and crossed my eyes but I don't think he saw. I held the pillow tight.

"What? Burning her scarf?"

"You cannot," he continued, "break into someone's apartment. You are breaking the law."

I was actually making him lose his cool. He was almost scolding me.

"I'm wearing her underwear," I said.

He didn't answer. His right foot started tapping the rug. He leaned forward. I imagined his hands folded under his chin, praying like crazy. It was really quiet and then there was a long squeak when someone turned on the water in the next apartment.

I wondered if he could order me to stop or whether therapists have to stay in the realm of suggestion. If they're bound to silence, like priests, or if they can go to the police.

"What do therapists do when their patients tell them they are contemplating murder?" I asked.

"What are you saying?" he asked. Now I knew he was thrown because he has to know I'd never contemplate killing Yvonne. Not seriously, anyway.

"Terry, listen to me. You've been anxious. Upset. People do things they wouldn't ordinarily do when they are upset."

I was getting him to talk a lot more than usual. It felt great to jolt him out of his careful questions and comments.

"You have got to promise to stop," he said. "Immediately."

I didn't say anything. I could hear him trying to collect himself. I knew that later he'd think of lots of interesting questions he could have asked. Like did I think Yvonne was another part of me and did I feel more like myself when I was calling myself Yvonne. Maybe he'd regret going to Cape Cod just as things were getting interesting. Maybe he'd give me his phone number.

"Who else knows this?"

I'd thought of taking Brian over there. To fuck him in her

bed. In the same bed she's been fucking my husband. But I knew I wouldn't. I knew *he* wouldn't.

"Brian," I said. "I took him there." I didn't know why I was saying it. Any of it. I started thinking maybe I was possessed.

"I don't believe you," Eric said.

Just like that. Like I'd said I'd never heard of the Beatles.

"Now just how much of this is true?"

He sounded angry.

"I thought," I said, "that in terms of therapy, what a patient believes is true is as important as what is actually true." I knew I had him.

"And what do you believe is true?"

I was tired, I was scared, and it was 12:30.

"It's true I've been going to Yvonne's," I said. "Only Sarah knows."

Eric turned on the light.

"Sit up," he said.

I sat up. It made me think of Father Dugan. I wondered if he'd give me penance.

He was wearing the brown shoes.

"I am going to give you a phone number where I can be reached," he said. He looked like he was thinking really hard. Like his mind was racing backward through all the textbooks he'd ever read, trying to figure out the right tack to take. "Please don't call unless it is absolutely necessary. But I want you to call me if you are planning to go back to that apartment."

I wondered if I should tell him that I was planning to go

right after the session. Maybe he'd keep me there. But I thought he might not give me the number. I promised. Eric wrote the number down. I memorized it immediately—in case he took it back.

· 1 8 ·

$\mathcal{E}$ric's gone. I called him and got his machine. "You have reached Eric Anderson. I will be away from the office until Monday, January second. If you need to speak to someone before then please call Raymond Stone . . ."

I dialed the Cape Cod number. I'm keeping it in my wallet and I also wrote it on the inside cover of my journal in case I lose the paper. No one answered. It occurred to me Eric might have given me the wrong number but I put the thought out of my head.

I called Brian. I knew I shouldn't, but I called him. I was trying to wait until I felt cheerful and upbeat, not so needy. But I called.

"What's up?" he asked. His voice sounded little, a little dry point of dread. Music was blasting in the background.

"Nothing," I said. "I just wanted to check in."

Hardly an enticing beginning.

"What did you say?" I asked. He was talking low and I couldn't hear him. I didn't recognize the music.

"How are things going?" he asked. Like a stranger. Like we hadn't just made love two days ago.

"How come you haven't called me?" I was going to say all

the wrong things, and I knew it. I knew I just should stay light and casual and fun. "Is something wrong?"

He wasn't saying anything. The other day I saw a copy of the *Duino Elegies* lying on his floor, opened out to the first elegy. Brian had underlined the parts about how much you miss when you're always distracted by the expectation of a beloved. About a soaring, objectless love. In turquoise marker he'd highlighted *Isn't it time we lovingly / freed ourselves from the beloved and, quivering, endured.* I remember because those same lines are underscored in my copy. Maybe everybody underscores those lines. But it looked like Brian really took them to heart. I'd looked around on his floor and table for a turquoise marker to see if he'd underlined them recently.

"Maybe I shouldn't have called," I said. I *knew* I shouldn't have called. I could see him looking at that new Chinese clock. He must have turned the music down because I couldn't hear it anymore.

"Terry," he said, "listen to me, I know you're having a rough time, but I feel like, I don't know, like you're using me to get across the street or something."

That beautiful Irish voice saying that. *Using me to get across the street or something.* I laid down on the couch and put my legs up on the wall. I rested the phone on my stomach, looked up at that painting of the puddle. Just stared at it. I thought of that kid Chris who had skated me across the intersection the other night. How sweet he was, a sweet helpful stranger. And I thought, Brian's right, I *was* using him. I like him a lot, but he is essentially a stranger. I've been using him—like a giant pacifier. And when it comes down to it, how well do I know him? What do I know about him? There's nothing familiar about him. His apartment never feels familiar. That dark, cavey room. That strange cumin smell. I never feel right in there, like I belong in there—the way I do with Mark. No, I don't know him very well at all. So how could I love him? And how could I expect him to love me?

"Terry . . ."

It's funny, how it just snapped into place. Just like that.

"You're right," I said. "You're right." I was almost relieved. "I'm so sorry," I said. "This isn't about you, I can see that." And it's true. It's not about Brian. It's about something, but it's not about Brian.

He seemed relieved, too. He started to sound more like himself. He told me about a movie he'd just seen and I didn't even wonder who he'd gone with. I said I'd call the next day, but I was pretty sure I wouldn't. It was over. I could see that.

I hung up. I lay there on the couch, my feet in the air, staring into that puddle, and when the scary thoughts came in I just let them go. I'm doing that a lot now. I had a yoga teacher who said that when unwanted thoughts come into your head you should acknowledge them and then let them go. So I let myself see the thought, really see it, and then I make it explode. When it gets really bad I write the things down and then throw the paper away.

THINGS I DON'T WANT TO THINK ABOUT:
Eric being away
Mark and Yvonne

Christmas without Mark
Student evaluations
Stacey
How much I am eating

THINGS I NEED TO THINK ABOUT:
Why I am crying so much
Screwing up at NYU
Telling Mark about Yvonne's
Going to Yvonne's
Reading the paper (there are more important things
    going on than your life)
Taking one day at a time

I thought of calling Eric's replacement, Raymond Stone,
but I want to save him for an emergency. I have to try to figure out some of this stuff for myself. I'm thirty-six, reason-
ably intelligent, it's almost the new year, and I can make a
new start. Make some early New Year's resolutions.

THINGS I WILL NOT DO:
Go to Yvonne's again
    (remember, one day at a time)
For today I will not go to Yvonne's
Cry in public
Call Mark
Call Yvonne
Call Eric
Call Sarah

Call my mother
Go home for Christmas
Read Mark's journal even though it's in his desk drawer

THINGS I WILL DO:
Spend one hour daily (at least) reading poems for next term
Stop eating in between meals
Meditate (at least 20 min.)
Stop talking to strangers
Send Mark a letter
Ignore Christmas
Clean the loft
Drink only one glass of wine a day
Go to the gym every day
Read the *Times* every day (*no* exceptions)
Think about people other than myself
Get Mark back
Tell Mark he left his journal here

· 1 9 ·

*M*ark is having an affair with Yvonne. I read it in his journal. It's funny, but I feel almost better knowing for certain. "Y again. Didn't think it would bother me," the journal said in black ink. "Thought I could keep it separate from feelings for T." Then a little later in green ink, "T strange & distant. Moody." A page later he wrote (black ink this time): "Y again." Then "Sold two ptgs: Rothenberg. Fischel."

There wasn't much more. Notes on paintings, figures. No dates anywhere. Mark's not big on journals.

So now I know. Maybe he wanted me to know. Maybe that's why he left the journal in his desk drawer. I hadn't meant to read it. Just that instead of cleaning the loft I decided to re-hang some of the drawings, make the place more mine, and the wires and hooks are in his desk drawer. I had his journal in my hand and I kept saying, *Don't open it. Don't open it.* Over and over. Then I opened it and saw Yvonne's name. Well, her initial. Y. *Y again.* I felt really sick but I couldn't stop. It's funny, it doesn't say anything *about* Yvonne. The way she looks, what kind of food she likes, how she moves. There are no specific details. Nothing. I think I know more about Yvonne than he does.

I've been sitting here, trying to figure out what to do. I thought of calling Raymond Stone but I can't imagine telling him the whole story. Maybe Eric left notes or files on all of his patients so Raymond could check quickly. What would my file say?

Spera, Theresa (Terry). After two years tells her "real name," 36. Married 5 years. Highly emotional. Has fantasies of being punished. Catholic. Believes husband having an affair. (Woman's name, Yvonne.) Calls self Yvonne at 12-step mtg. False pregnancy. Passed myself and family at Rockefeller Center, blocked it out, said she didn't see us. Afraid to be alone. Seems to be breaking into Yvonne's apartment. Having affair with a young student.

What would Raymond Stone make of that? Would he be able to construct a person out of that? How could he help me figure out what to do? Anyway it's Christmas Eve and he probably wouldn't answer the phone.

I kept telling myself it doesn't mean anything—Mark and Yvonne. That I just need to wait it out.

I called Yvonne's.

"Hi. Is Mark there?" I asked.

"Who is this?" I could hear her trying to sound calm. I wonder if she found the copy of *Crime and Punishment* in her oven. Maybe she's planning a big Christmas dinner and she'll set the apartment on fire.

"I want to speak to Mark."

"I'm sorry," she said, "you've reached the wrong number."

"Really? Is this . . ." She hung up.

I called Glenda and David. Their machine was on. I didn't leave a message.

My mother had called four times to see if we're coming tomorrow. I erased her messages.

Well, what doesn't kill you makes you stronger, Nietzsche said. The funny thing is, I felt almost calm. I stopped at the post office to pick up the mail and got a note from the head of my department at NYU saying he'd like to talk to me about the student evaluations. I didn't freak out or get upset. I was so calm, it's almost spooky.

"Honey, are you okay?" Sarah was looking at me so seriously I almost laughed. Dean & DeLuca was darker than usual, I think because they were going to close early for Christmas. Hardly anyone was there. Some of the chairs were already stacked on the tables. We were hunched over our cappuccinos in the back under the skylight.

"Yeah," I said, "I think I am. It's funny, but I think I'm okay."

"You don't look okay. You look kind of freaked out. You're pale." Sarah was staring at me intently, dipping her plastic spoon in and out of the milky foam. She had little bits of cinnamon stuck to her upper lip. "I think you should call Mark and talk to him," she said.

I laughed. "Right," I said. "I can say, 'Oh, honey, by the way, I was reading your journal and I realized it's true. You really are having an affair with Yvonne. Would you like to meet for coffee to talk about it?'"

I must have been talking loud because two people at the next table looked over at us. I glared at them.

"Let's try that scene again," I said to Sarah, to throw them off, but she hadn't seen them. "Anyway, I was thinking about it. It didn't actually *say* anything. It said 'Y again.' That's all it said."

It's true. That's all it said. Maybe he felt guilty just *thinking* about it. Just flirting.

Sarah leaned closer to me. "Terry, I'm worried about you, you know. About you going up to that apartment."

I'd finally told her the whole thing. Everything.

I liked how she said "going up to" and not "breaking into," the way Eric had.

"Well, I'm not doing it anymore," I said, and it's true. I haven't been there in a few days. I'd promised Eric and I was going to keep that promise. It was hard. I'd gone up to the neighborhood twice, walked around the block, but I did not go in.

"Well, that's good," she said. "Stay away from there." The way she was looking at me made me nervous.

"You think I'm losing it, don't you?"

Someone at a table nearby knocked his coffee over and yelled "shit." A busboy ambled over to mop it up.

"You just seem . . . upset . . . I mean, we've been through a lot together. I've seen you pull some crazy stuff. But honey, sometimes now I feel like you're crossing a line."

I didn't say anything.

"I mean I love you, Terry, I really do. You know that. But I'm worried. You need to calm down."

I leaned over and wiped the cinnamon from her lip. "I don't have your Christmas present yet," I said. "I've been ignoring Christmas."

"Dean & DeLuca will be closing in twenty minutes," the busboy announced. "Merry Christmas."

"It's okay," she said. "I don't have yours either. It's been a bad year." She licked the foam around the rim of her paper cup and put it down. "Some Christmas, huh?" she said.

We both just sat there looking glum. For someone who's Jewish, Sarah really takes Christmas to heart. It's something I've always loved about her.

"I have an idea," she said. Some Like It Hot is open late tonight. Let's go buy each other something wonderful. A little black silk will make us both feel better." Sarah always buys lingerie when she's feeling bad. I knew she was missing her old girlfriend, Karen, and things with Elly hadn't turned into more than friendship. Elly is definitely straight. Jealous as I'd been I still feel bad for her.

I went downstairs to pee. The scrawled penis was still on the wall but someone had scratched out the words, so that only the *God* was left. There was an arrow drawn from the word *God* to the tip of the penis with what looked like come spurting out. *God is coming*, I guess they meant. Really sick. On Christmas Eve.

I washed my face. I didn't think I looked so bad, just a little pale. I put on some blush, mascara. I added a touch of Scarlet Memory. I actually looked pretty good. "Merry Christmas," I said into the mirror.

Sarah just looked at me when I came upstairs.

"What?" I asked.

"Nothing," she said. She rubbed my cheek where maybe I'd put on a little too much blush. "Well, let's go."

We walked arm in arm over to the West Village.

"Too bad we can't marry each other," I said as we crossed

Seventh Avenue. We always say this when things reach a certain point.

"We're both too femme," she said. "It'd never work."

Inside the shop a few people were looking for last-minute gifts. Sarah started talking to this guy with a briefcase and Barney's bag who was trying to buy a silk slip for his girlfriend. "This one's nice," she said. "See, the lace is soft and won't scratch her." Men always trust Sarah.

I watched two transvestites fondle the lace bras and panties, giggling. It depressed me. It was Christmas, for God's sake. Something about seeing them, seeing that guy buying lingerie for his girlfriend, made me feel how far away from Christmas I was.

Sarah held a green silk chemise up against herself in the mirror. At the same time one of the transvestites placed a black fur brassiere over his "tits" and stood in a pin-up posture, looking at himself. When I saw the two of them framed in the same mirror, something, I don't know, something snapped. I saw my mother standing at her bureau, a fox piece fixed around her neck. Those tiny teeth biting the tail. My father behind her in the mirror looking at her, just looking. My own head bobbed behind Sarah and the transvestite. It looked like a ball that had detached from my body, just hanging there in all that lace. I moved to see that my head connected to my neck, shoulders, and I got a flash of myself balancing on Yvonne's chair, twisting and posing in front of her mirror, wearing only her panties. It seemed lewd. Something you'd see in a porno magazine.

I took out a tissue and wiped the lipstick off. This was no

place to be on Christmas Eve. I belonged in church. I needed to go to Mass. I could take a cab to Grace Church and
hear some music, and then, what the hell, I had no plans. I
could sit there and wait for Midnight Mass.

"Honey, I need to get out of here," I said to Sarah. "I'm
going to Grace Chruch to hear some music. Want to come?"

But Sarah said she'd rather go home and watch the Yule
log on TV.

The church was crowded. Hundreds of people dressed up for
Mass, the way we used to dress when I was a kid. Everyone
had children. Everyone was blond. All the women looked like
Liv Ullmann. I had wiped the lipstick off, combed my hair,
and tried to look as dignified as possible, but I think I was the
only one there in jeans. I fluffed Yvonne's scarf around my
neck to dress up my leather jacket, pushed my hair up and
under my beret. My hair is so dark I looked like an alien.

People kissed one another hello as the organ music played
"O Little Town of Bethlehem." Many of them looked like
they knew one another, like they came to Mass every
Sunday, not just on Christmas.

I'd picked up a handful of tracts at the door: *Introduction
to the Devout Life*, *The Spirituality of Waiting*, *Selections from
Kierkegaard*. I opened one of the tracts and skimmed quickly from one phrase to another: *One of the most pervasive emo-
tions is fear. People are afraid—afraid of inner feelings, afraid of
other people, afraid of the future.*

*A waiting person is a patient person, a person who believes this
moment is **the** moment.*

I wanted something more direct. Like *Here's what you should do about Yvonne.*

A tiny baby with a wrinkled red face cried in the pew in front of me. The mother rocked it and smiled up at her husband, who had his arm around her waist. It could have been me and Mark. Our baby. Where was Mark now? Was he with Yvonne? Had she persuaded him to go to hear music at some Upper West Side church? Was he at that stage of love where he would have agreed? When you do anything, even watch four consecutive nights of baseball, to be near the one you love. Had Mark *ever* been like that? Or Brian? Or is it only me that gets that way? Can't bear the time away. The time alone? And what about Yvonne? How lonely is she? Maybe she likes the nights she eats salad from a container in her living room reading one of those murder mysteries.

The priest walked up to the pulpit, dressed in red silk robes. It reminded me of the transvestites, but I put it out of my head. I wanted to pray, to think only pure thoughts.

Whatever doesn't kill you makes you stronger.

The congregation rose to sing the opening hymn. The priest made a motion to bless the crowd. He was an Episcopal priest, but it's close enough to Catholic. Catholic without the blood and guts. I kept reading. *A well-ordered love requires that we should love the soul more than the body.* Did I love Mark's soul more than his body? My own? How can you separate the soul from the body?

A kid behind me poked me with his hymnal and I realized I was still sitting. I stood up and joined the song. *"All*

is calm. All is bright," I sang. I took a deep breath and tried
to get calm. I was desperate to be calm. I sang loud. It felt
good to hear my voice blend in with the other people
around me. *It's the sound of your soul rising out of your sinful
body,* Sister Dominica used to say when we sang our hymns.
The sound of your souls rising together to Jesus. Together. I started wishing I were there with Mark or Sarah or Brian or *some-
body.* I made myself take a deep breath and sing even louder.
Surely, I told myself, I couldn't be the only person there
alone. The only sad person there. People lived through
tragedy, through losses and deaths and terrible disappoint-
ments. Some people love to be alone.

The music stopped and we sat down. The priest wel-
comed us and said something about tonight everyone was a
parishioner. There were no strangers and everyone was welcome. To bring all our joys and all our burdens into the arms
of Jesus. I liked that. I was glad he'd said Jesus and not God.
I've always found Jesus easier to picture than God. When I
was sixteen on one of those Christian Awakening retreats I
remember telling one of the counselors that I didn't know
how to pray. He was a really cute guy with long brown hair.
Gentle-looking with beautiful hands and a denim work-
shirt. He played the guitar. Robert Giralomo, his name was.
Robert said to make praying part of what you do. He said
he prayed while he played guitar. He asked me what I liked
to do. I said I liked to dance. Well, he said, pointing to a
small wood-paneled room with a light blue carpet, just go
inside there and dance with Jesus. And I did. It felt stupid
at first, but I did it. I imagined myself dancing a slow and

easy two-step with Jesus, who at that point bore a remark-
able resemblance to Robert Giralomo. I hummed and
swayed, eyes closed, leaning against the wall pretending it
was Jesus. Every now and then I wondered what, if anything, this had to do with praying. But it felt good. Pretty
soon I was completely turned on and went up to my room
to masturbate. I ended up with a terrific crush on Robert
and cried myself to sleep thinking about him.

We were singing again. A hymn I didn't know and had
to follow in the book. Something about resting in the gentle arms of Jesus. I still think of Jesus as looking something
like Robert Giralomo.

I want to rest in someone's arms. Anyone's arms. I'm
always so scared. I've always been so scared. And now Mark's
gone, and I can't call Brian, and Eric's away. He's only been
out of town a few days and already I feel like he doesn't exist
anymore. Think hard, Terry, he had said, about the fact that
you are so afraid to be alone. And now here I was, alone on
Christmas Eve. I could have stayed with Sarah. I could have
gone to my parents' house. I had no plans for Christmas. No
plans. I've never not had plans for Christmas. I could pretend it was nothing special and just go to the movies. Stay
home and read. "You're never alone when you're with God,"
Sister Judy had said. I tried to think about that, about
spending Christmas with Jesus, but it seemed like a pretty
poor consolation.

Mass ended. The congregation was singing an exuberant
"Joy to the World," exiting the church. I sang it too. I sang
it with such passion and conviction I almost convinced

myself I was joyous. I'd planned to sit inside and wait for Midnight Mass, but it was only 8:15 and, besides, I was pulled along by the movement of the crowd. People were kissing one another and smiling and saying "Merry Christmas."

"Merry Christmas," I said, and squeezed the hand of a little old lady who had smiled at me. She's alone, too, I thought. Pretty soon I was standing alone on Fifth Avenue without a clue as to what to do next.

I took a cab uptown.

· 2 0 ·

$\mathcal{F}$irst I stopped at the Korean vegetable stand. It was almost a relief to be somewhere that exhibited no sign of Christmas. Not so much as a paper Santa Claus. It was empty. I smiled at the old guy who never seemed to recognize me. For all he knew I could have been Yvonne. Maybe we all look alike to him: small dark-haired women coming in alone to circle the salad bar and concoct a quick dinner.

I made my way around the central display of pans and chafing dishes, prongs out, pausing by each tray as if this were to be my last meal. I saw myself reflected in a half-empty aluminum tray and stopped to fix my hair, then I continued. I picked out a vegetable sushi, some marinated ginger, a few yellowing broccoli florets that looked like bonsai plants. I tried to separate the broccoli from the sushi with a layer of ginger and a few bits of watercress, but once I added a piece of raw cauliflower the contents of the plastic container began to run into one another and the whole thing looked like a big mess. I skipped the dressing. I figured I could use Yvonne's. On impulse I stuck in two breadsticks which were probably stale, and closed the container. Mark and I always go out somewhere special for Christmas Eve and this container of raw food made me feel just the right level of sorry for myself. *I am alone on Christmas Eve, I am alone on Christmas Eve,* I kept saying to myself and almost had myself in tears by the time I hit the register. The old Korean guy pulled a rubber band around the container, and weighed it. He stuck in a plastic fork and spoon and napkin. I paid him. Outside I noticed that for the first time the sidewalk stand was not set up. That guy was probably home with his family wrapping presents.

Why are you so afraid to be alone? I could hear Eric asking. Well, *he* wasn't alone on Christmas Eve, was he?

I picked up a bottle of Chardonnay and headed to Yvonne's.

· 2 1 ·

*W*hat's funny is I never expected her to be there. As if the apartment I went to and the apartment she lived in existed in parallel universes. That it would be impossible for her to be there when I arrived. And yet if I think like that I could also say that the Mark she sleeps with and the Mark I sleep with, my husband and her lover, exist in parallel universes, so we're not sleeping with the same man. In a way, it's what Eric's been talking about: getting away from either/or thinking. Negative capability. What Yeats would call Unity of Being.

I wonder what Yeats's wife would have called it.

Let's face it. Yeats's wife didn't fool around. While her husband is banging his head on Madame Blavatsky's table, she figures out the perfect strategy and invents that stuff about automatic writing. On their honeymoon.

I guess I really didn't believe Mark was having an affair. Even after I saw it in his journal. *Y again.* He never actually said he *slept* with her. Maybe he's just thought about it. Maybe he feels guilty? I know about guilt. Guilt can come from just *thinking* about a thing. Anyway, he knows how I love Christmas Eve. He would think it cruel to be with his lover on Christmas Eve when his wife was miserable and alone.

Yvonne's apartment looked pretty much the same. Every pillow in place.

On the kitchen counter was a typed list:

CONCETTA COULD YOU PLEASE:
Fix the curtain
Take out garbage
Change lightbulb in bathroom (60 watt)
Clean refrigerator
Take in drycleaning (in basket)

This is for you ——————>
Merry Christmas, Y

(p.s. See you Jan. 8)

So she did have a cleaning woman. Next to each item was a checkmark in pencil. I figured Concetta had done that. Whatever Yvonne had left as a gift was gone.

I went into the bathroom. The lightbulb was changed. The soap was new. I wonder if Concetta puts fresh soap in every time she cleans, because the soap always looks new. I came back to the kitchen and stared at Yvonne's list. I stared at it until I was bored.

There wasn't much in the refrigerator so I guess she wasn't expecting guests. She'd hung a few Christmas cards along a black ribbon and strung it between the kitchen and living room. It looked pretty pathetic. I turned the corners back but the names meant nothing to me. *Wishing you peace in this sacred season*, one of the cards said. I crossed it out.

She'd probably never look at it again. Who looks at Christmas cards more than once? I threw my coat—her coat—over the couch and then sat down beside it.

I couldn't think of anything to do. I'd already tried on most of her clothes and anyway I didn't feel like changing. I had an urge to wreck the apartment, but I couldn't even muster the energy to mess up her books. *I am alone on Christmas Eve* I kept thinking. Alone. That's the thing. Just a couple of months ago it was Yvonne who was alone. Standing in her apartment, eating salad out of a plastic container. I remember the first time I followed her to the Korean vegetable stand—how alone she looked. Even then, miserable and afraid as I was, I was still looking at her from a relatively safe place. I mean I was still with Mark. I had only to get downtown and home to my husband. Now I realize how smug and safe you feel when you're with someone. Anchored. How you could be in some unfamiliar part of town and just have to picture home to start to feel safe. Someone there, waiting for you. How the minute you get in the cab you begin to feel safer as it pulls you closer and closer home. The first familiar thing you see, St. Mark's Bookstore or Dean & DeLuca, almost makes you completely peaceful.

And now here I was alone, in Yvonne's apartment, and she was safe somewhere with my husband. Now it was Yvonne, not me, who was safe and smug. And I had nowhere to go. I thought about Sarah. How had she stood it all these months without Karen? Why wasn't she on the phone with me continually, howling about being alone. How did she stand it?

How did Brian? Why hadn't he—Jesus, he's even in a strange country—why hadn't he begged me to spend Christmas with him? Now we would both be alone.

The apartment had never felt so quiet. I turned on the radio and switched to an all-news station so I wouldn't hear even a snatch of Christmas music. Then I turned on the TV. It was a little cold, so I pulled a sweater out of the closet and wrapped it around my shoulders. I opened the bottle of wine, poured a glass, and sat on the couch. On TV a small family was hugging one another and exchanging gifts—it was a commercial for batteries—every one of which needed several batteries to work. The father beamed and handed his son a battery-operated razor. The mother for some reason got a Walkman. When the husband gave a fond little squeeze to his wife, I thought about Eric and his wife and baby, warm and snug in their little house on the Cape. His wife wrapping last-minute presents while he held the baby, walked it around their cosy little living room, singing "O Holy Night" to put it to sleep. How could he understand how scared I was? How could he understand I felt as unanchored, as unmoored, as that ridiculous boat in his office? *You're afraid to be alone.* Of course I'm afraid. Only an idiot—or a hermit, or maybe a poet—would willingly spend Christmas alone.

The wine was making me tired and I had an urge to stretch out on the couch and sleep. Then it occurred to me *Yvonne* might have a journal. I'd never thought of that before. I started looking for it. All the likely places. The end table drawer was maddeningly neat. A spool of white thread, a spool of black thread, and a packet of needles. Scissors. A couple of photographs—no one I recognized. There was a number two pencil and one of those pens that has an image floating under its plastic case. A gondola slipping through the canals in Venice. When I was seven I found a pen like that in my father's drawer. A curvy woman in a strapless bathing suit and high heels. It was the first thing I ever stole. One side of the pen showed her from the front, the other from the back. When you tipped it, the ink passed out of the suit and she was naked. I used to sneak into my father's drawer and tip the pen back and forth. The suit sliding over her naked behind excited me. She didn't have any pubic hair, but I wouldn't have noticed that then. One day while I was watching Sister Thomas Aquinas write helping verbs on the board I started thinking that anytime, without any warning, my father could take that pen out of there, that I'd go for it and it would be gone. I ran home after school, snuck into his room, and took it. That night at dinner I couldn't look at him. I thought if I looked at him, he'd know it was me who had stolen that pen. Nothing happened that night. He didn't say a word. I waited. Days passed. Weeks. He never mentioned it. I'm sure now that he'd thrown that pen in there and never given it a second thought. But I didn't know that then. For months I couldn't look at him.

There were times I thought I should put it back, that it would make me feel better. Once I threw it under the couch so my mother would find it while she was cleaning and they'd both think it had gotten there by accident. But

before an hour went by I crawled behind the couch and
retrieved it.

Hiding it was a problem because there wasn't a drawer
my mother wouldn't open. I switched the hiding place every
day. I'd pull Valerie out (for some reason I thought of her as
Valerie), tip the pen back and forth, saying the word *ass* to
myself, and *bend over*. I pictured Father Murphy telling her
to bend over so he could spank her. I'd tip her suit up and
back. Then I'd crawl on the bed holding her, whispering
Valerie, Valerie, and rub myself until I was calm again. And
all that time I couldn't look at my father. I was embarrassed
by him. It's funny how something little, some misunder-
standing like that, something you imagine, becomes so real
it actually changes the course of your life. Maybe my father
and I could have been close. Maybe he would have teased
and joked with me, the way he did with my sisters. Maybe
it was me feeling so guilty and embarrassed that made us
both so awkward together.

Maybe it was me acting so weird now, so guilty and suspicious, that was pushing Mark away. Maybe I would *cause*
him to have an affair with Yvonne.

I put Yvonne's pen back. There was nothing else in the
drawer. The same for her desk. Nothing but the things
you'd expect to find in a desk. Not even an obsessive accu-
mulation of Wite-Out or Post-it pads. I checked the drawer beside her bed. No condoms. No diaphragm. Nothing
unusual. It was almost like she didn't exist. How could anyone be that uninteresting? That unreflective?

The radio was starting to get to me. And the TV. I felt

cluttered and full of static. I turned the radio off, turned the
sound down on the TV, and went back into the bedroom.
The bough I'd left in the window was gone. I wonder what
she thought when she found it. Maybe Concetta had found
it and thrown it out.

It was getting dark. All the lights were out so the TV
flickering in the living room made wavy blue-gray patterns
on the bedroom wall. I tried Eric again but there was no
answer. Where could he be on Christmas Eve? I was sure
he'd given me the wrong number. I was getting so anxious
that I made myself lie down to meditate. Most books on
meditation say not to lie down, to sit up so that your mind
is alert, so that you don't fall asleep. But I was tired from
that wine and I figure you can meditate in any position. I
mean, people who are paralyzed meditate.

I tried to clear my mind, but the more I tried the more
agitated I got. I saw Mark lying on his back with Yvonne
straddling his hips. Those moles on her thighs. I saw
Yvonne at the loft, sleeping in our bed, fucking Mark in the
back room of the gallery, meeting our friends. Sarah and
Yvonne becoming friends. Yvonne and Glenda going shopping for those big earrings they both wear. I saw a tree. A
tree in a living room. I could see the roots twisting under
the parquet floor. It started getting bigger. It kept growing
and growing until its tip pushed through the ceiling and
pieces of plaster started falling all over, speckling the floor.
But I couldn't see me there. Mark was there. He was looking up at the tree chanting and flicking his fingers in that
hocus-pocus gesture, as though he could make it stop grow-

ing. *Tree, tree, tree*, he kept saying. *Tree, tree, tree*. The more it grew the more you could see what kind of a tree it was. It looked like a Christmas tree, but it had a long bare trunk at the bottom and the body of it was round. It started shaking, as if it were dancing. Then I heard a long whistle.

It took a few seconds before I realized it was the phone. Yvonne's voice came on and said to leave a message.

"Eve? Evie, it's Mom," the voice was saying. "Honey, are you there?"

I tried to get to the machine but I'd been in such a deep sleep that I couldn't get my balance right away.

I watched the tape turn. I couldn't move. Eve.

"Dad can pick up you and your friend at the station in the morning, sweetheart. Just let us know what train you'll be on. I thought you might get the 9:11, which pulls into East Hampton at 12:32. Give a call tonight. We'll be at Midnight Mass, so you can call late. Merry Christmas, honey."

Honey. Sweetheart. She made me sick. I know mothers like that. I prefer my mother's *sonofabitchin'bastard*. I can trust that.

You and your friend. I had no doubt Mark would be there. East Hampton. It's perfect. All those art collectors. Now I realized how perfect a setup it was. Better than Brooklyn, anyway. I could see Mark sitting there on that 9:11 gearing up to sell some work. Yvonne filling him in on all those stupid WASP holiday traditions. Her mother probably has her own herb garden, makes her own decorative wreaths. It made me sick. Well, I would be on that 9:11 too.

I called the Long Island Rail Road to check the other times, just in case. I stayed on the line while a machine kept repeating how important my call was to them and not to hang up. I heard a recording of "Chestnuts Roasting on an Open Fire." I kept waiting. "Do You Hear What I Hear?" "White Christmas." When the recording switched to a sickening version of "Sleigh Ride," I was ready to scream.

"Calm down, Terry," I said to myself. I started singing with the recording. I picked up Yvonne's painting of the dog and stuck it in the end table drawer. I slammed the drawer shut as I shouted the alto parts I sang in high school glee club. *"Giddyyap, it's grand,"* I shouted, *"holding your hand."* I could see Yvonne and Mark and that whole stupid WASP family out riding in a sleigh through the Hamptons, singing and sharing hot chocolate. Cross-country skiing. I wanted to puke.

"Our cheeks are nice and rosy and comfy cozy are we," I was singing when I heard the door.

The TV was still on. My coat, Yvonne's coat, was on the couch. The bottle of wine was open on the counter. The lights, thank God, were out. I put the phone down. I heard voices. I yanked the coat off the couch and walked quietly toward the bathroom. I couldn't think of anything else to do. I was shaking and scared but I walked straight into the shower. I kept thinking about the bottle of wine open on the counter. Let her think Concetta left it there. I heard a laugh. A man's voice. I put on the coat. I stood behind the shower curtain, which was green with little fish all over it. At least she didn't have one of those frosted doors.

I put my bag down over the drain and tried to stay still enough to hear them in the living room. They were laughing. Then I didn't hear anything. Maybe they were kissing.

I could hear only muffled voices. I heard Yvonne say something about the TV. I heard her come into her bedroom. She must have been less than twenty feet from me.

"It's weird," she said, and walked back out. Then she came back into the bedroom, walked into the bathroom. I was shaking. I was sure you could see the shape of the black coat through the green shower curtain. I held my breath. She switched on the light. There was a pop and the light blew out.

"Shit," she said.

It was a new bulb. It must have been defective.

Yvonne walked out. Just like that. This woman walks into her apartment, the TV is on, a scarf is lying on her couch where she hadn't left it (I'd realized about the scarf after I got in the shower), a bottle of wine is open on the kitchen counter (I couldn't remember where I'd left the glass)—and she walks in and out of the bathroom without checking behind the shower curtain. I mean, I *always* check behind the shower curtain when I get home. Either she was drunk and careless or she is just really bizarre.

I was sweating and shaking. I could hear the man's voice. Mark's voice, was it? I couldn't hear enough to tell. You'd think after knowing someone for six years—living with them, being married to them—you'd be able to pick out that voice even in an earthquake. But I couldn't.

"I can't believe this," Yvonne was saying. *"The Spirituality of Waiting?"*

I heard her say something about knowing her for such a long time. I guessed she was talking about Concetta. Probably thinking she was a closet alcoholic who'd just discovered religion. Then it was quiet. I imagined Mark coming up behind her, kissing her, lifting her skirt. I tried to lean closer to hear, but the swish my coat made against the shower curtain stopped me.

The man's voice asked something. I really couldn't hear if it was Mark. Maybe I was too desperate to hear. And maybe it's just that men's voices are harder to hear than women's— more muffled.

"God," she said. She didn't sound panicky or upset. I would have been terrified. At least suspicious. I have been coming into this woman's life regularly for two months and she has not the tiniest bit of suspicion. I was getting furious. How could *anyone* be that unobservant? How could she be so oblivious to me? I mean, how much invasion can one person stand before they start to notice it?

"Eve? Evie, it's Mom . . ." When she started playing the messages back I almost felt ignored. I bet I could have walked into the living room at that moment and Yvonne would have had some kind of logical explanation for it. Where the hell did she think that scarf had come from?

I heard another laugh, both of them. Then Yvonne came back into the bathroom. She turned on the water and started brushing her teeth. She gargled. She was only about two feet from me, that curtain between us. Sweat poured down my body.

"Come *on*," she whispered. I could hear her feeling through the medicine cabinet. I remembered that's where she kept the condoms. How many packets had she bought since my first visit? I heard jars and bottles clinking, then something fell and smashed. It sounded like a glass.

"Shit," she whispered, then louder she said, "Don't come in here without your shoes."

So he had his shoes off. I half expected her to rush back with a broom and dustpan. She must have been pretty horny to let it go.

I didn't hear anything for a while. I had nothing to do but look at those fish. Big green fish. And little green seashells and conchs. Seahorses. Silvery, frosty white stuff that was supposed to look like seafoam. It was the kind of shower curtain you can get in a junk store for $3.99.

I was staring at a big puffy fish when I heard Miles Davis on Yvonne's cheap tape player. *Kind of Blue.* So they were going to fuck. The Miles Davis could have been a coincidence. I mean a lot of people listen to Miles Davis during sex. Mark used to say he always listened to Miles Davis when he was with someone new. After the novelty wears off he forgets about the music. He's still a great lover. With or without the music.

Impossible as it sounds now, after a while I began to realize I was pretty safe behind that shower curtain. There were moments when it felt like nothing more than stopping by a room where a TV is on and watching from the doorway for a minute. I thought that once they started to fuck I could probably even get out and sit on the toilet seat and watch. I have to say I was almost curious. I wanted to know how he would be with her. How loud or soft she would come. Whether Mark would force her to come louder, the way he had with me. *Scream,* he used to say to me, *you're keeping it inside you.* I wanted to see how tenderly he'd talk to her. Whether he'd be rough with her, the way he is sometimes, whether he'd go down on her. They were pretty quiet. I heard a moan. I think it was him. She might have just gone down on him. Mark really likes to start by getting sucked off.

They laughed. Both of them. So his cock wasn't in her mouth. I heard a gasp. I guessed he'd just penetrated her. It was like putting together a puzzle, guessing from the sounds of things. I couldn't see a thing. Only those fish. I didn't even know if all the lights were out.

Miles Davis was in the second track of *Kind of Blue.* It was almost cliché. I heard something drop, a shoe, maybe. And I heard things get louder. A few slaps. A laugh. Grunts. "Harder," Yvonne said. If this was Mark, things could go on for a long time. I must have been absolutely numb, because I definitely didn't feel freaked out or anything. I wasn't really thinking at all. I was transfixed. And not just because it was Mark and Yvonne. I think it must always be like that when you are watching or listening to someone have sex.

It went on and on. And then it hit me that I had to get out of there. My body wouldn't move. I felt like I was exist-

ing in two places at once. On the one hand I felt almost normal. On the other I was so numb I couldn't move my legs.
Even my crotch had fallen asleep.

I pulled aside the shower curtain. I saw flickering
lights. Candles. I saw feet. Yvonne's bed. I stepped down
and heard the crunch of glass under my foot. I stopped.
Held my breath. Nothing happened. I took one large step
onto the rug in Yvonne's room. Even then I thought if
they heard me I had the advantage. I was dressed. I could
run to the door and out before they realized. I came closer to the bed. I was within, I don't know, five feet of it.
Within five feet of knowing. But they were under the covers. That threw me. Mark never fucks under the covers.
Not even in the winter. This would have been a major
concession. I stepped on something soft that felt like
underwear. I stood there, I don't know how long, watching the rolling and moving. I say rolling and moving
because that's all I saw. That's it. Rolling and moving.
What looked like an ass under the sheets. I couldn't even
tell if it was a man's ass or a woman's. I did have the pres-
ence of mind to pick up whatever was under my foot. I
could check them when I was safe. I would definitely recognize Mark's underwear. I moved out to the living room.
I have heard stories in which a woman comes upon her
husband fucking someone else and confronts them.
Where a man decapitates the guy he finds fucking his
wife, sticks his head in a bowling bag. I could have
yanked the covers off them.

I didn't.

I didn't. I moved fast. I passed through the living room. Yvonne's bag was on the couch. I took it. I didn't think. I took it. I grabbed the scarf. I got to the door. I opened the door as quietly as I could. And then I ran.

· 2 2 ·

$\mathcal{I}$ ran. I couldn't wait for the elevator so I took the stairs. On the third floor I realized I'd look suspicious if anyone saw me coming out of the stairway, so I went into the hall and waited for the elevator. While I was waiting I noticed I was holding Yvonne's panties in a ball. I threw them across the hall. Just left them there.

I ran out onto Riverside Drive. I ran until I reached Broadway. I slipped in a patch of icy slush and almost dropped Yvonne's bag. It was small enough so I stuck it inside my own. I leaned against a bodega and closed my eyes. I could still see Yvonne and Mark in that bed. That rolling.

After a minute I crossed the street. That same guy was still selling Christmas trees. At 10:35 on Christmas Eve. Anyone buying a Christmas tree at 10:35 on Christmas Eve is succumbing to sentimental impulses as far as I'm concerned. He saw me and smiled. Joan Baez was playing again. I was almost out of breath.

"I'm still thinking of buying one," I said.

"Well, I could give you a really good price now," he said. He sipped coffee through a tear in the Styrofoam lid.

"They smell great," I said.

"Yeah, I never get tired of this smell," he said.

I touched a bough, closed my eyes, and breathed in the smell.

"What about your husband?"

He remembered.

"Fuck my husband," I said. I thought how appropriate that was at the moment. "Everyone else does."

"You need a tree," the guy said. I thought of my dream. The tree. It seemed like an omen.

"How much for this one?" The tree was about my height. He looked at it. Then he looked at me.

"How about fifteen?"

I knew it was a steal.

"Do you think it'd fit in a cab?"

"I'll get you one," he said.

On the way downtown I was so preoccupied with keeping the tree from getting crushed or bent that I almost forgot about Yvonne's bag. When I did think of it I forced myself to wait until I got home. The cab driver asked a few polite questions but I didn't feel like talking. I put my face in the branches to take in the smell of pine, to block out the picture of Mark and Yvonne in that bed, but my heart was pulsing like crazy and my head was like a slide show. Mark and Yvonne. Mark and Yvonne. Mark and Yvonne. I started doing this alternate-nostril breathing that's supposed to calm you down. I held one nostril closed and took a breath, held it for a count of eight, then closed that nostril and let the air out the other for a count of eight. The cab driver kept sneaking looks at me in the rearview mirror. By the time we

got to Spring Street it was midnight. All the Midnight
Masses would be beginning all over the city. "Merry
Christmas, Terry," I whispered.

The loft was freezing. Tony and Chico raced out to greet
me. "Merry Christmas, boys," I said. Then I remembered
the cat food. I'd forgotten it again.

I set the tree on its side and flipped on the phone
machine, which was blinking like mad. Mark. Sarah. My
mother.

Tony and Chico pawed and scratched my legs. "I'm sorry,
boys," I said. I poured them a bowl of Cheerios and filled
their water bowl, which was completely dry. They just
looked disgusted and followed me back out of the room.
They looked like they felt as bad as I did.

I picked up the tree. I hadn't considered how I would get
it to stand. I propped it up against the front window with a
couple of heavy books around the base. Tony and Chico
came over immediately and started rubbing themselves
against it. No matter how many times I pulled them away,
they ran back. I think they were really mad.

The phone rang.

"Terry, it's me. Are you there?" Sarah. It's funny how
many people leave messages saying "it's me." "I'm getting
sick of this Yule log. *Call* me."

I sat down and pulled Yvonne's bag out of my own. It was
soft black leather. A good bag, my mother would say. The
phone rang again. I held the bag behind my back and waited to see who it was. Guilt makes you think people can see
you over a telephone. It must be a Catholic thing.

"Treas, it's me. Are you there?"

Mark. I wondered if he was calling from Yvonne's. It was only an hour or so since I'd left them. I stared at the machine. "Terry, pick up the phone."

I picked it up.

"What?" I asked.

"You weren't going to pick up?"

"I was feeding the boys."

"You okay?"

"Great," I said. I hunched my shoulder to my ear to hold the phone and opened Yvonne's bag. It was crammed. I'd expected everything to be wedged neatly against everything else. "I'm great."

"You just get in?"

"Yeah."

I pulled out a Lancôme makeup case and put it on the chair beside me. I have the same one. It seemed like minutes went by.

"It's strange not being with you for Christmas," Mark said after a while. "I miss you."

I pulled out a gift box wrapped in the kind of wrapping paper they use in department stores. Little gold insignias on a white background. Little IUDs. I balanced it on my palm. I shook it. It sounded like earrings.

"Where were you tonight?"

"Yvonne's," I said.

"Terry don't start."

"Okay. I was in church. Where were you?"

Mark's strategy when he thinks I am being unreasonable

is to act as if everything is normal. To ignore any tension or weirdness. He takes long deep breaths and makes very reasonable statements.

"I went to a party with David and Glenda," he said.

I wanted to believe it. I wanted so badly to believe it. I pulled a wad of tissues from Yvonne's bag. A couple of green-tinted Christmas cookies shaped like a bell and a star fell out onto the floor. Tony rushed over and sniffed at them.

"Oh, where?" I asked. I leaned over to pick up the cookies and her phonebook fell out. I flipped to the H's. *Mark Holder.* It was there. The gallery number. So she didn't have our home number. There was only one name added after it so I guessed this affair was pretty recent.

". . . a great apartment. Three Rothkos," Mark was saying.

"Where was it?" I asked. I bit into the star. It was sweet. It tasted like Christmas. The cookies my mother makes once a year. Butter cookies with red and green food coloring. The kind you don't want to eat, but end up eating handfuls of.

"I told you, Sixty-sixth and Park."

"Right."

I bit the bell, crammed the whole thing in my mouth. I chewed it then spit it into the napkin.

"Terry, are you okay? You sound weird."

Weird. I considered the absurdity of being on the phone with my husband while I went through a pocketbook I'd just stolen from his lover as they were fucking. *That* was weird. A plastic spoon fell out of the bag and I remembered that container of salad I'd left at Yvonne's.

"I *feel* weird," I said. "I miss you." Then I wished I hadn't said it. I put Yvonne's pocketbook on the couch and walked the phone over to Mark's wine rack. I pulled out a bottle. "Any of these bottles you don't want me to open?" I asked, showing the bottle to the receiver.

"Terry, how much have you been drinking?"

Actually, that was a good question.

"I mean I guess half of all this is mine, right?"

"I don't give a shit what you open. You know that."

I was trying to open the bottle with the phone wedged between my ear and shoulder. I've never been able to open bottles of wine easily. If I was going to be alone I'd have to learn how to use a corkscrew.

I took a sip from the bottle, sat down, and pulled Yvonne's bag in my lap. It was soft. Like a tiny baby.

"Tree?"

Funny him calling me that now.

"Honey, I know Christmas Eve is a big night for you. Do you want me to come over?"

Mark saying *Eve* made me see Yvonne. Naked. That bruise at the top of her thigh. The moles. The curve of her ass. Did he call her Eve? Did even the sound of that syllable on his tongue right now get him excited? Make him feel guilty? Could he still feel her mouth on him, remember the taste of her? Could he have fucked her, come downtown, and sounded this calm? Was he capable of that?

"No," I said, then regretted it. It sounded harsh. "I need to go through this alone," I said. I looked down at Yvonne's bag and started to laugh.

"Listen, Terry," he said, "cut the self-pitying shit and talk to me."

Yvonne had forty dollars in her wallet. Bank cards, credit cards. Not one photograph. I thought about her trying to get on the Long Island Rail Road in the morning without any cash. Without any ATM cards. She'd have to stay home. We'd both be alone for Christmas. I could call her up. We could feel sorry for ourselves together.

"Terry . . ."

"*What?*"

"I'm trying to talk to you."

"Oh, right, okay. What do you want to talk about? Uh . . . let's see. How about Yvonne? Oops, that's right. We can't talk about Yvonne. So maybe we should talk about who you've been fucking. Oh *no*, we're back to Yvonne again. Boy, this is harder than I thought."

Mark didn't say anything. I couldn't hear anything in the background. For all I know he could have been at Yvonne's.

"You are being completely unreasonable."

"I read your journal," I said.

Nothing.

"I said, I read your journal."

"Terry, I am going to hang up."

But he didn't.

"Well," I said, and took another sip of wine, "you said you didn't give a shit what I opened."

He didn't say anything.

"*Whatever is done for love . . .*" I said.

Something crashed near the front of the loft. I walked the

phone over as Tony darted away from the Christmas tree he'd just knocked down.

"What was that?"

"Maybe I should read Yvonne's journal, too. But she probably doesn't keep a journal, does she? Or maybe she keeps it in her bag."

I sat on the floor by the tree, and dumped the rest of Yvonne's bag onto the floor. Nothing that looked like a journal or notebook. Only a letter she'd apparently forgotten to mail. The writing was almost illegible. I couldn't even make out the name. I slit it open.

"What if I told you I'd read your journal?" Mark asked.

I didn't know if he meant that he *had* read my journal, or he was asking how I'd like it if he had.

I didn't say anything. I was torn between reading Yvonne's letter and trying to remember what I had said in my journal. A lot of it was coded. Poems. I'd copied out Sylvia Plath's poem "The Rival" last week and tried to write one like it. Maybe he'd think the poem was mine.

"I always have my journal with me," I said.

Chico sat in my lap. I held him close and continued to read. Yvonne's handwriting was so hard to read that I could stare at the letter and literally not make out a word. *I saw green ducks in summer land.* I glanced quickly down looking for Mark's name. *Playing in four graves.* Either Yvonne was a completely irrational letter writer or I just couldn't crack the code. No one could read that chicken-scratch.

"Terry?"

I took a mouthful of wine. It tasted good. It tasted like dinners with Mark, like opening presents, like sex.

"Anyway, I know you wouldn't do that," I said.

"How do you know?" he asked.

A black picnic the size of hamlets. We ate [are?] dogs. I was never going to find anything out from this mess. I was almost glad she *didn't* keep a journal. She could scrawl this stuff on billboards and still be assured of privacy.

"Terry . . ."

"I know you," I said. And I do. I looked at the picture of Curly above our bed. I thought of Mark. The way he holds me after we fight, knows my moods. Forgives anything. I knew he hadn't read my journal. Or maybe he had. I guess I don't know what to think anymore. When did everything become so uncertain?

He didn't say a word. The phone beeped for call waiting, but I ignored it. I don't know why, but I thought of the police. For the first time I thought of how many traces I'd left in Yvonne's apartment. All my fingerprints. For the first time I realized this could have repercussions beyond me and Mark and Yvonne. The world could become involved. Police. Investigations. I would have to get rid of Yvonne's stuff. I'd have to get rid of the keys and any evidence. It was all hitting me at once. *Whatever is done for love occurs beyond good and evil.* Try telling that to the police.

"I'm scared," I said. "I'm really scared. Please come home," I said.

Mark didn't say anything. The phone beeped again.

"At least come home tomorrow," I said.

"I'll call you in the morning," he said. "Get some sleep."

The phone rang after we hung up. The machine clicked on. It was 12:30. My outgoing message ended. The tape switched on. No one was there.

I tore Yvonne's letter into tiny pieces and tossed them— my own little snowstorm. I opened the present. A pair of those big ugly earrings Yvonne wears. Turquoise. I put them on.

There was the rest of the wallet to go through, nothing else in the bag. Only two pens. How could someone carry only two pens?

I found nothing unusual—charge cards, a cash card, two stamps, her NYU I.D., a punched-out card to Crunch, and a bunch of business cards, none of them Mark's. The only odd thing was a St. Jude prayer card. That impressed me. Maybe she was doing a novena to get Mark to leave me.

I propped St. Jude against the tree. If it came to a choice between me and Yvonne, I know he'd pick me.

· 2 3 ·

I decided to ignore Christmas completely. I planned to wake up, have coffee, and stay inside all day reading the new biography of Yeats. For backup I had a listing for special Christmas day Al-Anon meetings. If things got bad I could always go.

The Christmas tree was lying on the floor. It had fallen again. I set it up against the window. It smelled good. It smelled like childhood and hope and expectation. I've always loved Christmas and I have to say I have had some near perfect "Christmas moments" in my life: Caroling with friends, snow falling through the streetlights, one Christmas Eve when I was seventeen . . . Sitting on Santa Claus's lap in Macy's telling him I wanted the Lennon Sisters Colorforms more than anything. And getting them. Him remembering . . . Running into the living room, a blue two-wheeler—I knew it was for me—leaning on its kickstand beside the lit-up tree . . . red felt Christmas stockings along the fireplace. It was an imitation fireplace that my mother had fitted with brick Con-Tact paper, but it didn't matter. It was a fireplace. To make the fire, my mother (she still does it) sets up a bunch of tiny red electric lights behind the logs. Over the lights she balances a tin plate that revolves when the heating lights push the plate around. And the red light flickers over the logs like real fire.

I pulled out a set of Christmas lights Mark and I had hung at a party we gave a few years ago. I popped off all the bulbs except the red ones, and plugged it in. I bunched up the bulbs and wires under the tree, stuck a pie plate over it, and waited for the lights to heat. I watched it. I waited. I started to long for Christmas at home. With cookies and presents, my family and Mark. Tradition. I wanted to be part of something.

I made a cup of hot mint tea. I decided if it took me all night I'd figure out what to do. I sipped the tea and was staring into space, thinking about Yvonne and Mark in that bed, when I realized I was staring at the *I Ching*. I pulled it down.

What should I do? I wrote. I held the pennies in my hand until they got warm. I held the question in my mind, and then I threw. Broken, broken, solid. One hexagram down and I hadn't thrown a changing line. I threw again. Broken. I had only two more throws. I needed to throw a changing line—it makes me feel like I have an extra chance. That I'm not in a fixed and static state. I threw a nine. Two changing lines. Two chances.

The first hexagram was #39: *Obstacles*. I read the text, underlining what applied. Something about a dangerous abyss lying before me and a steep inaccessible mountain rising behind me. I figured my life was the abyss, Yvonne and Mark the mountain. It said that these obstacles are part of my path and must be overcome. *Seek advice*, it said. *The struggle takes place within the self.*

This was getting me nowhere. I wanted something more specific. I turned to the changing hexagram, #52: *Meditation (Keeping Still)*. Now it said to meditate and focus on achieving a quiet heart. That once my mind is calm I will transcend my inner turmoil. Act in accordance with the cosmos, it said. *The future cannot be mapped out.*

I shut the book. It's pretty pathetic when a self-help book tells you to seek advice. *Act in accordance with the cosmos.* What is that supposed to mean? I thought maybe the answer would come if I meditated and kept still like the *I Ching* said. I sat on the floor and tried to breathe but I couldn't stay still. Then I remembered an exercise from *Hope for Your Nerves*, a book Sarah had lent me. The four-step approach: (1) FACE, (2) ACCEPT, (3) FLOAT, (4) WAIT IT OUT. I sat there trying to face and accept the anxiety. My stomach pulsed. I couldn't stay still. I walked back and forth through the apartment, trying to breathe, trying to face it, float in it, and all I could see were those two bodies rolling in Yvonne's bed.

I called Mark.

"Honey, it's one-thirty."

So he wasn't at Yvonne's.

"Do you want to go to my parents' tomorrow?"

"Are you kidding?"

"Do you have other plans?"

I thought I was going to start screaming and shrieking over the phone.

Mark didn't say anything. If he was "the friend" Yvonne's mother mentioned then he was weighing possibilities. It's not beyond Mark to pull out last minute. I knew he could easily call Yvonne and cancel. And when he heard about her bag being stolen he'd be glad to avoid the conflict. Mark hates it when things get complicated. That is, if it *was* Mark. What still throws me is the blankets. Mark never fucks under blankets.

"Are you doing something else?" I asked. I could feel my voice getting too big and wide to fit in the phone wires. Like it was going to blow them apart.

"Could we talk about this in the morning?"

"I need to know *now*," I said.

Mark mumbled something.

I couldn't tell if the room was smoky or my lenses were getting dry.

"It smells like a fire in here," I said.

"You always smell fire when you're nervous," he said. And he's right. I've summoned Italian hotel managers at three in the morning to complain about smoke. I've called the fire department more than once, convinced the loft was on fire.

"I mean it, Mark," I said. "It smells like, I don't know, like when you melt crayons on lightbulbs . . . oh Jesus, the lightbulbs!"

Smoke was billowing out from under the pie plate, filling the front end of the loft. I couldn't see Tony and Chico. I heard a pop, the lights started sparking.

"I can't see the boys! I can't see the boys!"

"Salt, Terry, salt," Mark said. "Get the salt over the sink. I'll stay on."

I ran. I kicked over the bowl of Cheerios and the boys' water bowl and almost slid across the floor. I hurled and tossed the salt. Tons of it. Luckily there were two boxes because I had to use it all. By the time I put it out there was salt all over the floor, the tree, the clock, the pile of lights, and the contents of Yvonne's bag. I tossed a handful over my left shoulder, just in case, then I fished out St. Jude. The whole place reeked of burnt plastic.

"Terry, you can't just plug in old lights without testing them," Mark said. But I felt good. There'd been a fire and I put it out. I did it myself. I took care of it. Alone.

"Come to my parents'," I said. I waved away some black smoke. "Please."

"Treas, it's late. Call me in the morning," he said. "Honey?"

"Okay," I said.

And it was okay.

I hung up. I opened the window a little. I turned on the ceiling fan. I picked up Tony and Chico and held them in my lap, brushing the salt off their fur. Everything felt different. It doesn't matter, I thought. None of it matters. I thought about how much we always feel we have to know. But maybe it's like the mysteries you grow up with. Like the Trinity, or the Resurrection, or Jell-O. You spend a long time thinking about how it works, trying to figure it out, and then, I don't know, what gradually becomes certain, something you know for sure, is just the fact of that mystery. That it will always be a mystery. Maybe that's all Nietzsche and Foucault meant. To let life keep its mysteries. I could let Mark keep his mystery. I could let Yvonne remain a mystery. Myself a mystery. You can't know everything. Maybe there are terrible things that *almost* happen to us all the time. These close calls throughout our lives. Times we just miss being knifed or jumped, hit by a car, pushed off a subway platform, and we never know about them. Like Yvonne never knowing about me. Right there in the middle of her bedroom.

I woke up in the chair. Tony was in my lap. My back hurt from the position I'd slept in. When I put my foot down the salt crunched beneath it. It was 8:09. Christmas. The phone rang and I sat and watched the tape turn. I reached to answer. Mark's voice went on and on. I don't even remember what he said.

Books were scattered all over the floor. And salt, and Cheerios, and half-drunk glasses of wine and cold tea. Yvonne's wallet and keys and makeup. I picked up her bag. I thought of her trying to get to East Hampton without cash. I wondered if she had an extra set of keys. Even then I thought it was funny that I had two sets of Yvonne's keys.

I dialed her number, listened to the message. She didn't answer. I hung up. I dialed again. The message played. She didn't answer. I did it over and over. Then I just started hitting redial. I must have done it thirty times, alternately cursing her for not picking up and figuring she must have left for Penn Station. Maybe she keeps a stash of money in the apartment somewhere—although I've never seen it. Maybe she borrowed money from whoever it was that was in her apartment last night. Maybe it hadn't been Mark. And there was only one way I was going to find out.

I took a cab to Penn Station. I fixed my hair in the ride up. I rubbed the leftover eyeliner from below my eyes, which made the circles darker. I hadn't changed my clothes. I hadn't even thought to brush my teeth. And I was still wearing those big earrings. I took them off and tossed them out the window. The cab driver said nothing. He didn't even look at me.

The streets were quiet, deserted. A grim chill hung over the city. One old man rummaged through a trash can on Houston Street, filling a garbage bag with empty bottles. Usually I hate it when it's damp and gray on Christmas morning, but today it was almost a relief. Like God felt as bad as I did.

Penn Station was crawling with people, everyone carrying shopping bags. Some dressed for Christmas and the usual lot of disheveled transients checking the coin returns in all the telephones. I don't know which I looked more like. "Jingle Bells" played over the scratchy loudspeaker and a Salvation Army Santa Claus waved a bell up and down for donations.

I was carrying only a few dollars in Yvonne's coat pocket and her leather bag. I bought coffee and a corn muffin at one of those stands that sells Life Savers and porno magazines. The muffin was so dry the crumbs caught in my throat and I started to choke. I threw it out. I took a few sips and tossed the coffee as well. There was a mirror on the wall but I knew how pale I'd look in the fluorescent light, so I checked my reflection in the black window of the Station Bar. I rubbed a napkin across my teeth. I needed to find Yvonne.

It was 8:52. I found the track number for the 9:11 to East Hampton but I didn't see Yvonne anywhere. People had begun to board. I got on the first car and started looking. In every seat. I kept checking my watch. If the train started I'd be stuck for the ride. I didn't have enough cash to cover a round-trip, but I could use Yvonne's forty dollars.

People guarded their seats as I looked, wanting, I know, to keep an empty seat beside them. Once I got so annoyed I made as if to sit down, just to scare the woman sitting there, then I pretended to look her over and change my mind.

At 8:58 I still hadn't found Yvonne. I decided to have her paged. I made up a story and convinced the conductor—an older guy with curly gray hair who smiled a lot and was saying "Merry Christmas" to everyone—that it was an emergency.

I stood outside the front car holding Yvonne's bag. I heard the announcer say her name. *Yvonne Adams. Will Yvonne Adams please come to the front car.* People were still boarding. Everything was jumping inside me. The way it does when you're about to see a new lover and you know it will be minutes. Even seconds. The way your body knows, leaps and leaps inside.

No one showed up. I stood there waiting. At 9:03 I began to think she wouldn't come. I clutched her bag and looked at anything moving toward me.

"Looks like she's not here, miss." The conductor stood

looking at me. His hands fidgeted helplessly around him.

"It's an emergency," I said. I could feel the panic pushing up through me. Little shivers of blood forcing into my heart ventricles. I was having trouble keeping still. It was cold and Yvonne's coat wasn't really warm enough.

"Are you sure you got the right train?" He was about my father's age. He looked concerned. Like he would have concocted her out of plaster of paris if that would have made me happy.

"Please . . ." I said.

And then she was there. I don't think she saw me at first. I know she didn't.

She was alone.

She looked like she hadn't slept. Her hair was pulled back in a clip and there were dark circles under her eyes. It was the first time I'd ever seen her looking messy. She had a run in her stocking, a leather tote slung over her shoulder.

She was alone.

"Your sister . . ." the conductor said.

Yvonne looked at me. She seemed to try to place me. She looked confused.

I hadn't thought at all about what I'd do or say. I'd made up no plan of action. *The future cannot be mapped out* the *I Ching* said.

I stared at her. She stared at me. I held out her bag.

"Yvonne . . ." I said.

She just stood there looking confused. Then she looked at the bag.

"Oh my God," she said.

"Yvonne . . ."

"I don't understand . . ."

"We have to talk," I said. I tried to smile at her.

I guess I was thinking that we could talk it out. Like adults. Go somewhere and have a coffee and I could explain how upset I'd been. That she would feel shame. Remorse. That we'd decide what to do. The two of us together. Like Norma and Adalgisa.

"Why do you have my bag?" she asked. "How did you get my bag?"

"I can explain," I said.

She looked at the bag as though it were a bomb. She did not reach for it.

"All aboard," someone yelled.

"It's about Mark," I said.

Several people ran down the station stairs and past us into the car.

"Excuse me, miss. Two minutes," the man who'd helped me said. He approached us.

"I have to get on that train," Yvonne said. She was beginning to shake. She had on the big garbage can lid earrings.

I moved toward her. She moved back.

"Please . . ." I said. I was so hot my body felt like a furnace in that coat.

"How did you get my bag?" she almost shouted, as if she'd say anything to keep me from talking.

She moved back onto the train. I followed. Those big earrings were dangling from her lobes. I was so close I could have yanked them out.

"Were you with my husband last night?"

She moved back another step, gripping her shoulder bag in front of her with both hands.

"Are you crazy? You *are* crazy."

Her little squeaky voice was getting higher. I realized this was not going to be like Norma and Adalgisa at all. She didn't sound remorseful in the least.

"Is something wrong?" someone called out.

I stepped closer to Yvonne.

"*Were* you with Mark last night?"

Someone moved behind me.

"Miss," he said. He put his hand on my shoulder.

"*Don't. Don't. Don't.*" I yanked away.

He backed off. I turned to Yvonne.

"I need to talk to you," I said calmly. It was like trying to approach a frightened animal. I was trying not to make any sudden movements.

Yvonne was shaking pretty hard.

"Miss," the conductor said.

"This is personal," I said.

I moved toward Yvonne, to touch her. To calm her down.

"Get away from me," she said.

I was getting mad.

"I just want to *talk*." I was almost shouting. I don't really remember how it happened but I do remember we were off the train at that point. On the platform. I remember thinking if I could just get her to shut up I could explain everything.

"I'm going to call the police," she said.

"Just *listen*," I said. I grabbed her coat. She pulled back, called to the conductor.

"I am not going to talk to you like this," she said.

I hit her. I hit Yvonne. I didn't mean to but she wouldn't listen.

Yvonne just stood there looking stunned. I hit her again. I'd seen it coming. I couldn't stop. It was like my body was moving somewhere apart from my head. Taking over. Like when you're having sex and you start doing and saying things that aren't in your head at all.

Someone grabbed me from behind.

"*Miss*, are you getting on that train?" the conductor asked Yvonne.

"I don't know, I don't know, I don't know," Yvonne moaned. She was looking at me. A policeman asked if anything was wrong. He looked like he was still in high school. Yvonne pushed back some loose bangs. She took her hair out of the clip then clipped it back again. Her hair looked dirty.

"What's going on here?" an older cop asked. He'd pushed through the small group of people. He held my shoulder.

I started thinking of the cops finding all the signs of me at Yvonne's. All the clues. Talking to the woman at the Korean vegetable stand. The guy selling Christmas trees. I pictured myself in prison. The lawyers questioning Eric. Tough, crazed guards forcing me to have sex. Losing all my friends.

"Please," I said, looking at the older policeman.

"This woman has my bag," Yvonne said quietly to the other cop.

I looked at her. Her stupid bag. I could have slapped her again.

"This woman is fucking my husband," I said calmly to my cop. "This woman is *fucking* my husband," I said it louder this time. "This woman is *fucking my husband,*" I started shouting over and over.

Now it was her turn. Now Yvonne was trying to calm me down.

"Stop it. Stop it," she said. She looked pathetic and embarrassed. All these people had gathered around us. Both cops were trying to talk at the same time. The older one was still holding me. I noticed the younger one trying not to laugh.

"Deny it," I said. "Say you're not fucking my husband. Say it. *Say* it," I was shouting.

WASP that she is, it was just too much outside Yvonne's sense of things to hear me screeching like that. Like embarrassment was the worst indignity she could imagine. She calmly explained to the policeman that she was on her way to "visit her folks" in East Hampton. Could they please hold the train. Officer this, and Officer that. She pulled out every respectable stop. She'd moved onto the train and stood in the doorway. It must have seemed to her the height of adventure to hold the train like that.

Several people were shouting about getting the train going.

"Some *fucking* Christmas," this guy with two Bloomingdale's shopping bags was saying. He was leaning out of the same doorway Yvonne stood in.

"*Shut* up," I said. I looked at Yvonne. "*You*," I said, ripping away from the cop, "you have no soul. You could *never* understand Yeats," I said. "You stupid bitch. Your stupid neat little apartment."

I turned to the cops. "Even her *toothbrush* is neat," I said. "'Concetta, could you please fix the curtain.' 'Oh Concetta, wash the soapdish.'" I mimicked her to the cops. They just stared at me.

I've read about people—quite normal people—suddenly becoming unlatched. Murdering their husband or killing their mother. Someone who'd just returned library books or gone grocery shopping that afternoon. Then just snapped. Like there's a valve that suddenly gives. That all the pain, all the loss and anguish, all the anxiety and disappointment and hurt you've felt, or tried not to feel, bursts out in one long rush. I think temporary insanity is kind of normal given the way we live.

I rushed at Yvonne. I grabbed her off the train and started shaking her. "You have no soul. You have no soul," I kept saying.

· 2 4 ·

I don't remember exactly the course of events, but we wound up in the cops' station right off the waiting area. Yvonne was sobbing and shaking, asking if she could call "her folks" and tell them she'd be late. Asking if she could call Hampton Jitney to find out when the next one left.

"Both a youse just sit tight," the young cop said. "Yeah, yeah. Merry Christmas," he said and waved off some old guy who was rubbing his beard on the doorway, mumbling. He sipped a coffee through a rip in the Styrofoam lid. I was dying for a coffee.

I tried to take deep breaths. I wanted to call someone, too, but I couldn't think of who I'd call. I guess I could have called Sarah. I just sat there, pulling pieces of stuffing out of the ripped office chair, reading the cartoons and sayings that were plastered all over the walls. Schedules. Mug shots. I imagined my face on that wall. A picture of me and Mark on our honeymoon in Florence. Outside in the waiting area a group of black guys was harmonizing a jazzy version of "O Come, All Ye Faithful." I was still holding Yvonne's bag.

Now that we were sitting alone I didn't know what to say to Yvonne. The way you run out of small talk with a colleague or acquaintance you see at a party. I don't think either of us knew what to do next.

"Let me have that bag," the older cop said. Giordano, his name was. Officer Giordano. I handed him the bag. He looked at it as if he had no idea how to proceed.

My lip was bleeding. I must have bitten it. I pressed it with a tissue I found in Yvonne's coat pocket. Yvonne hadn't said a word about my references to her apartment. I don't even know what she heard.

"Where did you get this?" Officer Giordano asked me, holding out the bag. "Larry, commere. Take this down," he said.

Larry shook his head and put his coffee down. "Jeez, Joe, this is a circus," he said. He leaned against a file cabinet and held his clipboard and pen.

Officer Giordano looked at me.

"She left it at my house," I said. I checked my lip. It was still bleeding.

Yvonne didn't say a word.

"It was on the couch when I got in last night," I said. I felt inspired. Like God was speaking through me, guiding whatever I had to say.

"I'd suspected she'd been having an affair with my husband," I said. I looked at Yvonne. "I'd been *told* she was having an affair with my husband"—I waited to see what I'd say next—"but I really didn't believe it was possible until last night."

Larry snorted. Officer Giordano shot him a look.

I don't know why I was so sure Yvonne wouldn't contradict me. I knew she'd just go along with it. I suppose something that sordid couldn't fit into her vision of life. That she shuddered at the thought of court appearances and newspapers, confronting Mark—all of it.

"She's lying," Yvonne said.

I looked at her. I'd almost been believing myself.

"I'm not," I said.

"Listen," Larry said, "you girls want to get your story straight."

I swear he looked fifteen. Yvonne looked at him in disgust.

"Larry," Officer Giordano said.

"Larry, why not let the adults take care of this," I said.

Yvonne almost laughed.

"Listen, Joe, why don't we call the husband."

Now this was something I think neither of us had considered. I don't know what was going on in Yvonne's mind but I didn't want Mark around for this.

"I don't have to sit here," Yvonne said suddenly. "I've had it. Give me my bag," she said. She stood up. "I want to go."

The cops looked at one another.

"You wanna just drop this?" Officer Giordano asked.

"It's Christmas," she said. "I want to go home."

"You can press charges," Larry said. What a small-minded little weasel.

"Can I call Hampton Jitney from here?" Yvonne asked.

Officer Giordano shrugged.

She walked to the desk and dialed. The black guys were singing that drummer boy song that goes "par-um-pum-

pum-pum" all the way through. I checked under the tissue. The bleeding had stopped. I picked off tissue fibers that were stuck to my lip and looked at Yvonne. That run in her stocking. She'd probably have a long wait this time Christmas morning. She lit a cigarette. That surprised me. I'd never pictured Yvonne smoking, never seen a cigarette in her apartment. I'd never even smelled smoke. Maybe she only smokes when she's nervous. I felt bad for her. I started thinking. Maybe that hadn't been Mark in her bed. Maybe it had been someone else. Maybe Yvonne wasn't as alone as I'd imagined her to be. Maybe she had a lover. Several of them. She did say she had a date the other night. And I was with Mark. I mean, when it came down to it, what proof did I have that Yvonne and Mark were having an affair? None. No real proof. *Make sure you have all the facts*, my father used to say. But facts can be misleading. *A little bit of knowledge is dangerous.* I could hear my mother: *That kid has some imagination.* And I know it's true. I thought about all the times I'd imagined fires at the loft—and the thing is, I'd really smelled smoke. I really had.

"I can't get through," Yvonne said. She was beside me. Just another woman. She didn't even look much like me after all.

She looked around, then put the cigarette out on a coffee lid that was lying on Officer Giordano's desk. Mark hates cigarettes. "I'm sorry," she said. She was twisting the butt onto the plastic to make sure it was out.

"No, *I'm* sorry," I said. I stood up.

I heard Larry mutter something.

"It was nothing," she said. "Nothing. I didn't realize, I mean . . . you never connect . . ." She pushed her hair out of her face. "It's over," she said. "We ended it."

I was just looking at her. Her mouth was moving and she was saying things, but I couldn't get them in sync. She seemed really far away. She moved toward me.

"Mark was . . . I mean, it didn't mean anything," she said. "To him. I mean, he really loves you."

She was looking at me the way you look at a small rabbit that got hit by a car.

"You had an affair with Mark?"

My voice felt really tiny. I was so hot it felt like steam was seeping out of my coat.

"You and Mark had an affair?"

Yvonne just stood there. I could see it now. She didn't look like me in the least.

"When?"

· 2 5 ·

I could say it's all a blur, what happened next, but I remember it all: Me just standing there. Yvonne looking so guilty and sympathetic and strange—exactly the way Sarah had looked when she first told me about her. The two cops shaking their heads. The cigarette butt smeared with Yvonne's Scarlet Memory and smashed into the plastic lid. The black guys singing that drummer boy song. I remember it all. All of it. I took a cab home, I remember that.

The loft was a mess. Salt and books, half-filled teacups and wineglasses, Cheerios, cookie crumbs, newspapers, clothes—stuff all over the place. It looked like we hadn't cleaned in months. That damned tree was on the floor again, tangled up in the curtain that must have come down from the front window when the tree fell. Tony stretched across it scratching at the bark, Chico beside him. The floor was covered with crushed pine needles and salt. The string of burnt-out Christmas lights. I remember thinking that the loft looked the way my mind felt. All jumbled up.

I called home. Before my mother could start talking I told her not to ask any questions. That I loved them all, and I'd call later on, but I needed to figure some things out.

Maybe it was something in my voice, but she didn't argue. "I love you, too," she said. "Make sure you call."

Then I called Mark. David and Glenda recited a jokey Christmas message saying to "leave a jingle at the . . . *beep.*" The beep sounded to end their sentence.

"This is a message for Mark," I said. "I know everything. And you knew I knew." Then I hung up.

I stood there looking at the phone for a while, barely able to move. I looked around the loft. All that mess. I thought if I did some cleaning up it would help me think.

I put on Maria Callas singing Puccini and I started with the big stuff. I shook out and rehung the curtain. I picked up the tree, brushed it off, and stuck it in a terra-cotta pot. I surrounded the base with crushed tinfoil so it wouldn't fall. I found a wad of garbage bags I'd taken from Yvonne's and began to throw things out. The lights, the wrapping paper, Yvonne's letter. I found Brian's tape wedged between the couch cushions. "The Cliffs of Dooneen." I put it in my bag so I wouldn't lose it and I made a note to call him later, too, to see how he was. I thought he might be lonely.

By the time Maria Callas was singing *Manon Lescaut,* I'd shelved the books, put the dirty glasses in the sink, dumped the clothes into a wicker basket by the bathroom, and made a pile for the dry cleaner. It was Christmas so no place would be open, but I could bring them the next morning. "*Sola, perduta, abbandonata.*" I picked up Mark's journal and stuffed it in the garbage bag.

Why had I thought I needed to know? I mean it's always better to remain uncertain. At least you have a little hope. When I was a kid I used to think it was really strange that no one talked about Curly when he wasn't in a particular episode. One day there was Curly and the next day Shemp. I kept waiting for someone to mention him. Say why he wasn't there. Why didn't Larry ask where Curly was? Were we supposed to think Shemp was Curly? Were we supposed to pretend that Shemp had been there all along? I tried to figure it out. I thought about it for a long time before I asked my mother. Even she had never mentioned the fact that sometimes Shemp was there instead of Curly. When I finally asked her she told me Curly had died. And that made it even worse. I couldn't picture Curly dead. And then whenever he was on the show I saw him as a dead man.

The garbage bag was almost full. I tossed in Mark's T-shirt. The one I'd used to polish my boots.

When the floor was clear enough I swept up the salt and Cheerios and pine needles. I washed the wood with Murphy's Oil until it gleamed. I made the bed. "*Io la deserta donna.*" I tried to ignore the song. It made me think too much. It made me think about Maria Callas. How her whole life fell apart after she left her husband. How she lost her voice. Lost everything. Did she have any idea what was going to happen when she was recording that song? In 1954? Did she know she'd lose all that weight and have a twenty-two inch waist, that Ari would leave her for Jackie, that she'd end up alone and desolate, just like the song says. Had she known? Is that why she sounds so tragic? When she got to the part about not wanting to die alone I'd had it. *"Non voglio morir, non voglio morir,"* she kept singing. It ripped me apart, the way the music stops and she keeps singing, her voice all alone and naked. Sarah says she killed herself, but Sarah always thinks people killed themselves. She believes all that tabloid stuff. That JFK was sleeping with Marilyn Monroe, that he had her killed to keep her quiet. Sarah says that if Callas didn't kill herself why did they skip the autopsy and rush to bury her?

I didn't want to think about Maria Callas killing herself. I switched to Cecilia Bartoli singing Mozart. That beautiful voice makes you feel like even the sad, hard things are manageable. Cecilia Bartoli would never kill herself.

Maria Callas is just too tragic and hopeless sometimes.

I made six big piles of old *New York Times*. It was Mark's job to tie up the newspapers and put them out, so the fact that I could make those bundles made me feel pretty good. It took a while to figure out the best way to wrap the cord to make a tight bundle. One that wouldn't open. I wrapped and tied the cord as if with each bundle I was getting rid of something, clearing something out of my life. By the last pile I'd gotten pretty good at it and I was sorry there weren't more to tie up. I picked up a Book Review. October 5. The one with the Yeats/Maud Gonne letters on the front page. *Save*, I'd written at the top. *Save*. It seemed like another life. Before the gallery opening. Before Sarah had told me about Yvonne. Before I'd ever set foot in Yvonne's apartment. I closed my eyes and I swear I could see me and Mark sitting at the table on that Sunday morning drinking coffee and reading each other bits from each section. Art reviews. A sale at Barney's. Profiles of figure skaters. And had it already started? The affair. Mark and Yvonne. Was he already sleeping with her? Had he already been thinking about her when he told me about the new biography of Yeats? I didn't want to think about it. It occurred to me that it had been just about the only thing I *could* think about when I hadn't known for sure—and now that I knew, now that Yvonne had confessed, it was like I didn't want it in my head at all.

I ran up and down the stairs about eight times to get rid of all those stacks of newspapers and bags of garbage. I was out of breath but the loft was starting to look pretty good. I ran down again and picked up two cans of tuna for the boys. They raced over and climbed up my legs while I opened the cans and I could barely get the food into the bowls. They ate so quickly the bowls kept scraping along the floor, then they just hunched there, licking.

Cecilia Bartoli was singing this beautiful aria about what could be causing her heart's agitation. Anger? she asked. Fear, jealousy, love? Well that about covers it, but I knew she'd be okay. And I knew she knew. It was painful but she wouldn't give up. She seems downright cheerful compared to Maria Callas. Maybe that's why Mark doesn't like her. He thinks Cecilia Bartoli is too sunny. He likes his women tragic, which is pretty funny since he never seems to be able to stick around for the tragic part. It's too messy. Like when he went to see *Casablanca* with me while his old girlfriend, Isabelle, was in the emergency room. No, Mark likes to keep things neat and separate. At least in his head. I picture everything in Mark's head stacked and tied in separate bundles. Like those newspapers. Mark just doesn't get things like Cecilia Bartoli and Mozart—the way the sadness and happiness are all jumbled up together.

I started on the bathroom. I thought I could spend the whole day cleaning, maybe go out and get some higher-watt lightbulbs. Mark always buys 60 watt, which is pretty dim. I was thinking that Yvonne had the right idea, keeping her apartment so neat. It feels better when things are neat and orderly. It's easier to think. I even regretted for a second that I hadn't gotten Concetta's phone number, but you can always find someone to clean things up. And it felt good to do it myself. I ran water into the bathroom sink, threw in my blouse and Yvonne's scarf and panties and rinsed them out. Green dye seeped out of the scarf as I wrung it out and hung it on a hanger to dry. It dripped green across the bathroom floor which I'd already mopped. It always happens like that: you make things messier as you're trying to clean them up.

I washed the sink, really scrubbed it. I picked out the crusted soap along the bumpy nubs of the soapdish. I washed the mirror, the tiles, the pipes beneath the sink. I shook Ajax into the bowl and swished it out. I sponged and dried every bottle, jar, and tube. I found stray pieces of hair curled onto the sides of the sink. Ordinarily I wouldn't think about it, but I kept wondering if it was my hair or Mark's. Or Yvonne's. Could she have been here? No. I knew at least that. Or I was relatively sure. That's the thing, I can't be sure of anything now. Like when you notice a tiny speck of green mold on a piece of cheese and then start seeing it all over and have to throw the whole thing out.

I beat the mat and dumped the towels, emptied the toothbrush cup and threw out the old brushes. I took the brush I'd been using, the green one with silver sparkles I'd bought the day I went to Yvonne's for the first time. I sprayed it with Fantastik and used the splayed bristles to brush around the spigot and cock.

Then I turned on the shower and watched the mirror steam. I watched my face slowly disappear. I rubbed the steam to see myself, then watched me disappear again. I did it over and over. *Yet always when I look death in the face / when I clamber to the heights of sleep / or when I grow excited with wine / suddenly I meet your face.* But it was my own face I kept seeing. I wonder if it had ever occurred to Yeats to say *my face. Suddenly I meet my face.*

By the time I got in the shower I was already drenched. I made the water hot. As hot as I could stand it. I peed into the tub, something Mark hates. I watched the stream of urine run down the white porcelain, into the drain. I sang. My voice rose up and out of me, a full, round voice filling me up and pouring out. I could feel my breath reaching through me, to my fingertips and toes, filling every part of me. And then it poured out. My voice just washed out of me, singing Mozart.

Steam blew around me in hot, airy drafts. I washed my hair. I scrubbed my skin with the loofah mitt until it turned bright red. Then I rubbed Neutrogena sesame oil all over and wrapped myself up in a big green towel.

I didn't want to get dressed. It was Christmas and I usually dress for Christmas, but it looked like I wasn't going to be going anywhere. It made me think about that Christmas with Mark, when we'd spent the whole day in bed. That tiny gold ring he'd tongued out of me. I'd been okay, I think, until I thought of that. Christmas with Mark. That great bottle of wine. Chevalier-Montrachet.

The phone rang. I thought it might be Mark. I turned the volume all the way down and watched the red light hold, then start blinking when whoever it was hung up. For a minute I thought about calling Eric. But what could I say? That Mark was having an affair with Yvonne? He already knew that. And it would take too long to explain. That I had known but not really known.

The phone rang again. Right away. And I knew it was Mark, that he'd gotten my message. I turned up the volume.

"Treas, it's me," he said. "Please pick up."

I just stood there.

"Come on, Terry, please pick up the phone. I know you're there. Honey, I want . . ."

I turned the volume down again and I knew he was still talking.

Let him wait. Let him wait and worry and guess. Just like I had. Let him wonder. And feel sick and crazy and depressed.

The machine clicked off and the light started blinking.

I stared at the phone thinking of who I could call. And then, it's funny, I pulled out the plug. I pulled out the plug and looked at that dead phone just sitting there.

The keys.

It's a little voice inside telling you what to do.

I took Yvonne's keys out of my bag. I went into the bathroom, threw them in the toilet, and flushed. I watched them
spin, heard them clang against the bowl, and go down. I
waited until the water was still, and I flushed again.

Then I went back inside. I sat in the big chair and looked
at how clean everything was. Tony and Chico approached,
tentative at first, pawing the towel a little. I could smell the
tuna on Chico's breath when he jumped in my lap.

It was quiet. I hadn't noticed the music end. I knew the
phone wouldn't ring. I think it was the most silent moment
I've ever experienced. *There are many kinds of silence. A lot can
happen in silence.* I felt comfortable in that silence. My whole
body felt quiet. I just sat there. Just sat and sat.

And then it happened. A movie moment. Suddenly I felt
so real in that chair. Dense and substantial. I can't really
explain it. It was like I was watching myself. Watching the
way that big fluffy green towel wrapped around me, cover-
ing all of me. The way the floor looked so clear and clean,
that warm woody cello color spreading out in every direction. I think that if it had been a movie a cello would have
been playing. Just one lone cello. Calm and quiet. Adagio.

For the first time in a long time things seemed to fit into
themselves. My breath fit in my body. My thoughts fit in
my head. I think there are times when what's inside you gets
too big and it's all there pulsing and rocking in you trying
to find a way out. I think there are times you can't just meditate and push it all back.

The bells from St. Anthony's rang for one o'clock Mass.
One solitary gong. It was only three hours since I'd left

Yvonne. I didn't know what I was going to do for the rest of the day. I didn't know what I was going to do about me and Mark. I breathed and breathed and sat there looking at how clean I had made the loft. Thinking about how I didn't know anything. That maybe I would just sit there and breathe. For hours. I didn't know. And it was okay. It really was. I was quiet. I was inside myself.